SQUIDDING AROUND

CLASS CLOWN FISH!

KEVIN SHERRY

WITH COLOR BY WES DZIOBA

graphix

AN IMPRINT OF

SCHOLASTIC

To Erin Nutsugah,
a true catch and my reel love

Library of Congress Cataloging-in-Publication Data Available

ISBN 978-1-338-63671-0 (hardcover)
ISBN 978-1-338-63670-3 (paperback)

10 9 8 7 6 5 4 3 2 1   21 22 23 24 25

Printed in China   62

First edition, May 2021
Edited by Jenne Abramowitz
Book design by Steve Ponzo
Creative Director: Phil Falco
Publisher: David Saylor

CHAPTER 1

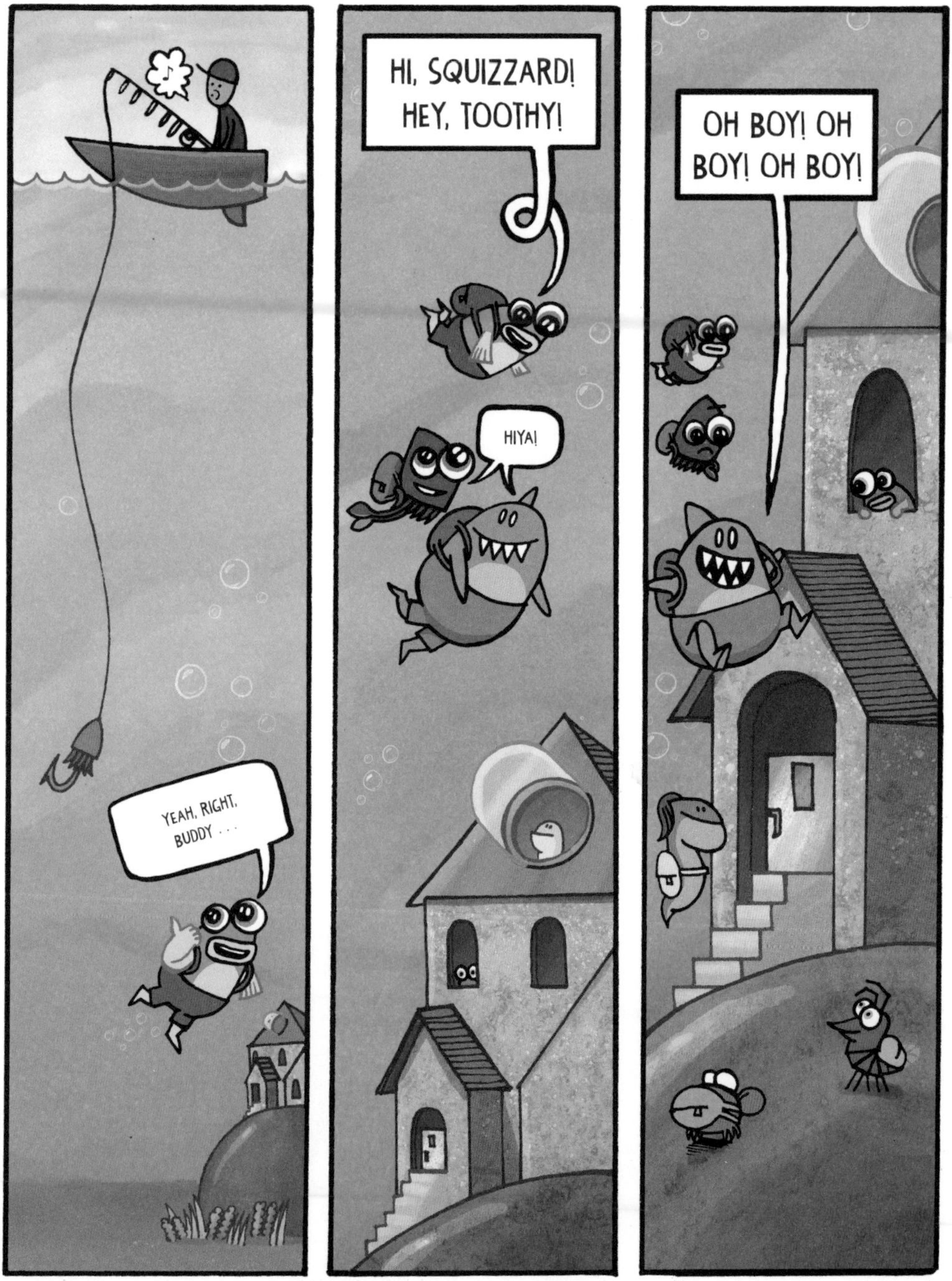
YEAH, RIGHT, BUDDY . . .
HI, SQUIZZARD! HEY, TOOTHY!
HIYA!
OH BOY! OH BOY! OH BOY! OH BOY!

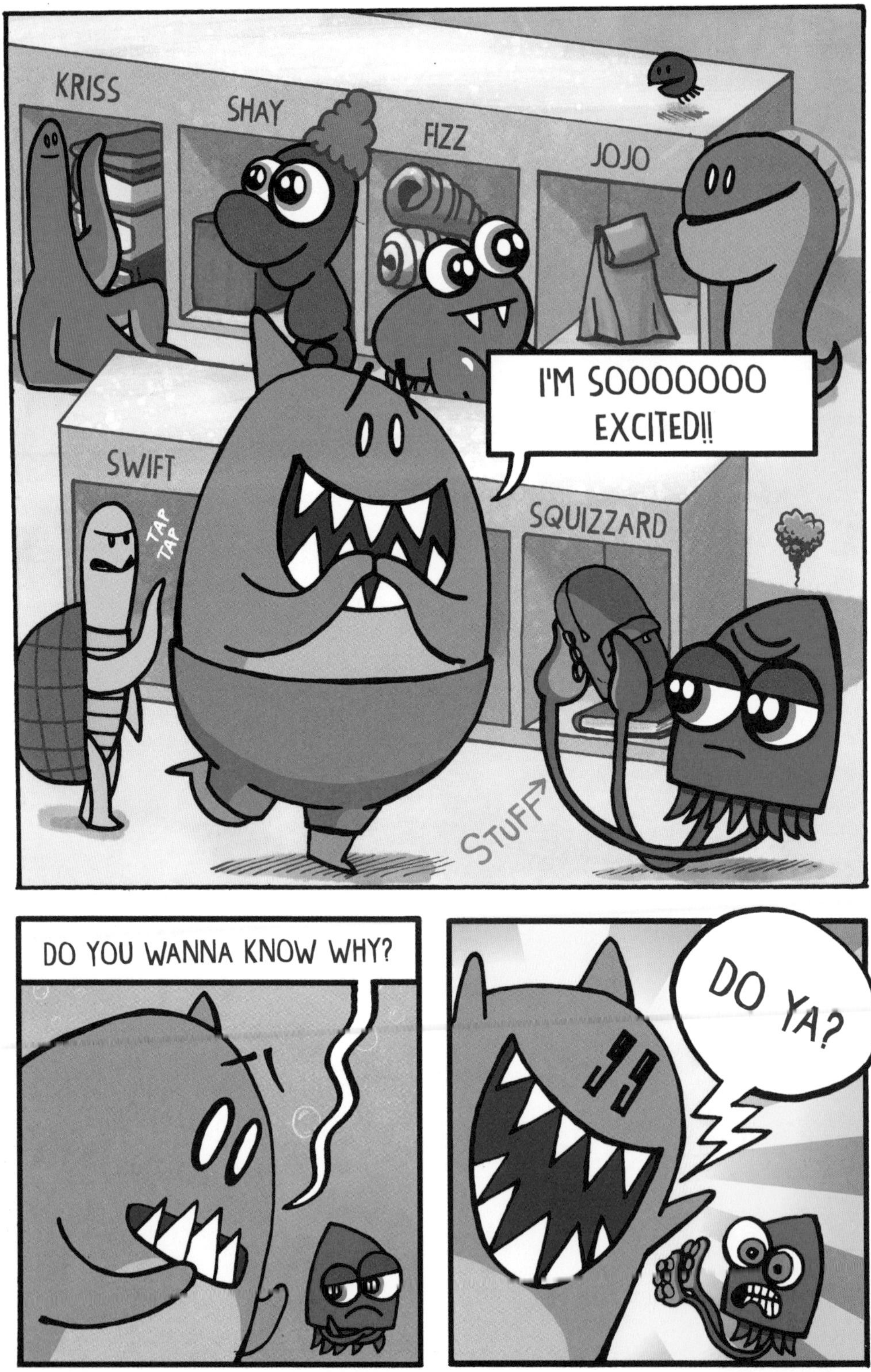
KRISS
SHAY
FIZZ
JOJO
SWIFT
SQUIZZARD
I'M SOOOOOOO EXCITED!!
TAP TAP
STUFF
DO YOU WANNA KNOW WHY?
DO YA?

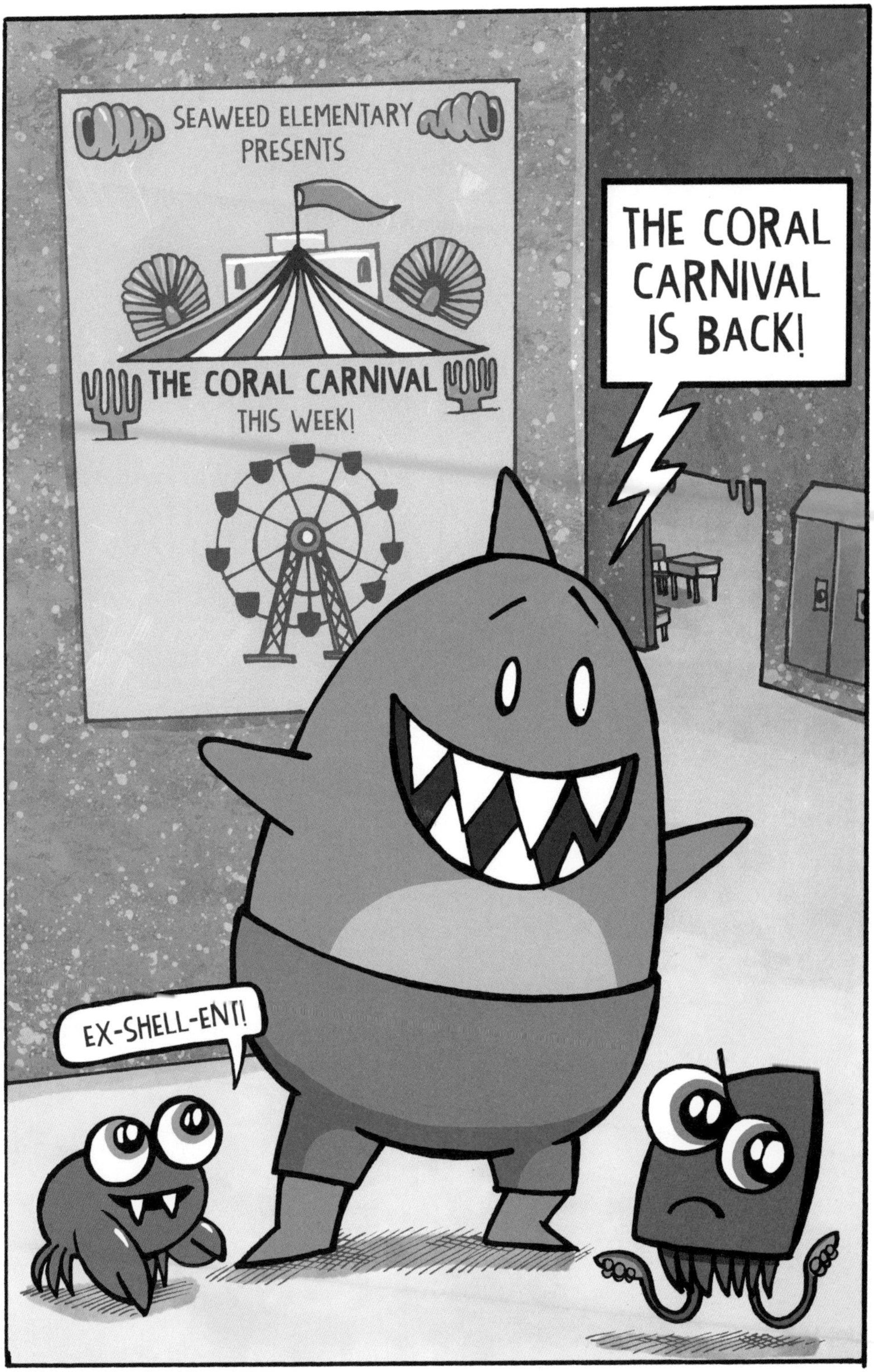
SEAWEED ELEMENTARY PRESENTS
THE CORAL CARNIVAL
THIS WEEK!
THE CORAL CARNIVAL IS BACK!
EX-SHELL-ENT!

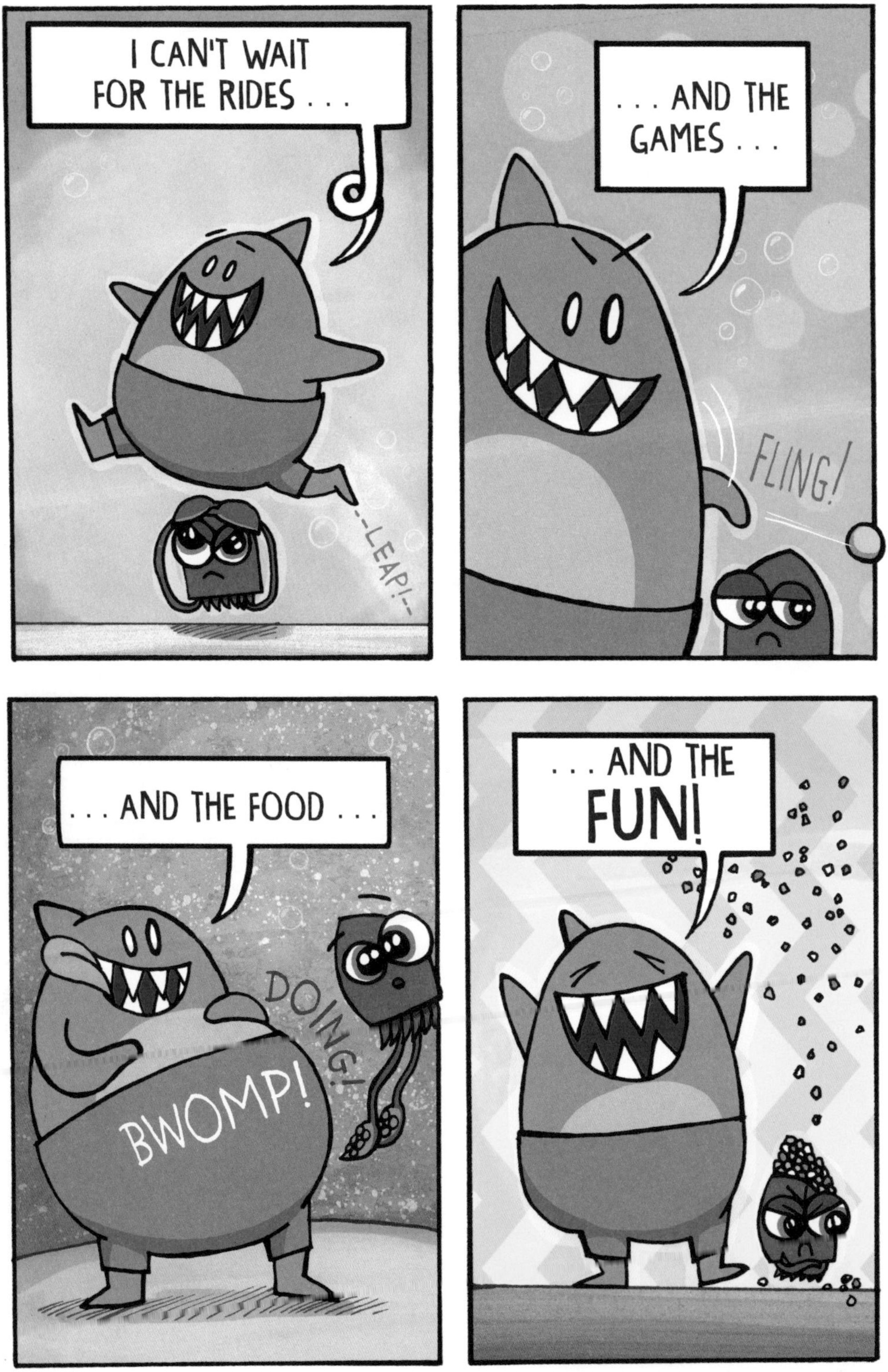
I CAN'T WAIT FOR THE RIDES . . .
LEAP!
. . . AND THE GAMES . . .
FLING!
. . . AND THE FOOD . . .
DOING!
BWOMP!
. . . AND THE FUN!

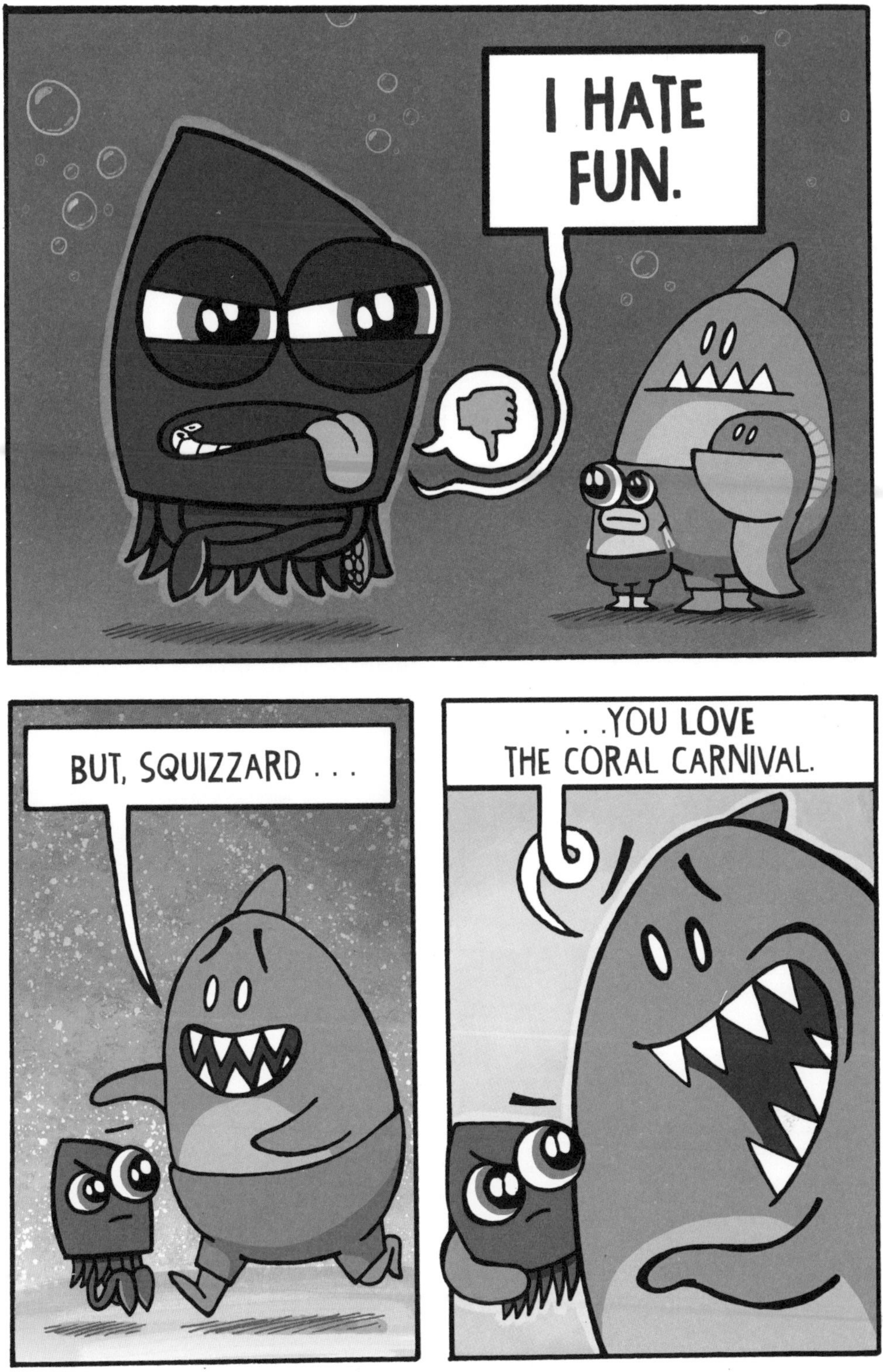
I HATE FUN.
BUT, SQUIZZARD . . .
. . .YOU LOVE THE CORAL CARNIVAL.

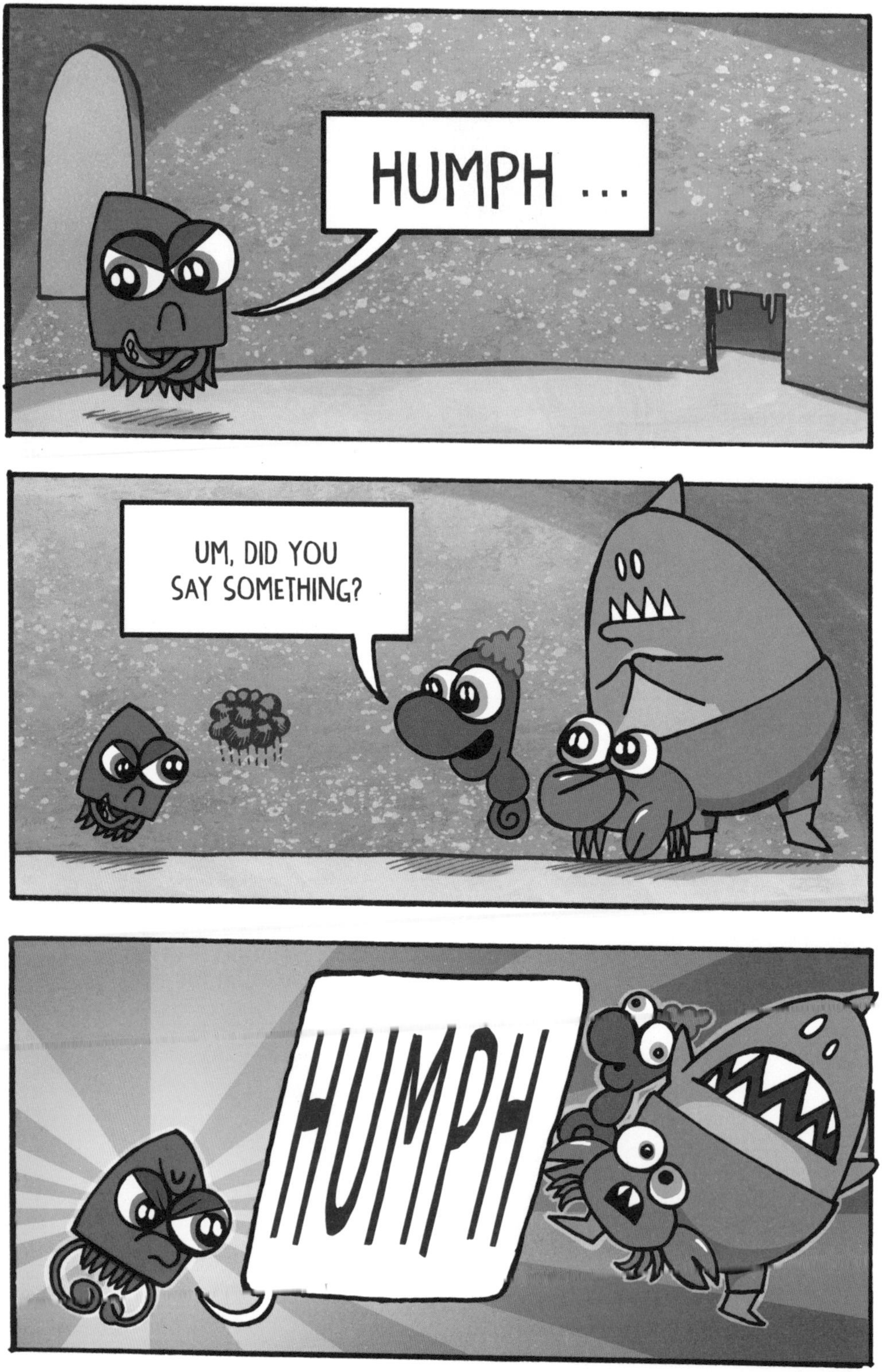
HUMPH ...
UM, DID YOU SAY SOMETHING?
HUMPH

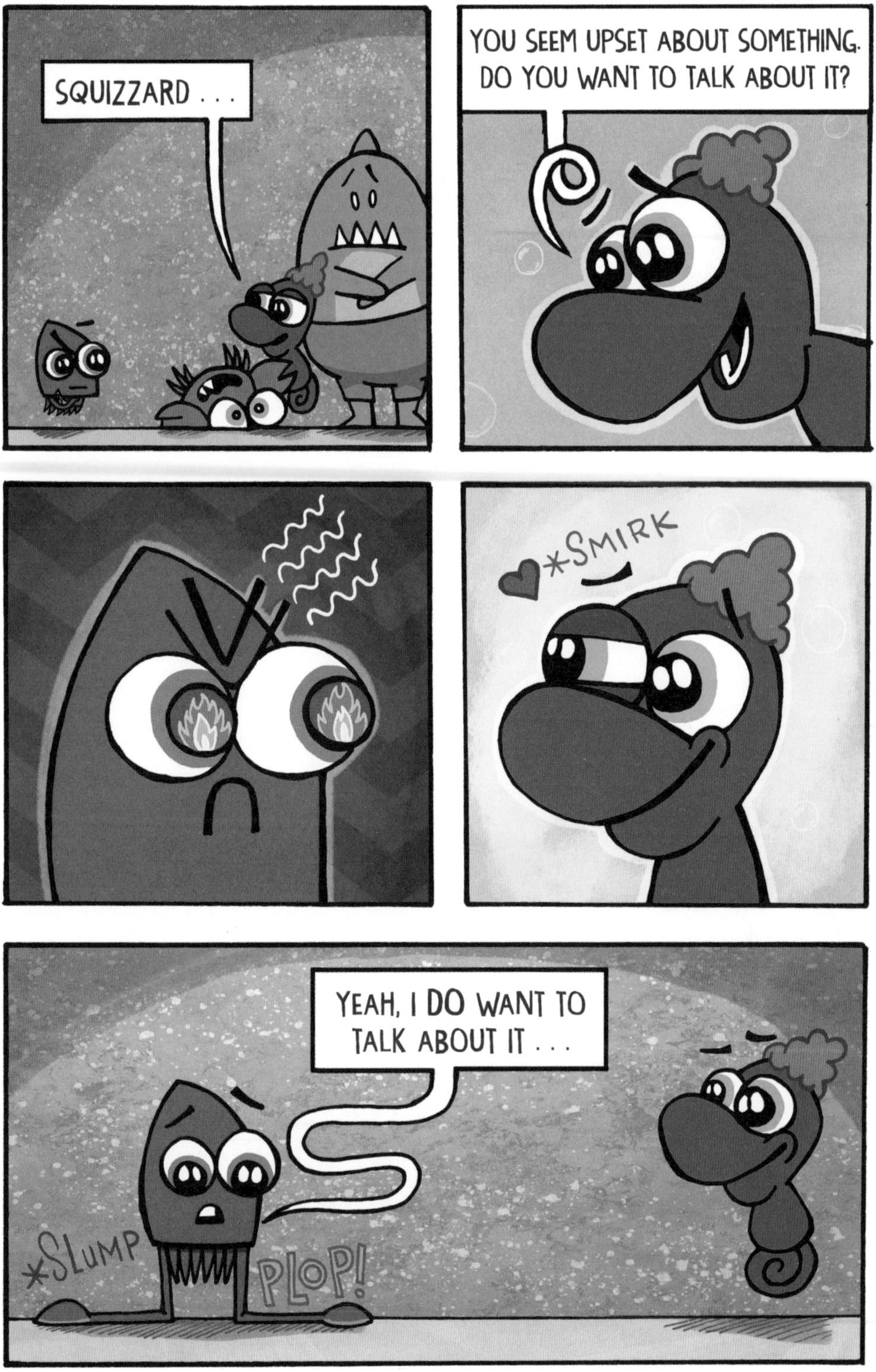
SQUIZZARD . . .
YOU SEEM UPSET ABOUT SOMETHING. DO YOU WANT TO TALK ABOUT IT?
*SMIRK
YEAH, I DO WANT TO TALK ABOUT IT . . .
*SLUMP
PLOP!

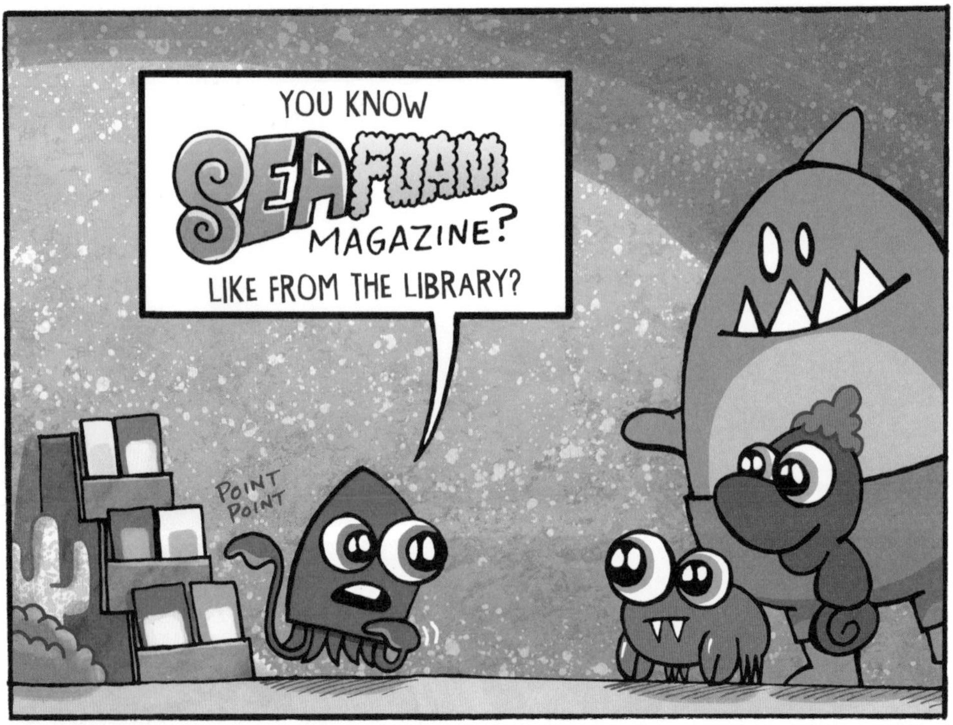
YOU KNOW SEAFOAM MAGAZINE? LIKE FROM THE LIBRARY?
POINT POINT

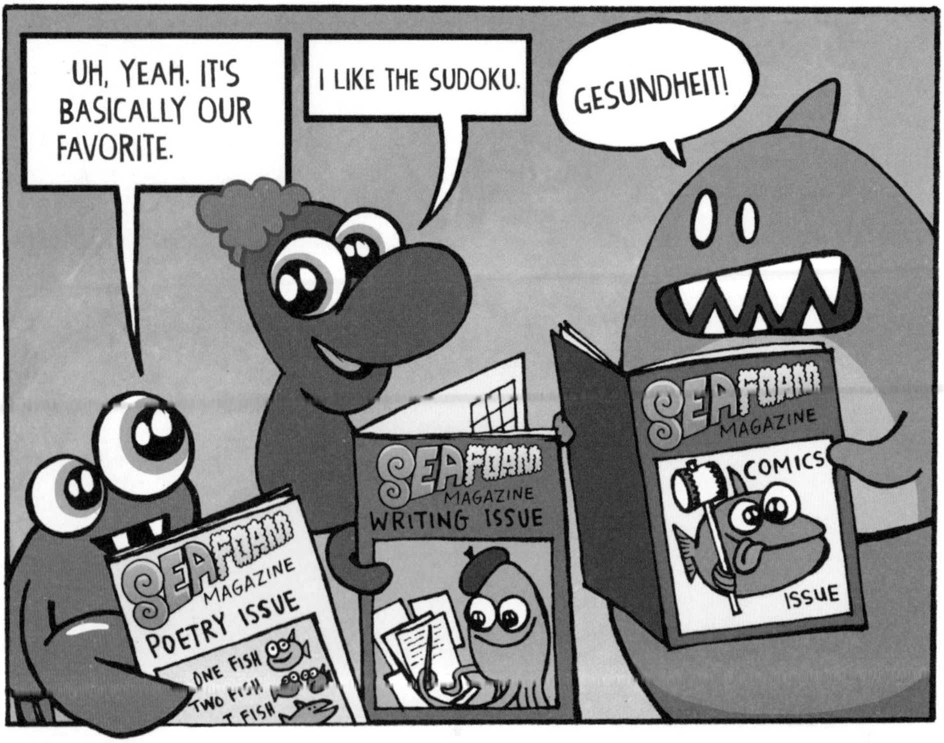
UH, YEAH. IT'S BASICALLY OUR FAVORITE.
I LIKE THE SUDOKU.
GESUNDHEIT!
SEAFOAM MAGAZINE POETRY ISSUE
ONE FISH TWO FISH
SEAFOAM MAGAZINE WRITING ISSUE
SEAFOAM MAGAZINE COMICS ISSUE

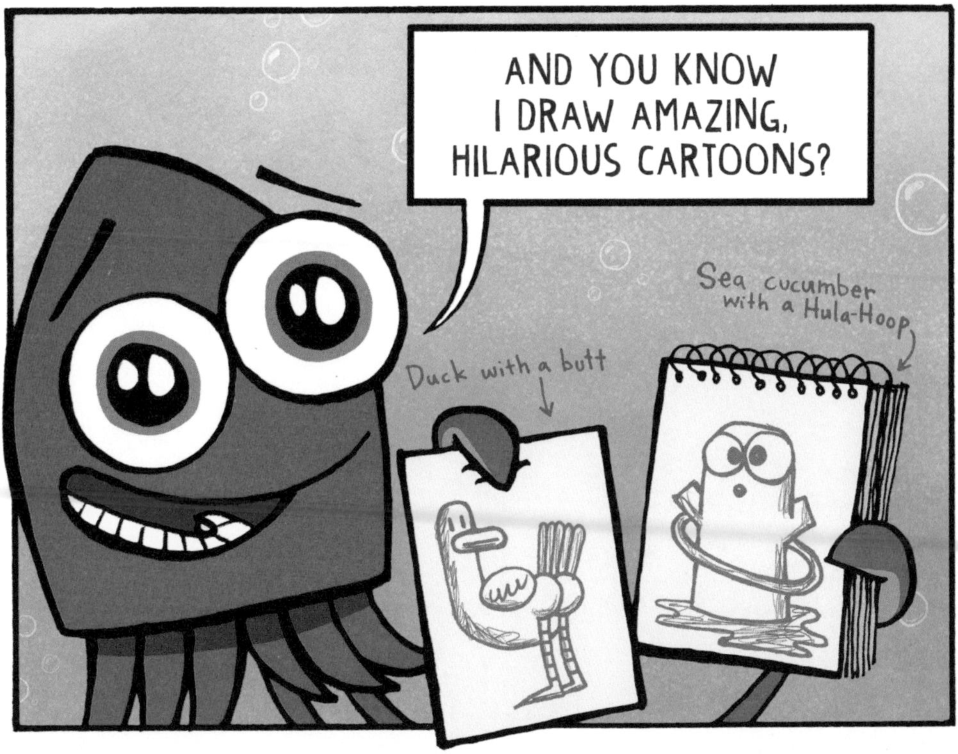
AND YOU KNOW I DRAW AMAZING, HILARIOUS CARTOONS?
Duck with a butt
Sea cucumber with a Hula-Hoop

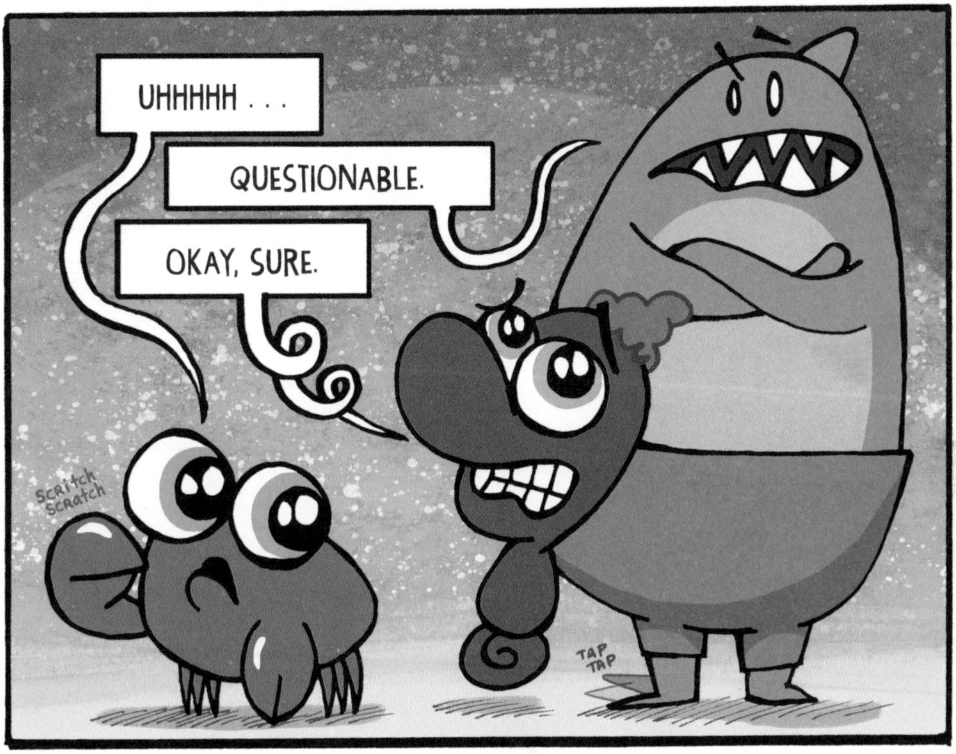
UHHHHH . . .
QUESTIONABLE.
OKAY, SURE.
SCRITCH SCRATCH
TAP TAP

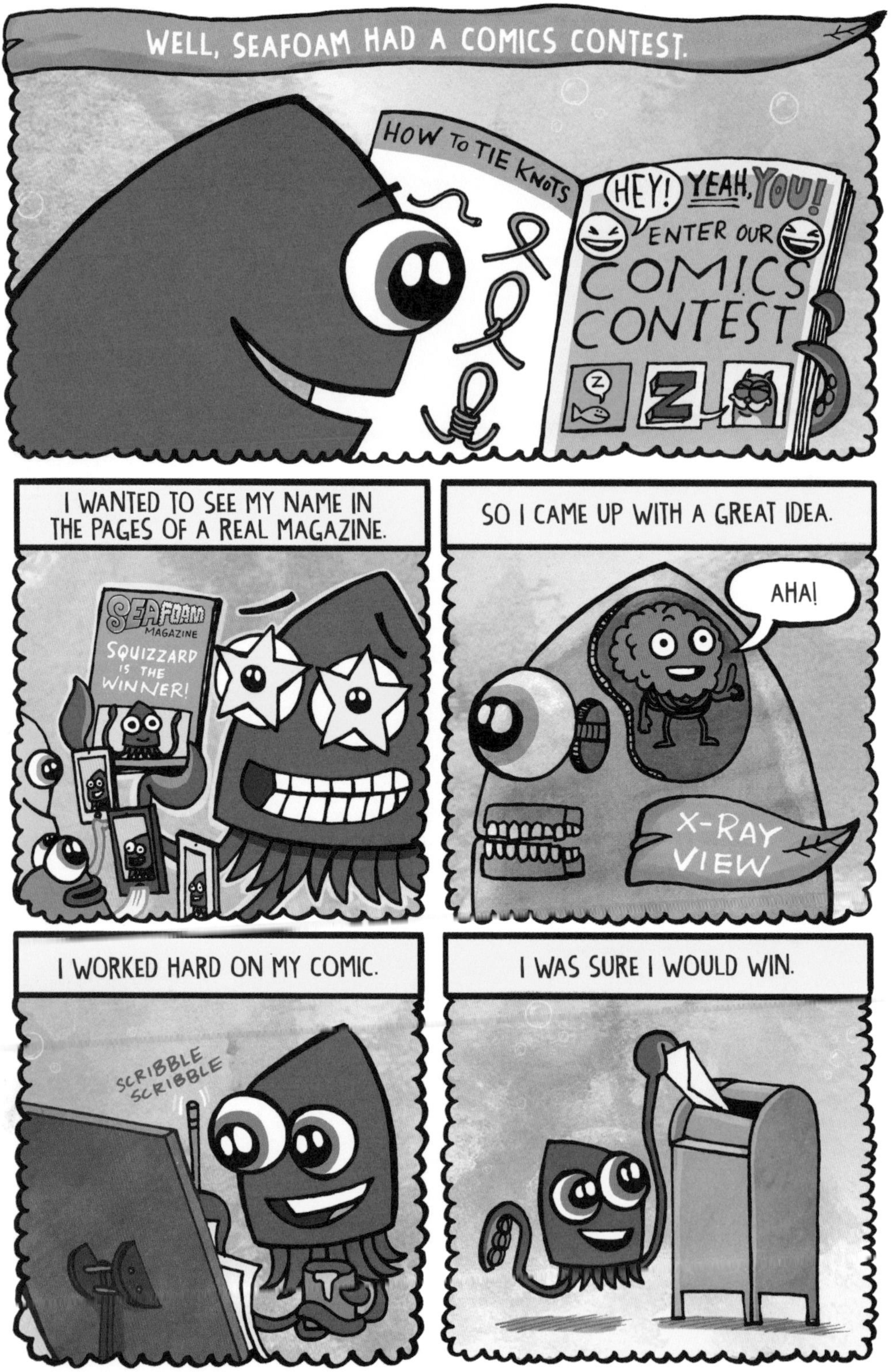
WELL, SEAFOAM HAD A COMICS CONTEST.
HOW TO TIE KNOTS
HEY!
YEAH, YOU!
ENTER OUR COMICS CONTEST
I WANTED TO SEE MY NAME IN THE PAGES OF A REAL MAGAZINE.
SEAFOAM MAGAZINE
SQUIZZARD IS THE WINNER!
SO I CAME UP WITH A GREAT IDEA.
AHA!
X-RAY VIEW
I WORKED HARD ON MY COMIC.
SCRIBBLE SCRIBBLE
I WAS SURE I WOULD WIN.

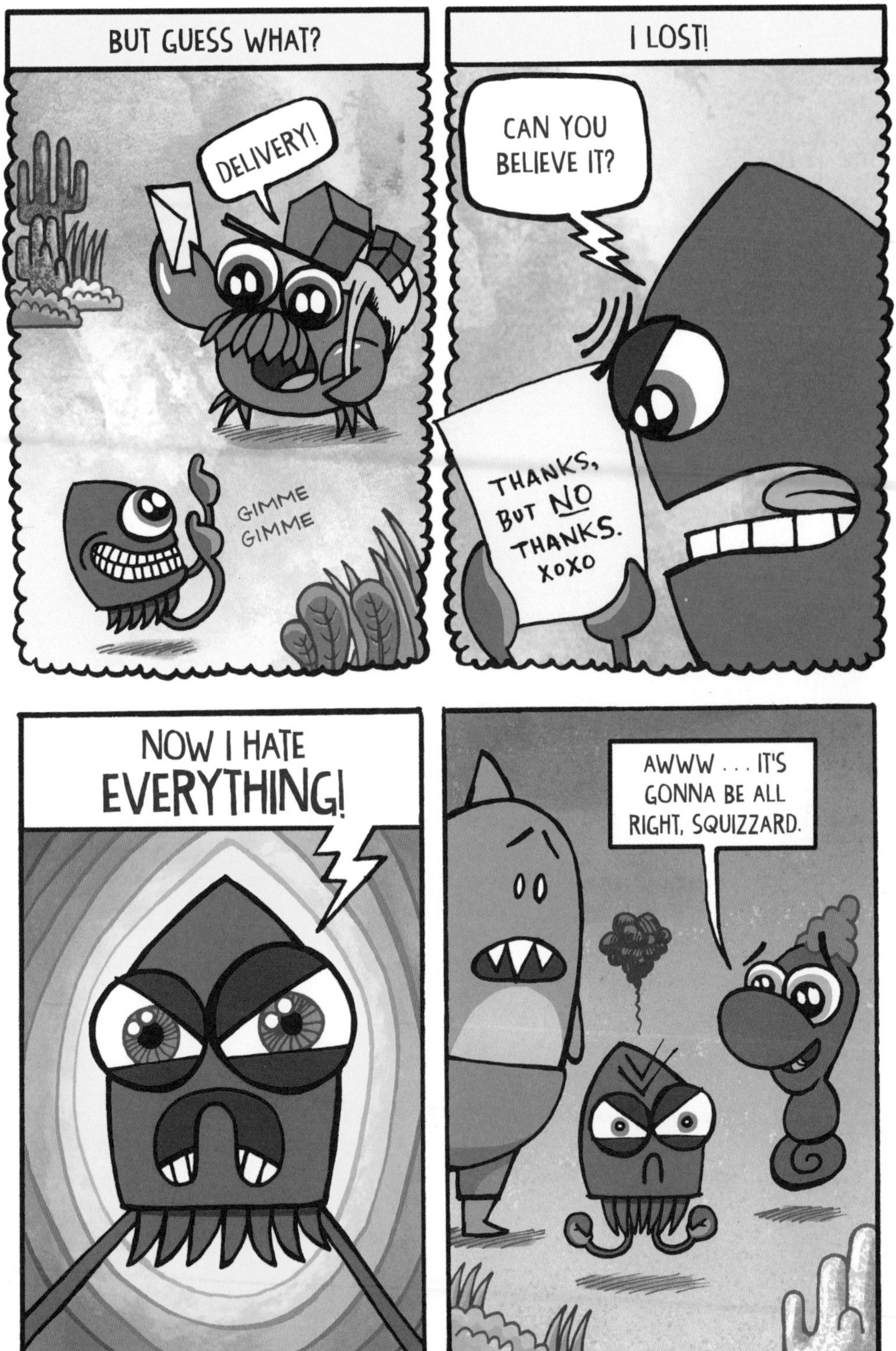
BUT GUESS WHAT?
DELIVERY!
GIMME GIMME
I LOST!
CAN YOU BELIEVE IT?
THANKS, BUT NO THANKS. XOXO
NOW I HATE EVERYTHING!
AWWW . . . IT'S GONNA BE ALL RIGHT, SQUIZZARD.

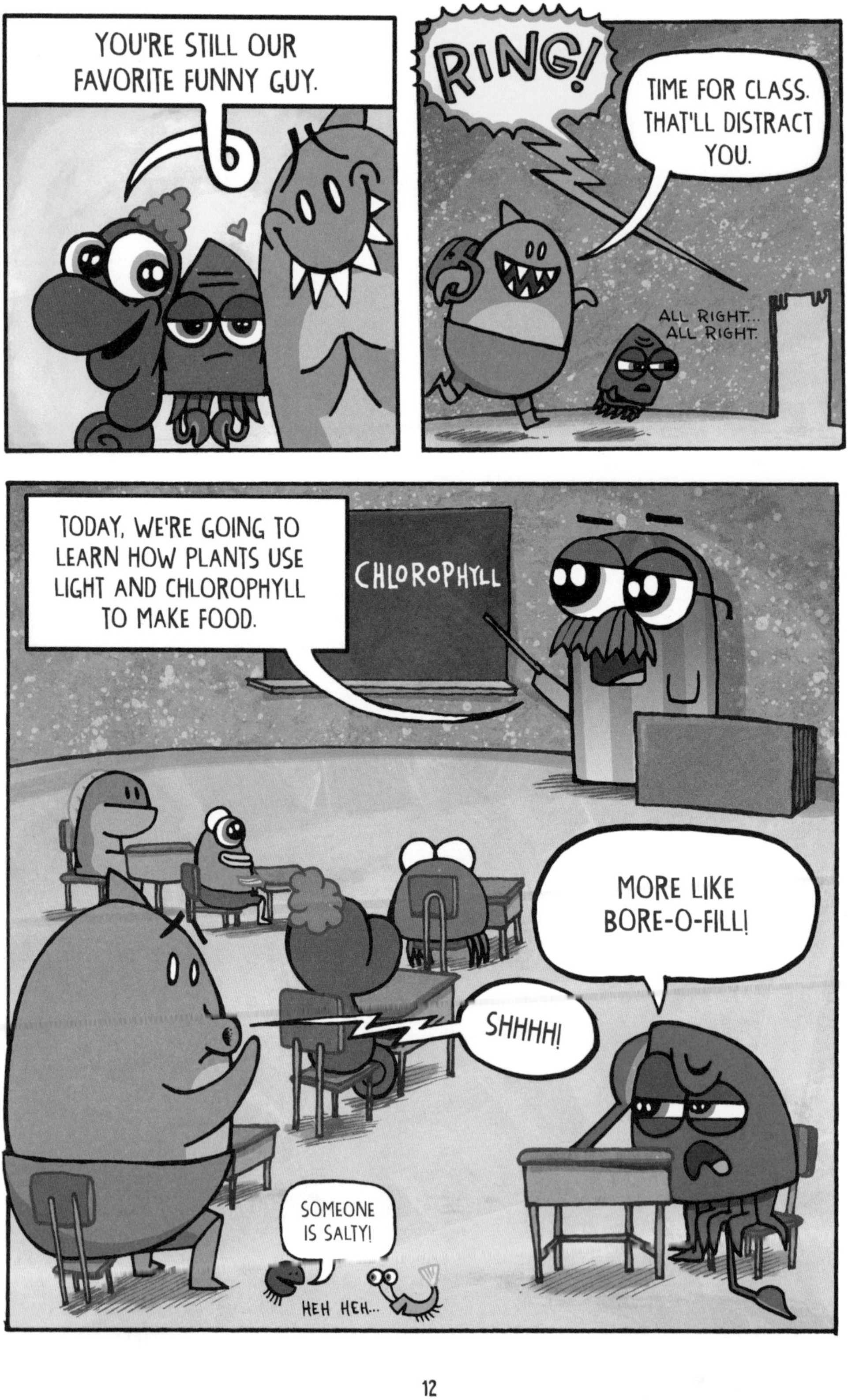
YOU'RE STILL OUR FAVORITE FUNNY GUY.
RING!
TIME FOR CLASS. THAT'LL DISTRACT YOU.
ALL RIGHT... ALL RIGHT.
TODAY, WE'RE GOING TO LEARN HOW PLANTS USE LIGHT AND CHLOROPHYLL TO MAKE FOOD.
CHLOROPHYLL
MORE LIKE BORE-O-FILL!
SHHHH!
SOMEONE IS SALTY!
HEH HEH...

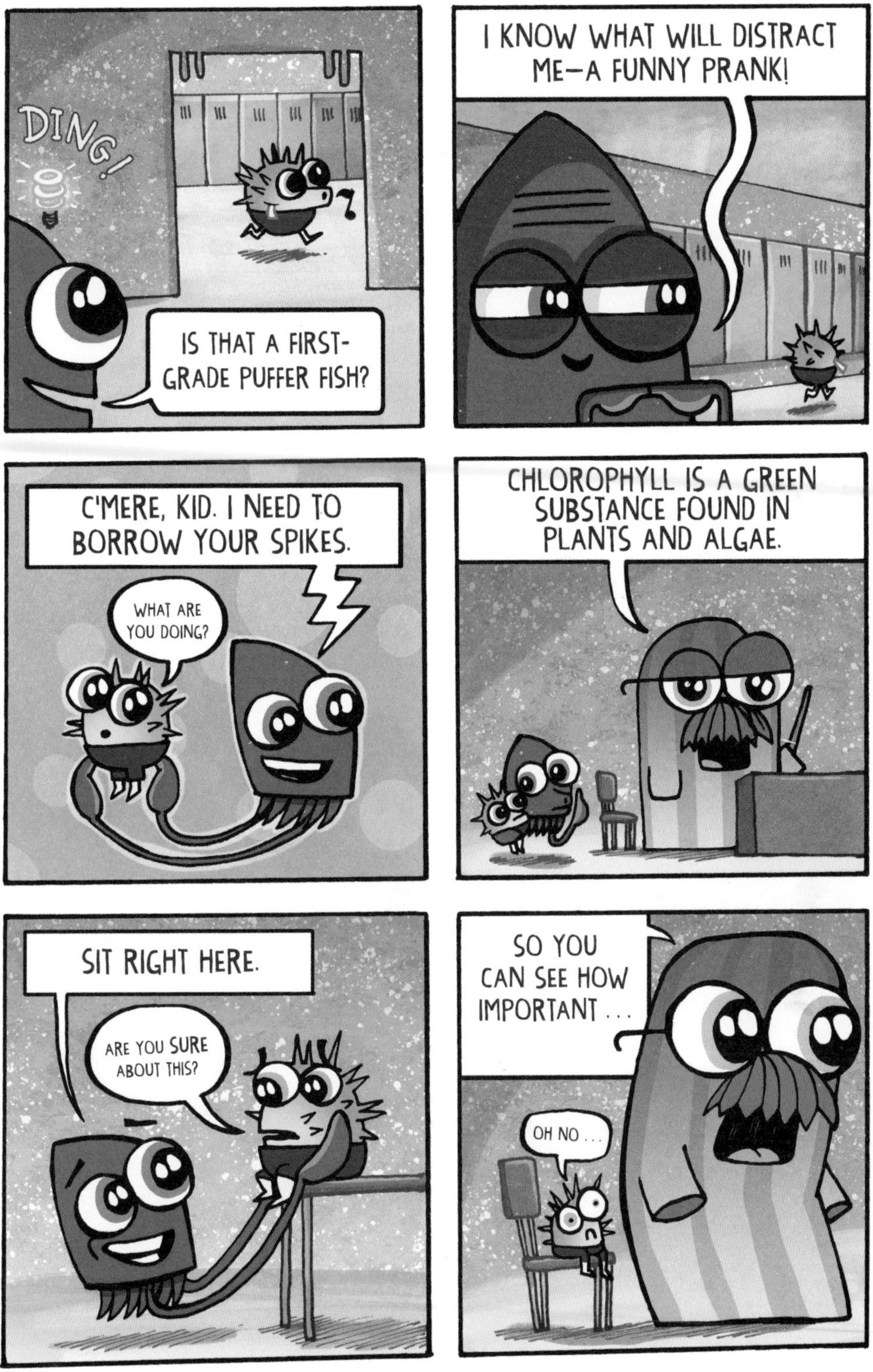
DING!
IS THAT A FIRST-GRADE PUFFER FISH?
I KNOW WHAT WILL DISTRACT ME—A FUNNY PRANK!
C'MERE, KID. I NEED TO BORROW YOUR SPIKES.
WHAT ARE YOU DOING?
CHLOROPHYLL IS A GREEN SUBSTANCE FOUND IN PLANTS AND ALGAE.
SIT RIGHT HERE.
ARE YOU SURE ABOUT THIS?
SO YOU CAN SEE HOW IMPORTANT . . .
OH NO . . .

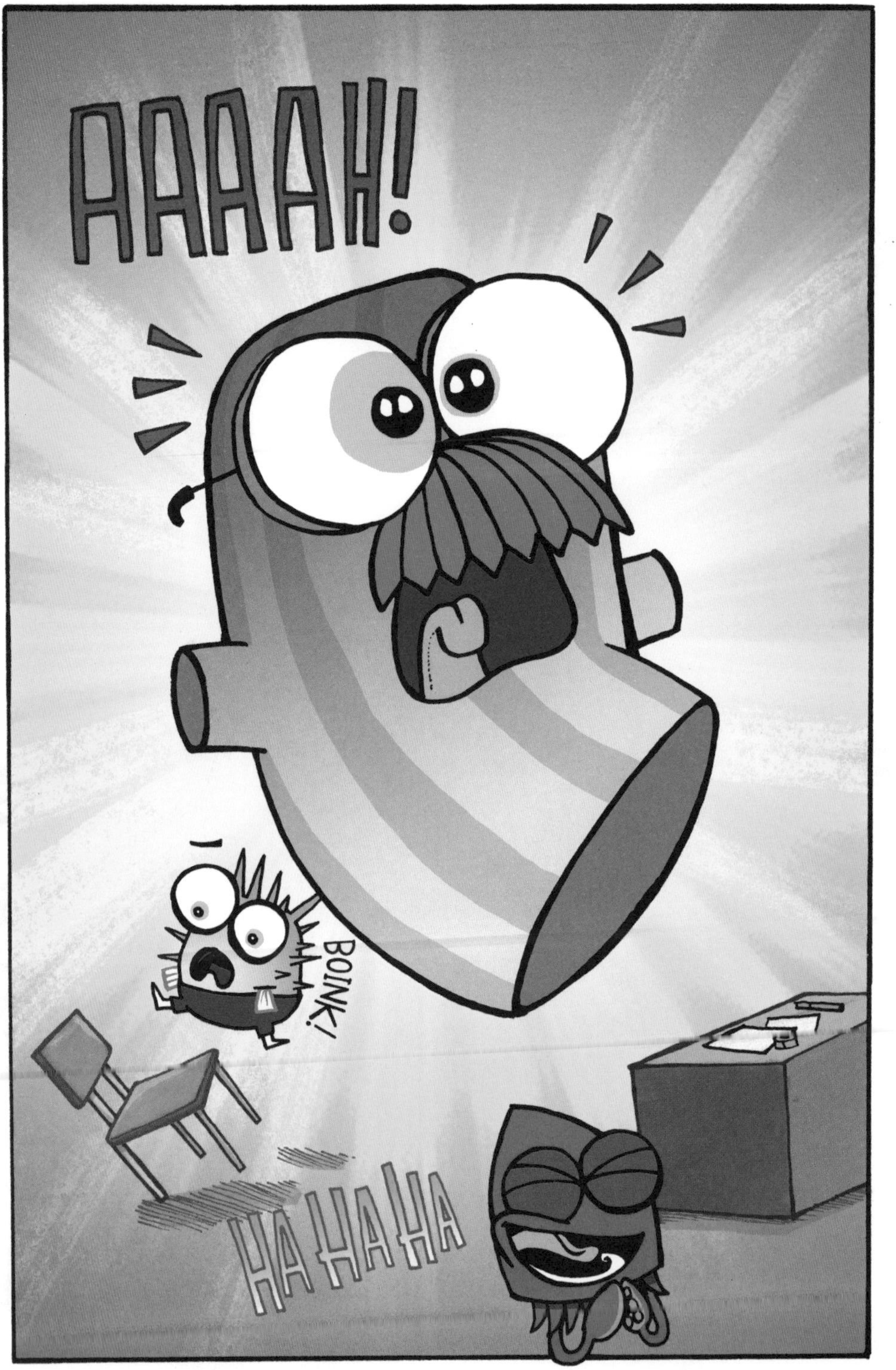
AAAAH!
BOINK!
HA HA HA

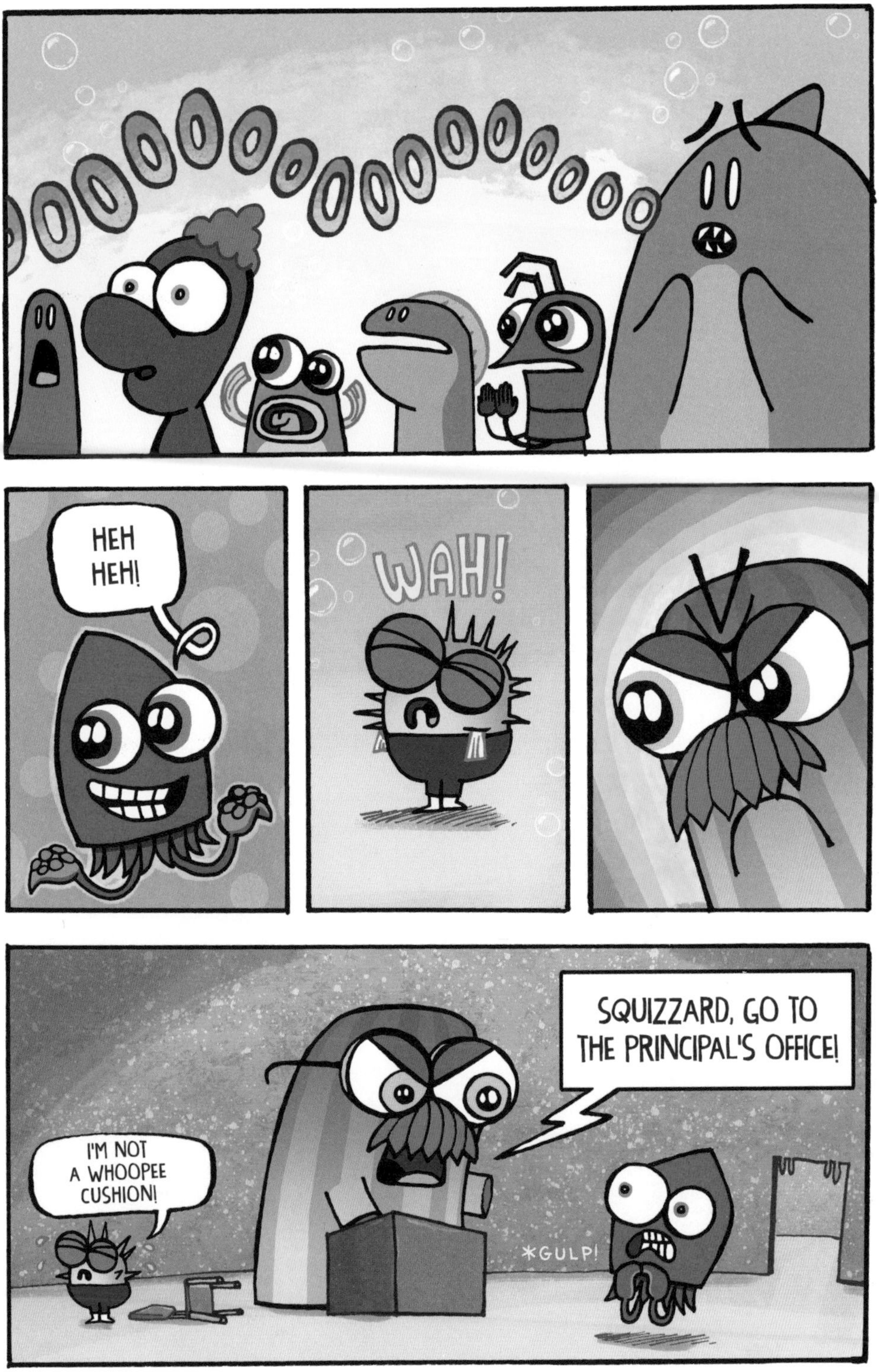
OOOOOOOOOOOOOOOOOO
HEH HEH!
WAH!
SQUIZZARD, GO TO THE PRINCIPAL'S OFFICE!
I'M NOT A WHOOPEE CUSHION!
*GULP!

CHAPTER 2

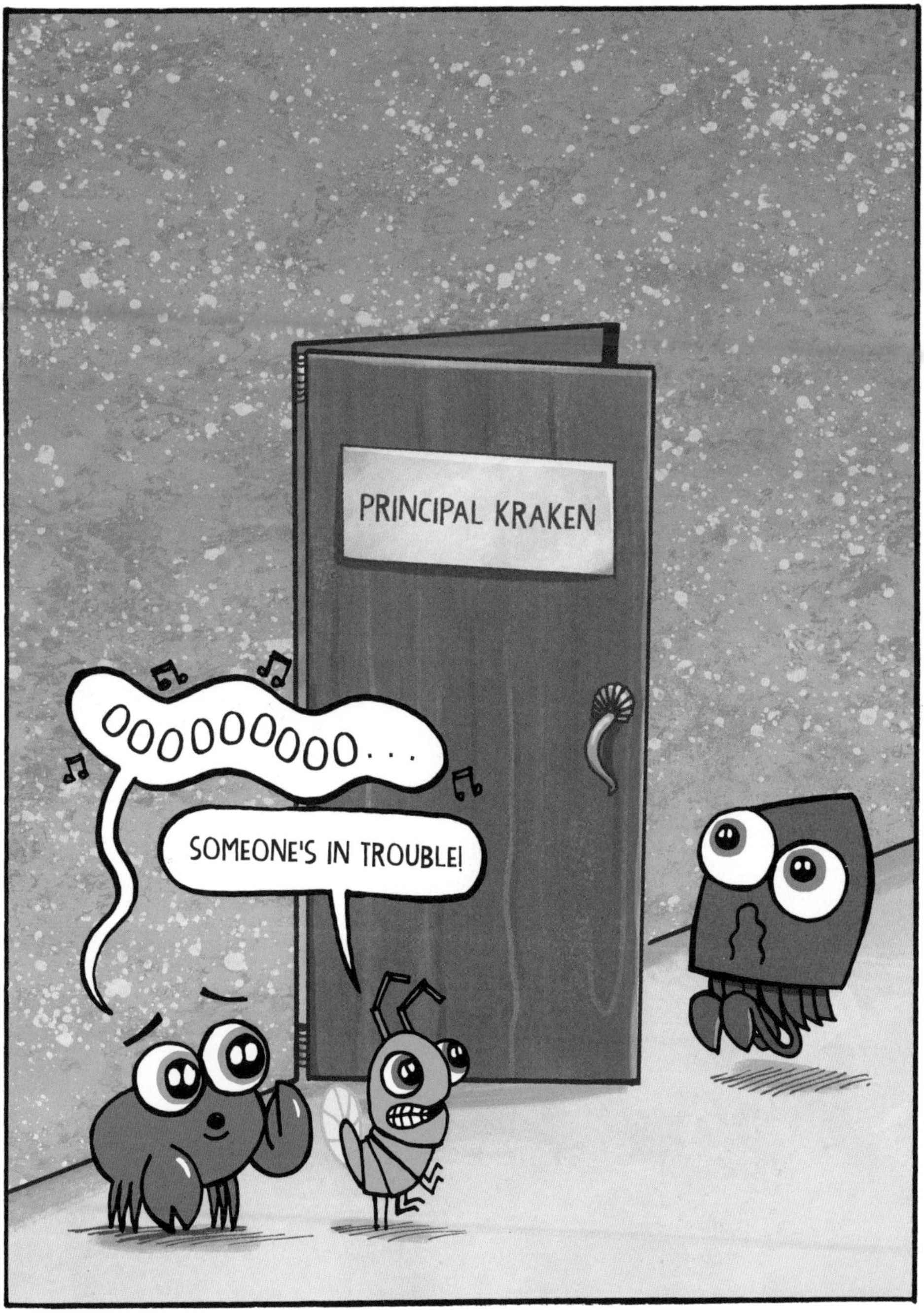
PRINCIPAL KRAKEN
OOOOOOOOO . . .
SOMEONE'S IN TROUBLE!

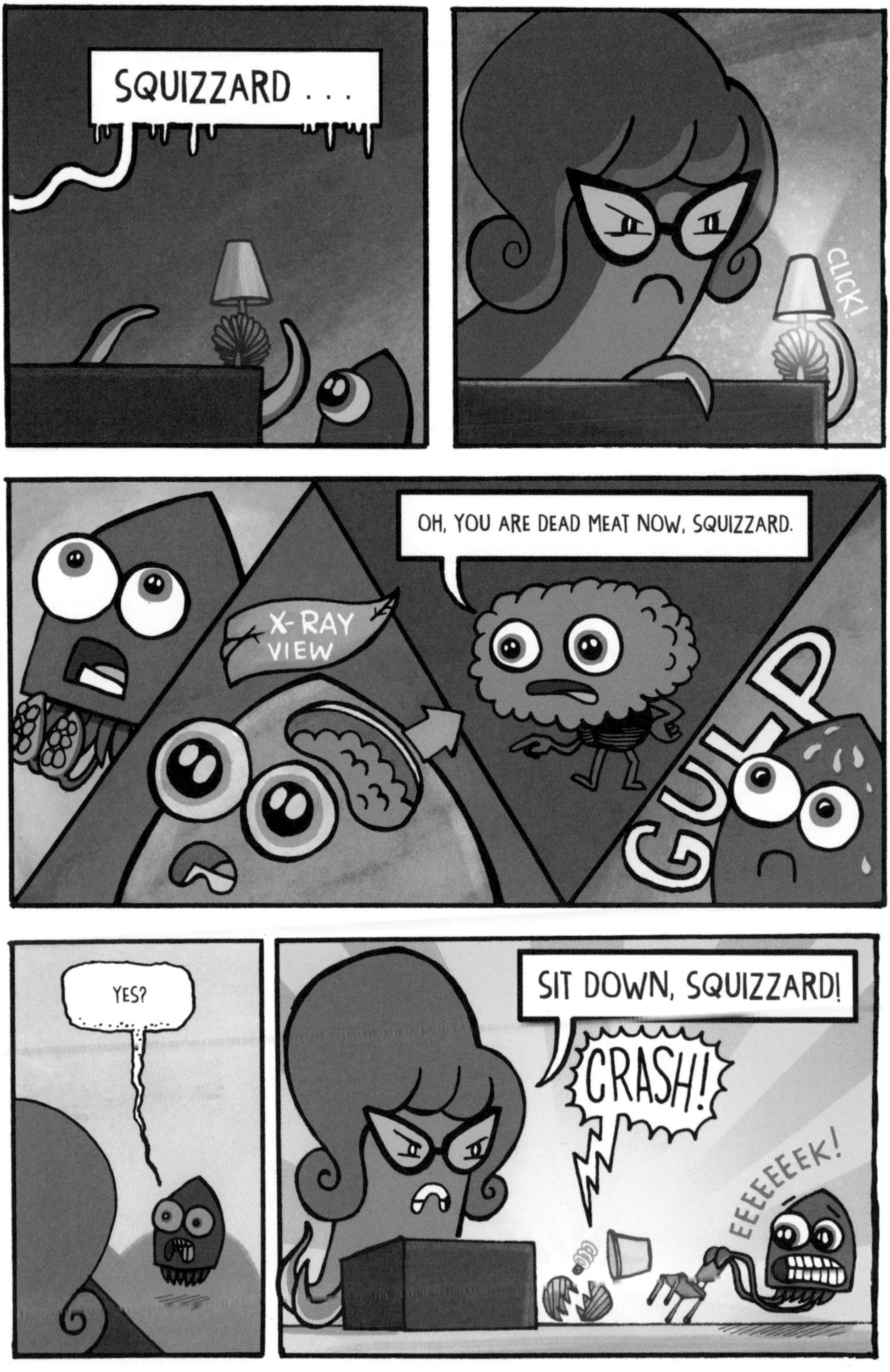
SQUIZZARD . . .
CLICK!
X-RAY VIEW
OH, YOU ARE DEAD MEAT NOW, SQUIZZARD.
GULP
YES?
SIT DOWN, SQUIZZARD!
CRASH!
EEEEEEEK!

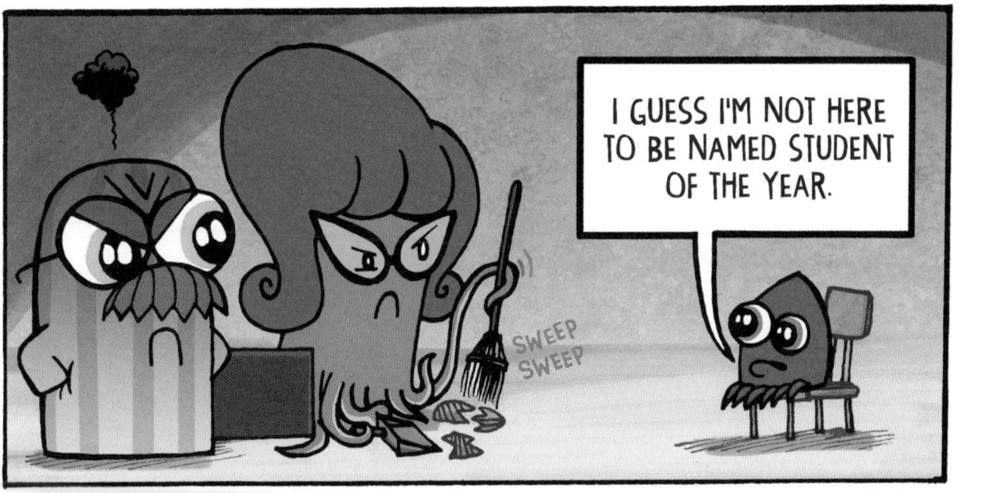
I GUESS I'M NOT HERE TO BE NAMED STUDENT OF THE YEAR.
SWEEP SWEEP

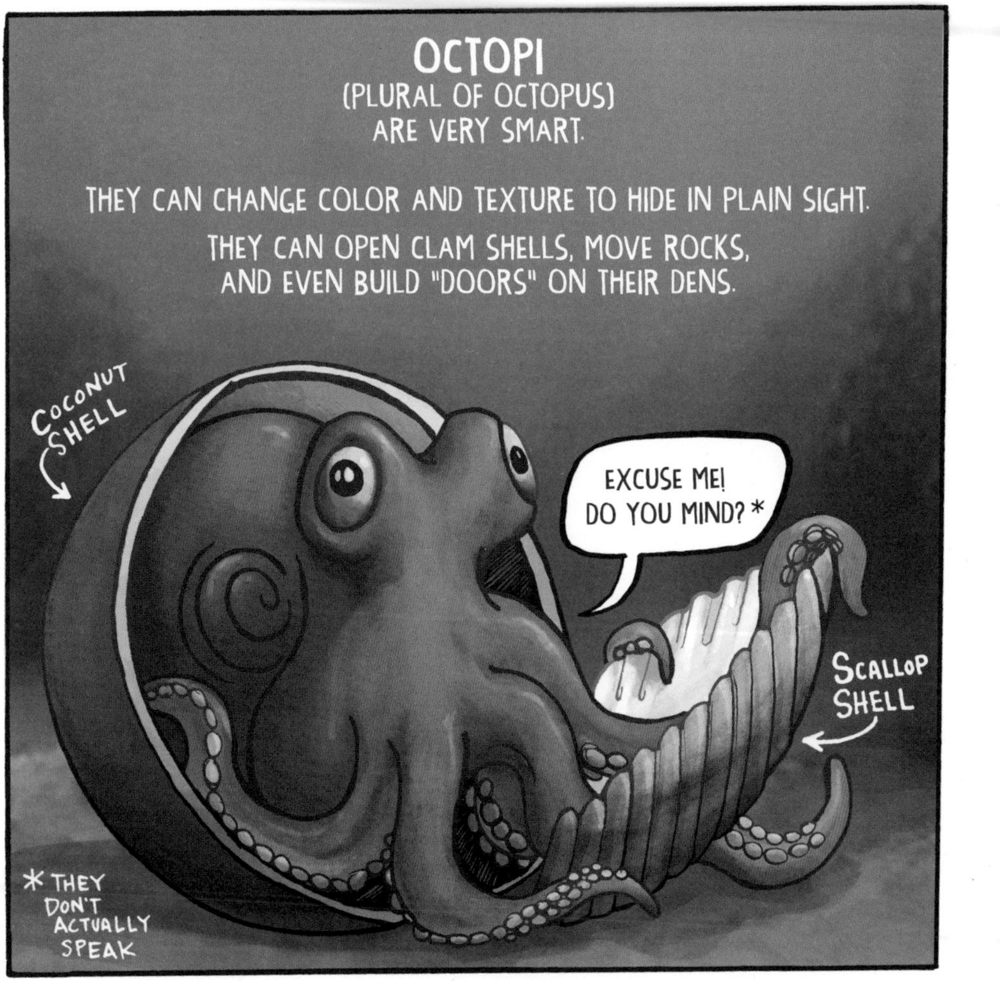
OCTOPI
(PLURAL OF OCTOPUS) ARE VERY SMART.
THEY CAN CHANGE COLOR AND TEXTURE TO HIDE IN PLAIN SIGHT.
THEY CAN OPEN CLAM SHELLS, MOVE ROCKS, AND EVEN BUILD "DOORS" ON THEIR DENS.
COCONUT SHELL
EXCUSE ME! DO YOU MIND? *
SCALLOP SHELL
* THEY DON'T ACTUALLY SPEAK

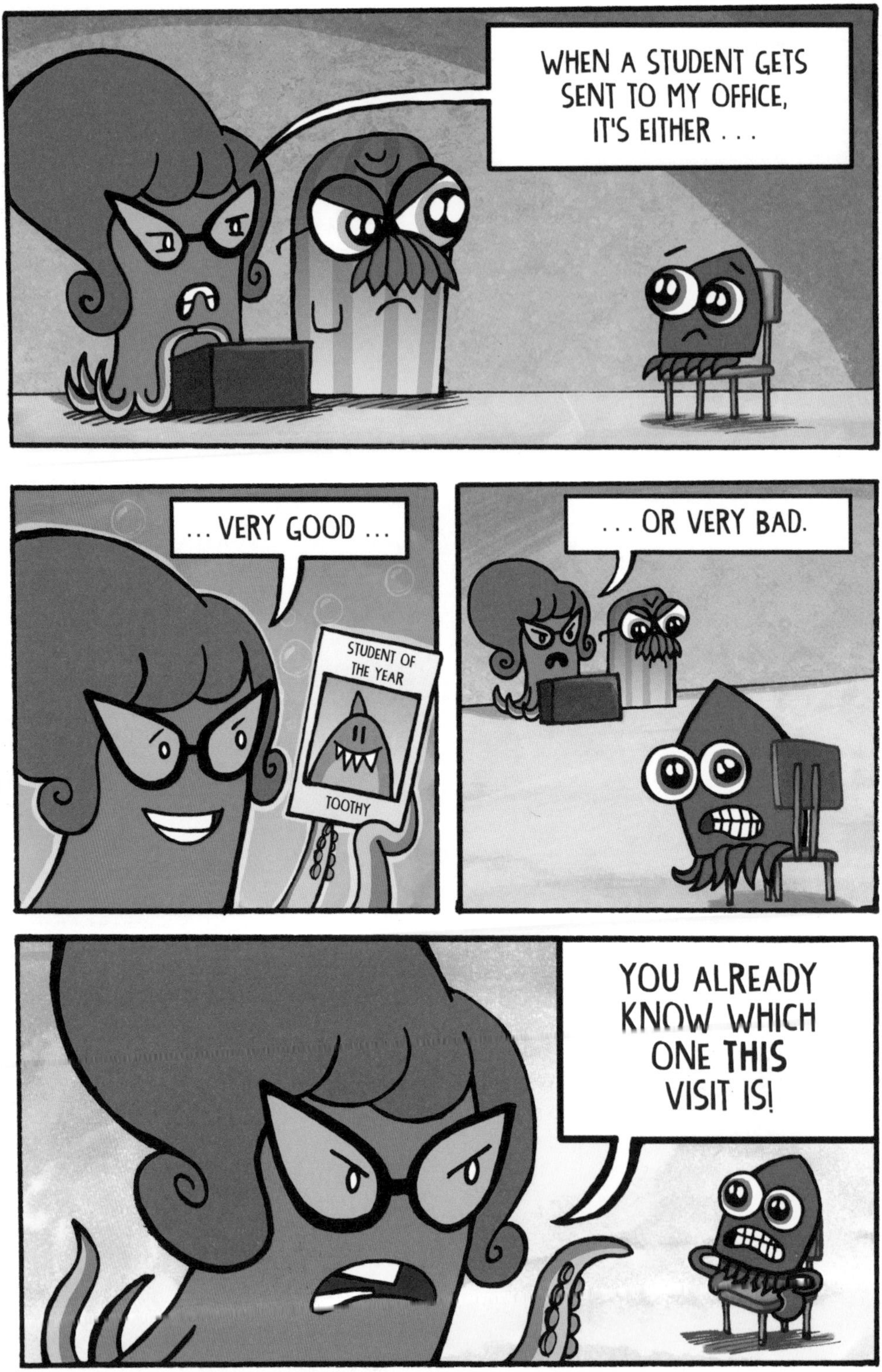
WHEN A STUDENT GETS SENT TO MY OFFICE, IT'S EITHER . . .
... VERY GOOD ...
STUDENT OF THE YEAR
TOOTHY
. . . OR VERY BAD.
YOU ALREADY KNOW WHICH ONE THIS VISIT IS!

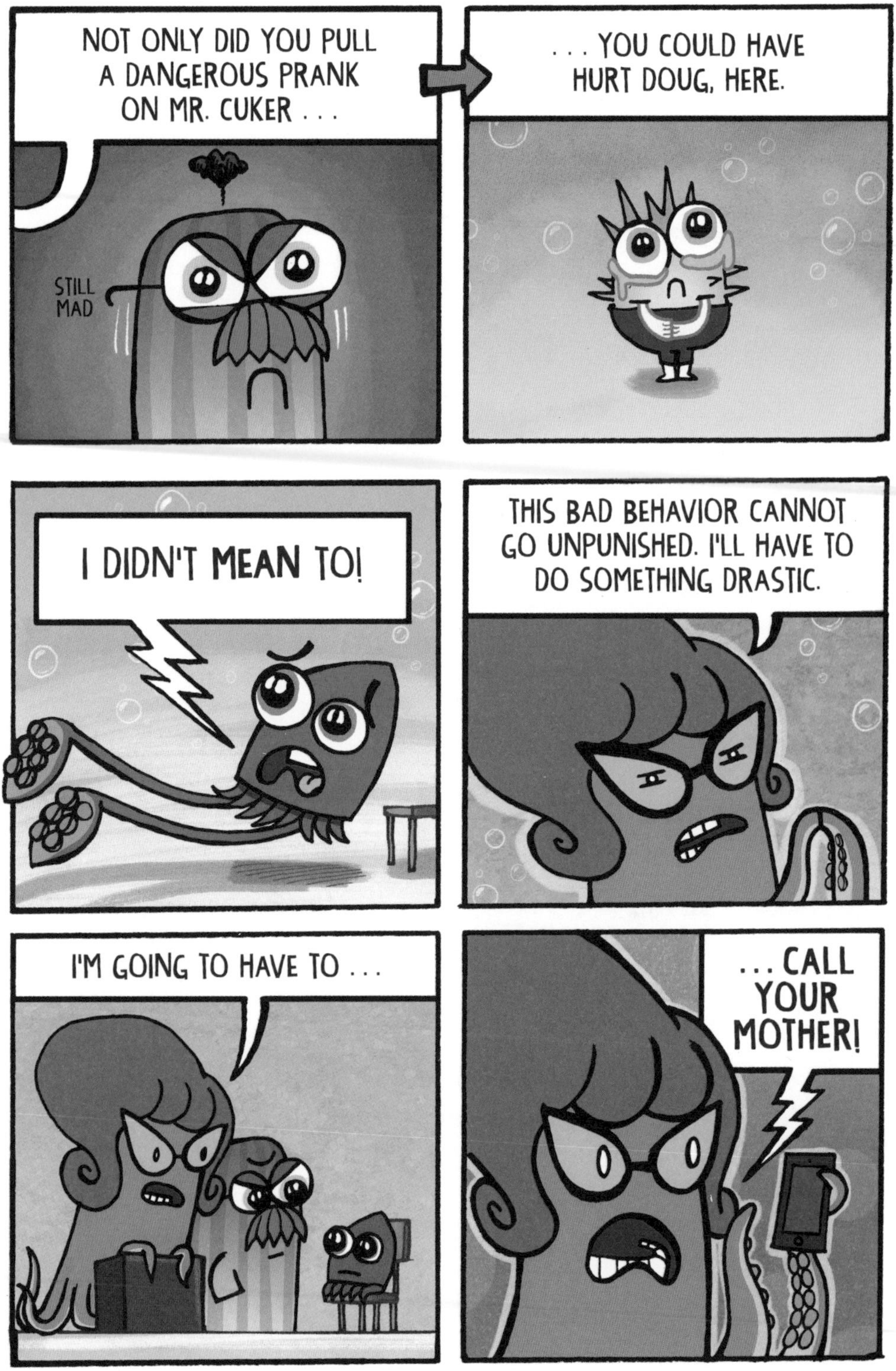
NOT ONLY DID YOU PULL A DANGEROUS PRANK ON MR. CUKER . . .
STILL MAD
. . . YOU COULD HAVE HURT DOUG, HERE.
I DIDN'T MEAN TO!
THIS BAD BEHAVIOR CANNOT GO UNPUNISHED. I'LL HAVE TO DO SOMETHING DRASTIC.
I'M GOING TO HAVE TO . . .
. . . CALL YOUR MOTHER!

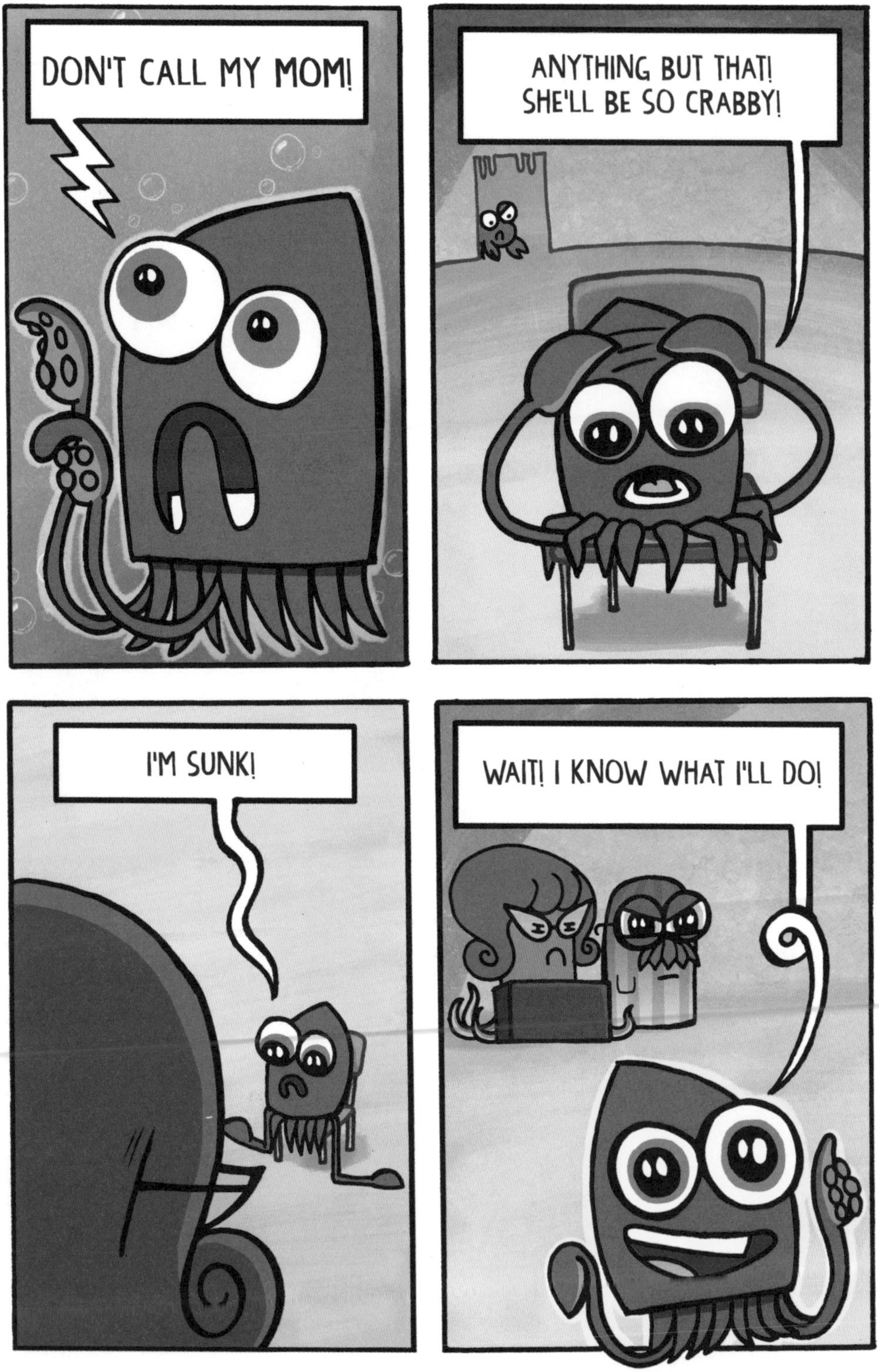
DON'T CALL MY MOM!
ANYTHING BUT THAT! SHE'LL BE SO CRABBY!
I'M SUNK!
WAIT! I KNOW WHAT I'LL DO!

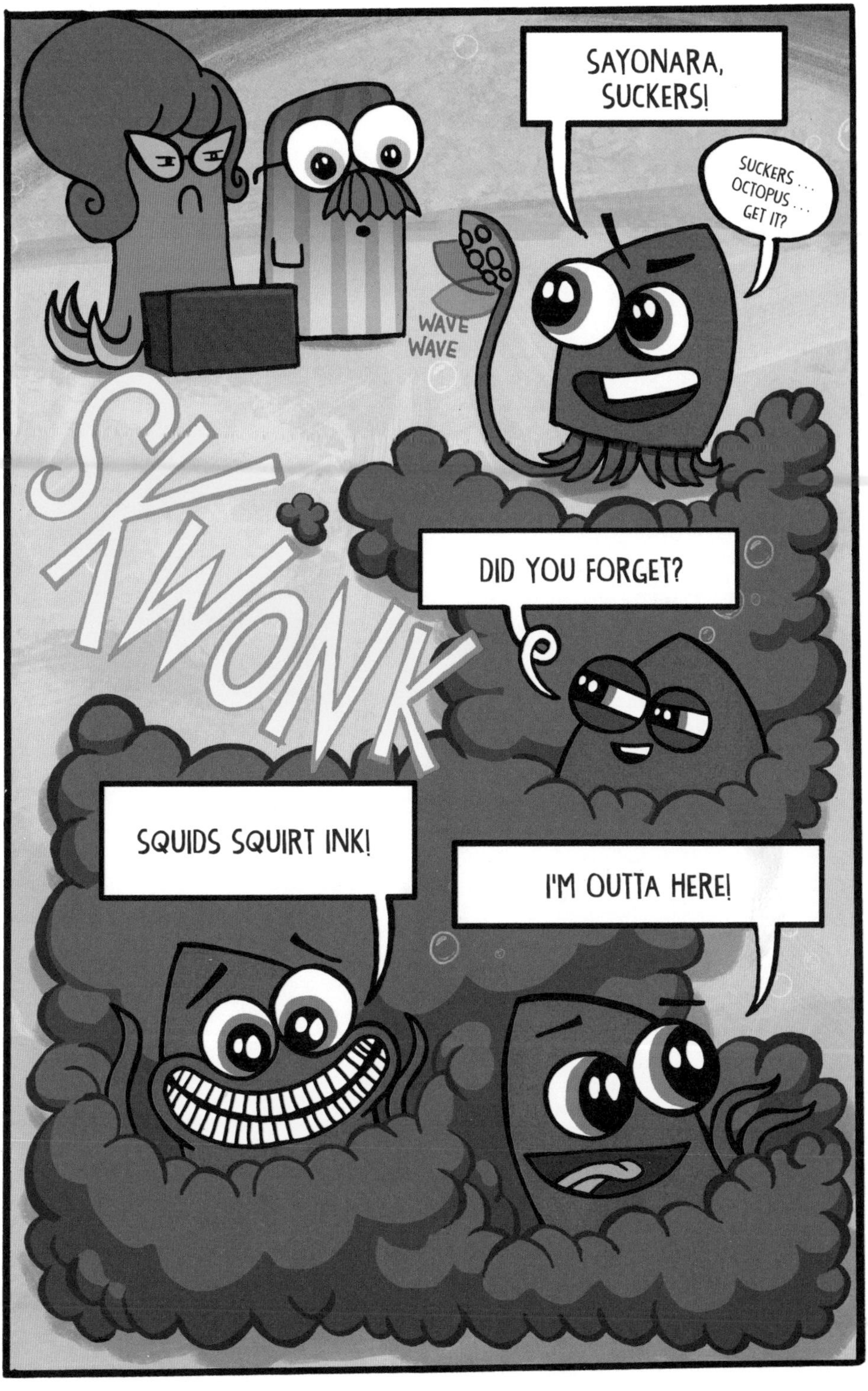
SAYONARA, SUCKERS!
SUCKERS . . . OCTOPUS . . . GET IT?
WAVE WAVE
SKWONK
DID YOU FORGET?
SQUIDS SQUIRT INK!
I'M OUTTA HERE!

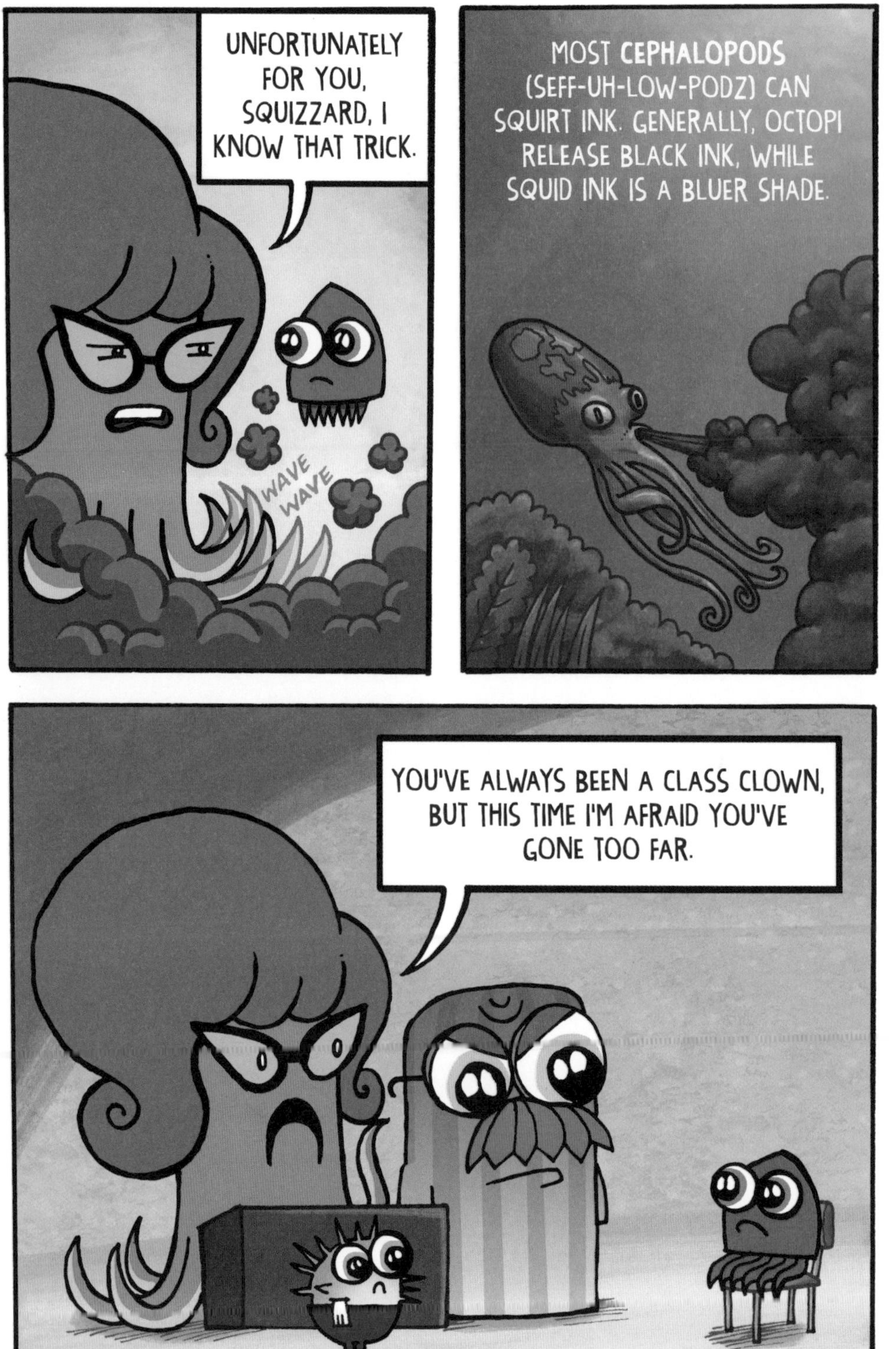
UNFORTUNATELY FOR YOU, SQUIZZARD, I KNOW THAT TRICK.
WAVE WAVE
MOST **CEPHALOPODS** (SEFF-UH-LOW-PODZ) CAN SQUIRT INK. GENERALLY, OCTOPI RELEASE BLACK INK, WHILE SQUID INK IS A BLUER SHADE.
YOU'VE ALWAYS BEEN A CLASS CLOWN, BUT THIS TIME I'M AFRAID YOU'VE GONE TOO FAR.

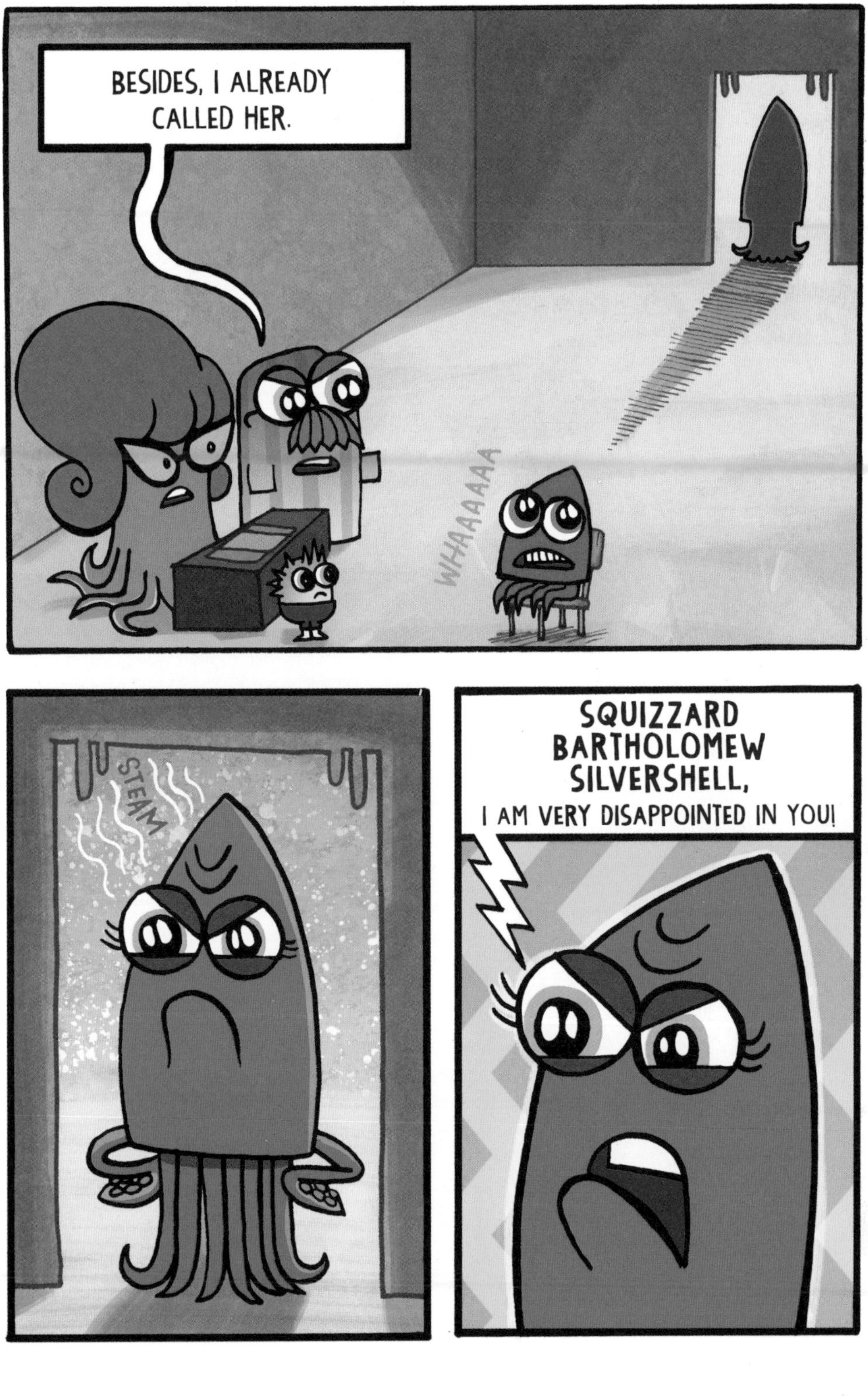
BESIDES, I ALREADY CALLED HER.
WHAAAAAA
STEAM
SQUIZZARD BARTHOLOMEW SILVERSHELL,
I AM VERY DISAPPOINTED IN YOU!

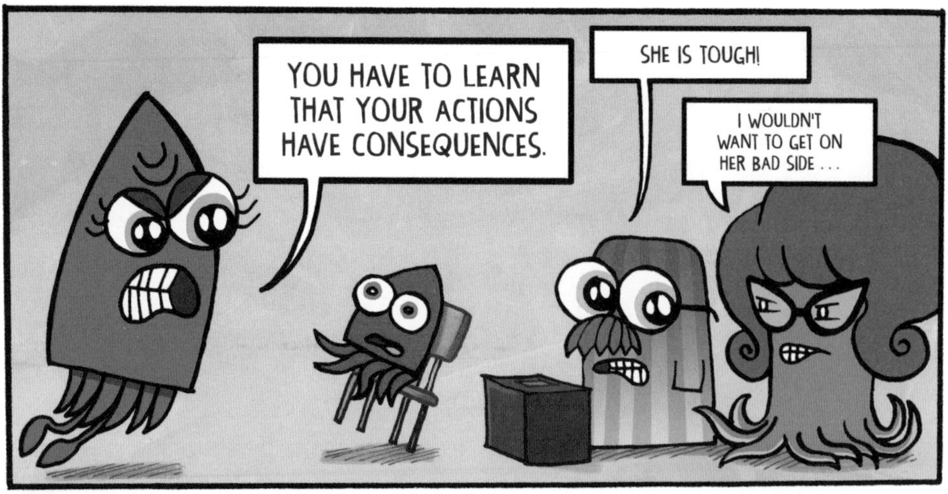
YOU HAVE TO LEARN THAT YOUR ACTIONS HAVE CONSEQUENCES.
SHE IS TOUGH!
I WOULDN'T WANT TO GET ON HER BAD SIDE . . .

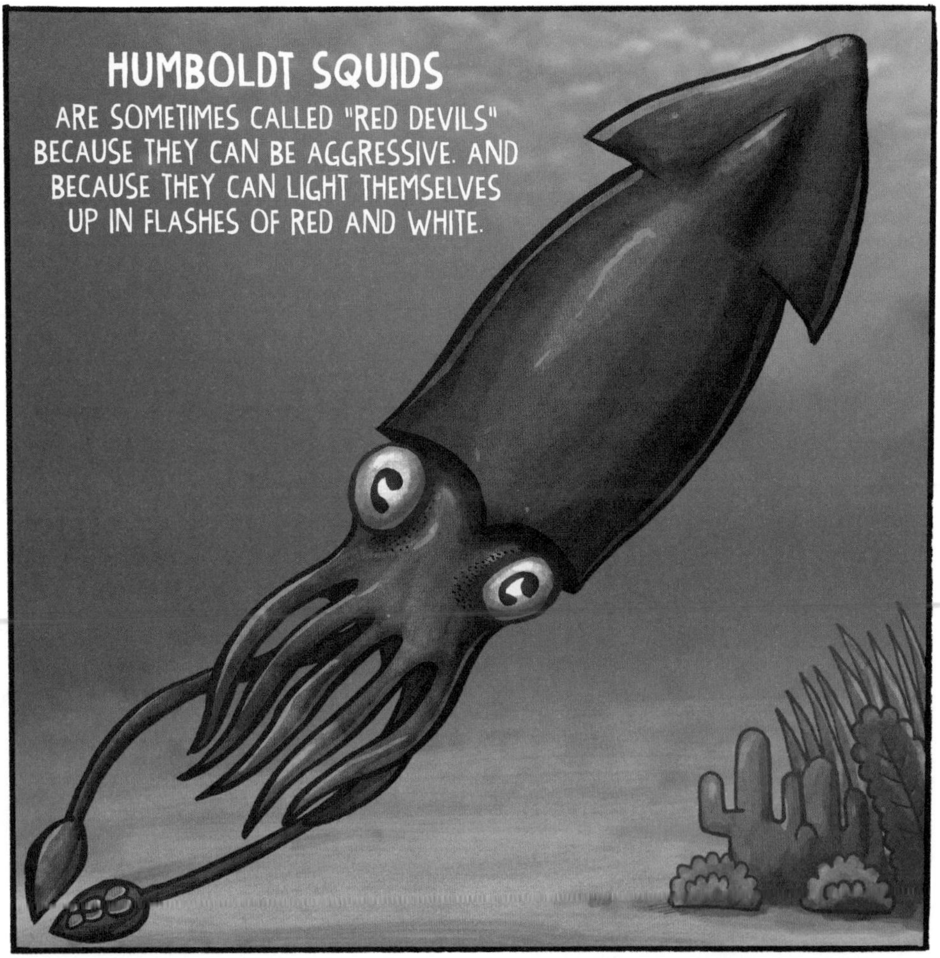
HUMBOLDT SQUIDS
ARE SOMETIMES CALLED "RED DEVILS" BECAUSE THEY CAN BE AGGRESSIVE. AND BECAUSE THEY CAN LIGHT THEMSELVES UP IN FLASHES OF RED AND WHITE.

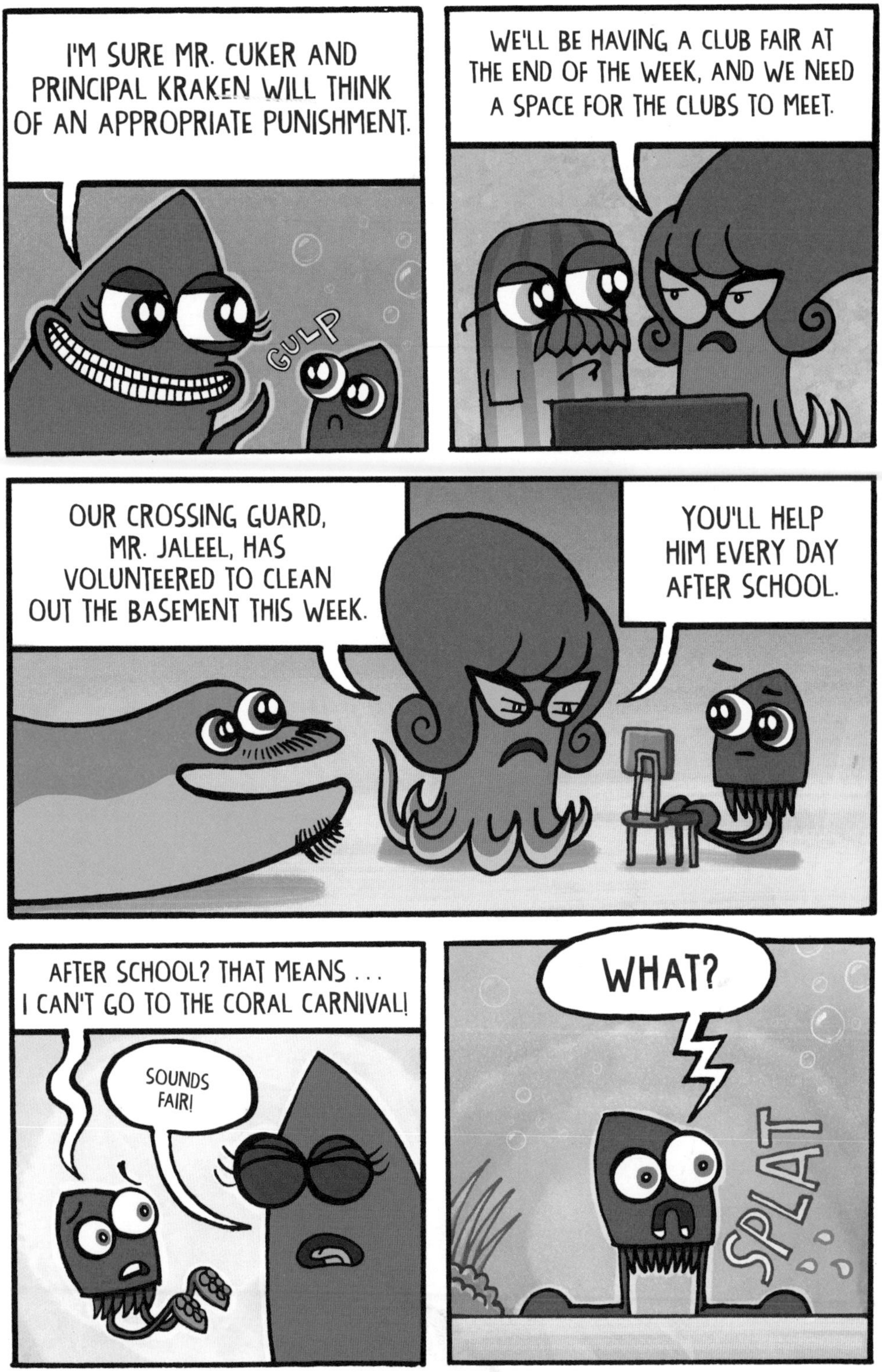
I'M SURE MR. CUKER AND PRINCIPAL KRAKEN WILL THINK OF AN APPROPRIATE PUNISHMENT.
GULP
WE'LL BE HAVING A CLUB FAIR AT THE END OF THE WEEK, AND WE NEED A SPACE FOR THE CLUBS TO MEET.
OUR CROSSING GUARD, MR. JALEEL, HAS VOLUNTEERED TO CLEAN OUT THE BASEMENT THIS WEEK.
YOU'LL HELP HIM EVERY DAY AFTER SCHOOL.
AFTER SCHOOL? THAT MEANS . . . I CAN'T GO TO THE CORAL CARNIVAL!
SOUNDS FAIR!
WHAT?
SPLAT

CHAPTER 3

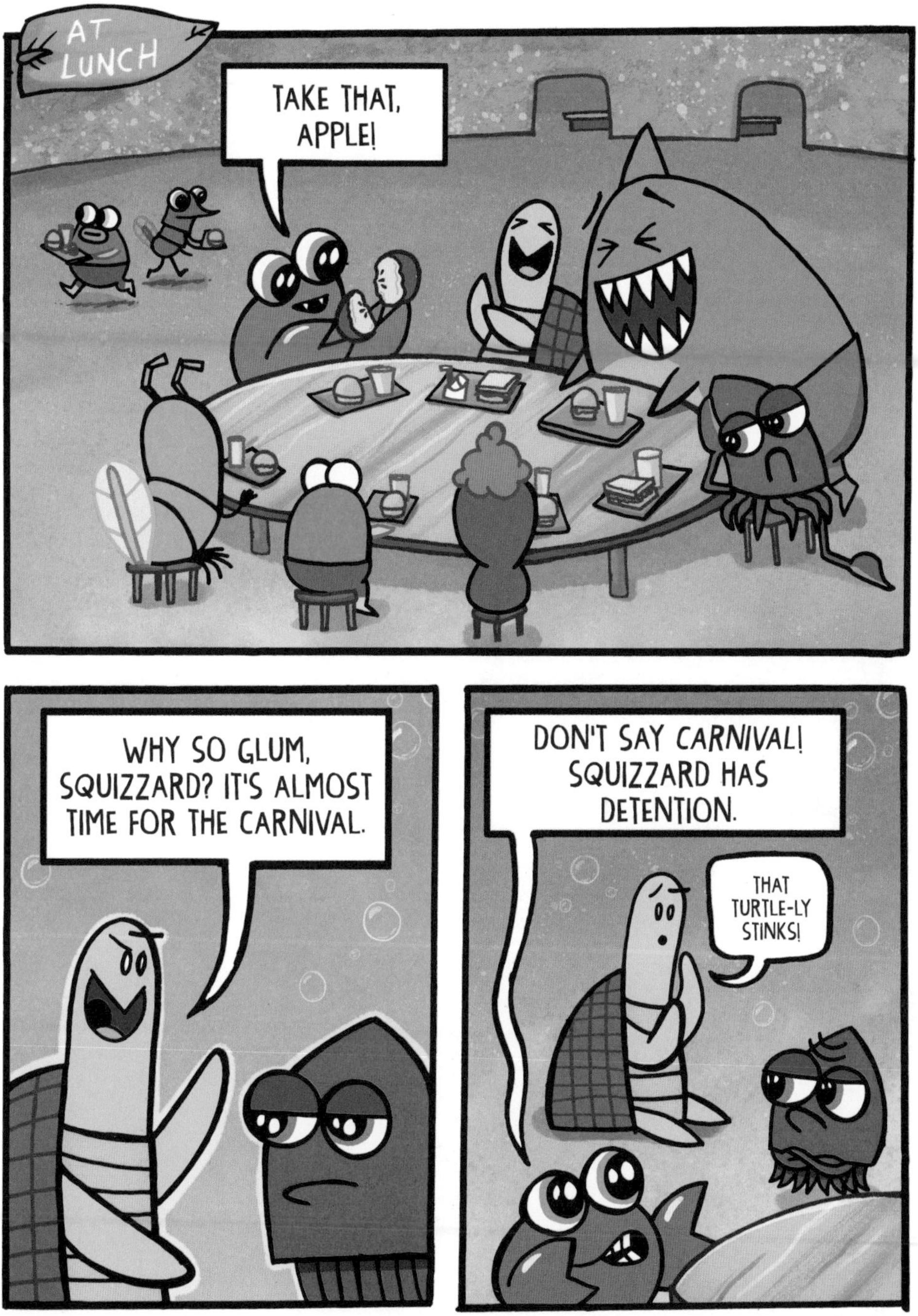
AT LUNCH
TAKE THAT, APPLE!
WHY SO GLUM, SQUIZZARD? IT'S ALMOST TIME FOR THE CARNIVAL.
DON'T SAY CARNIVAL! SQUIZZARD HAS DETENTION.
THAT TURTLE-LY STINKS!

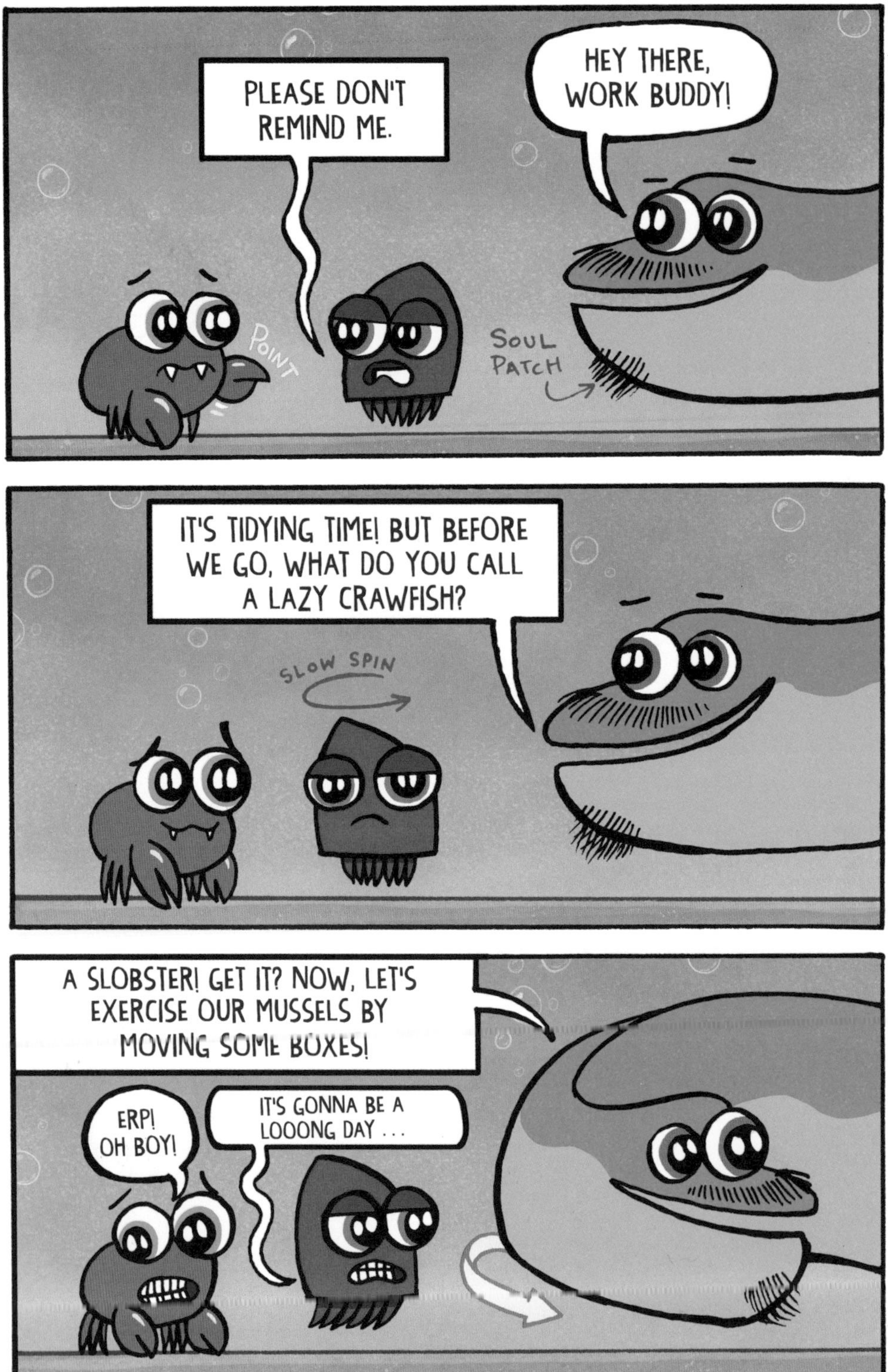
HEY THERE, WORK BUDDY!
PLEASE DON'T REMIND ME.
POINT
SOUL PATCH
IT'S TIDYING TIME! BUT BEFORE WE GO, WHAT DO YOU CALL A LAZY CRAWFISH?
SLOW SPIN
A SLOBSTER! GET IT? NOW, LET'S EXERCISE OUR MUSSELS BY MOVING SOME BOXES!
ERP! OH BOY!
IT'S GONNA BE A LOOONG DAY . . .

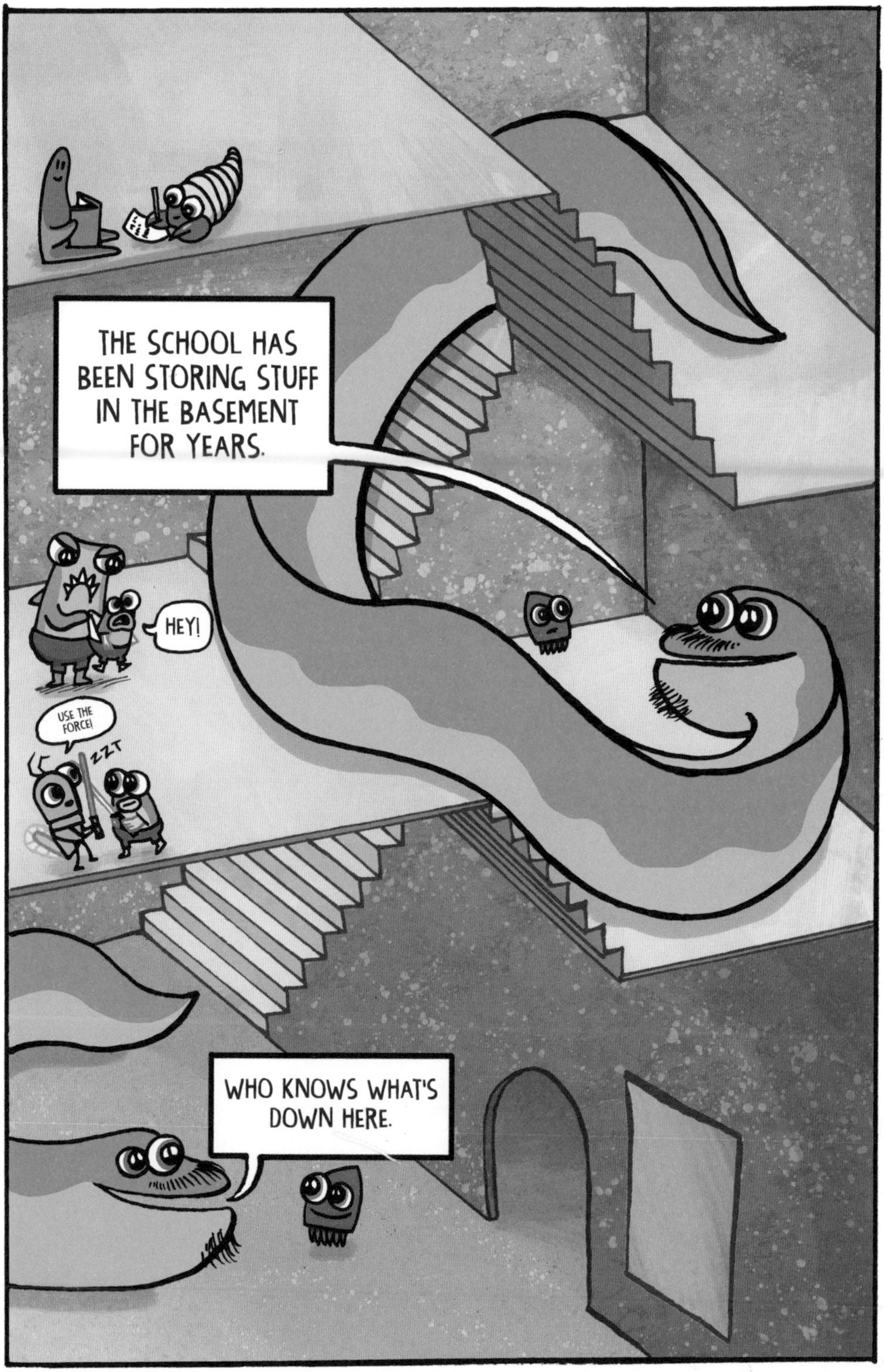
THE SCHOOL HAS BEEN STORING STUFF IN THE BASEMENT FOR YEARS.
HEY!
USE THE FORCE!
ZZT
WHO KNOWS WHAT'S DOWN HERE.

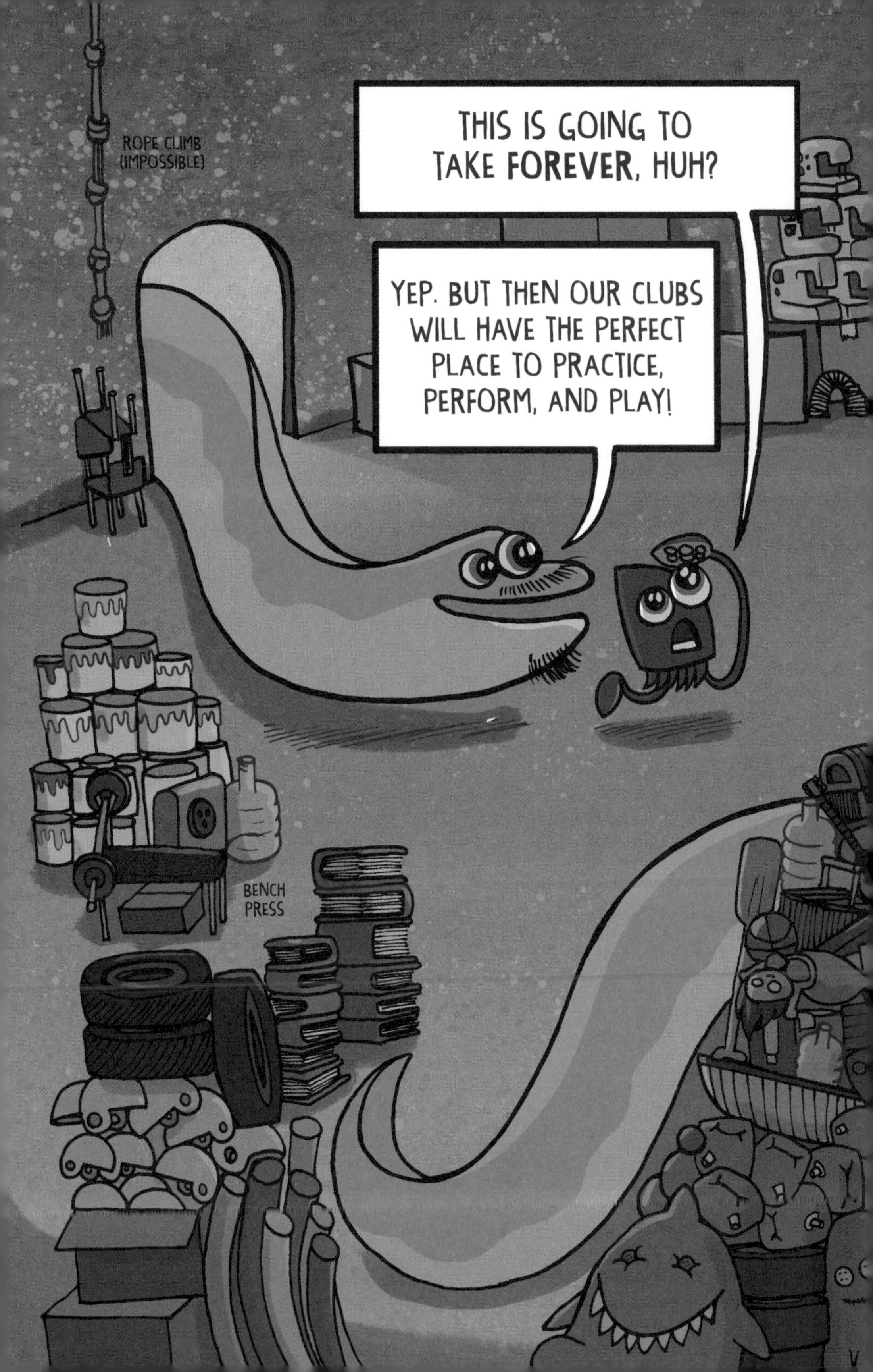
ROPE CLIMB (IMPOSSIBLE)
THIS IS GOING TO TAKE **FOREVER**, HUH?
YEP. BUT THEN OUR CLUBS WILL HAVE THE PERFECT PLACE TO PRACTICE, PERFORM, AND PLAY!
BENCH PRESS

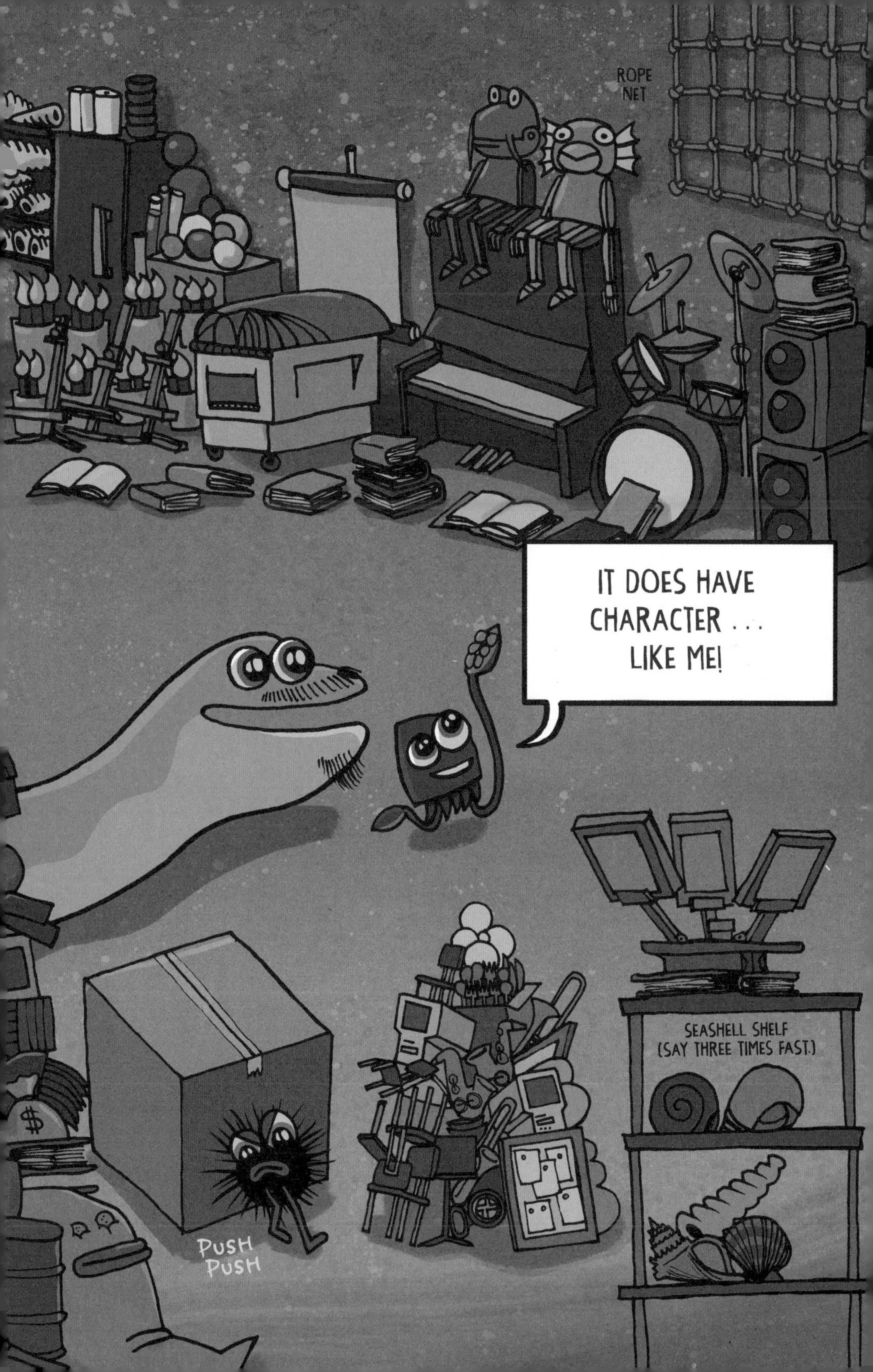
ROPE NET
IT DOES HAVE CHARACTER . . . LIKE ME!
SEASHELL SHELF (SAY THREE TIMES FAST.)
PUSH PUSH

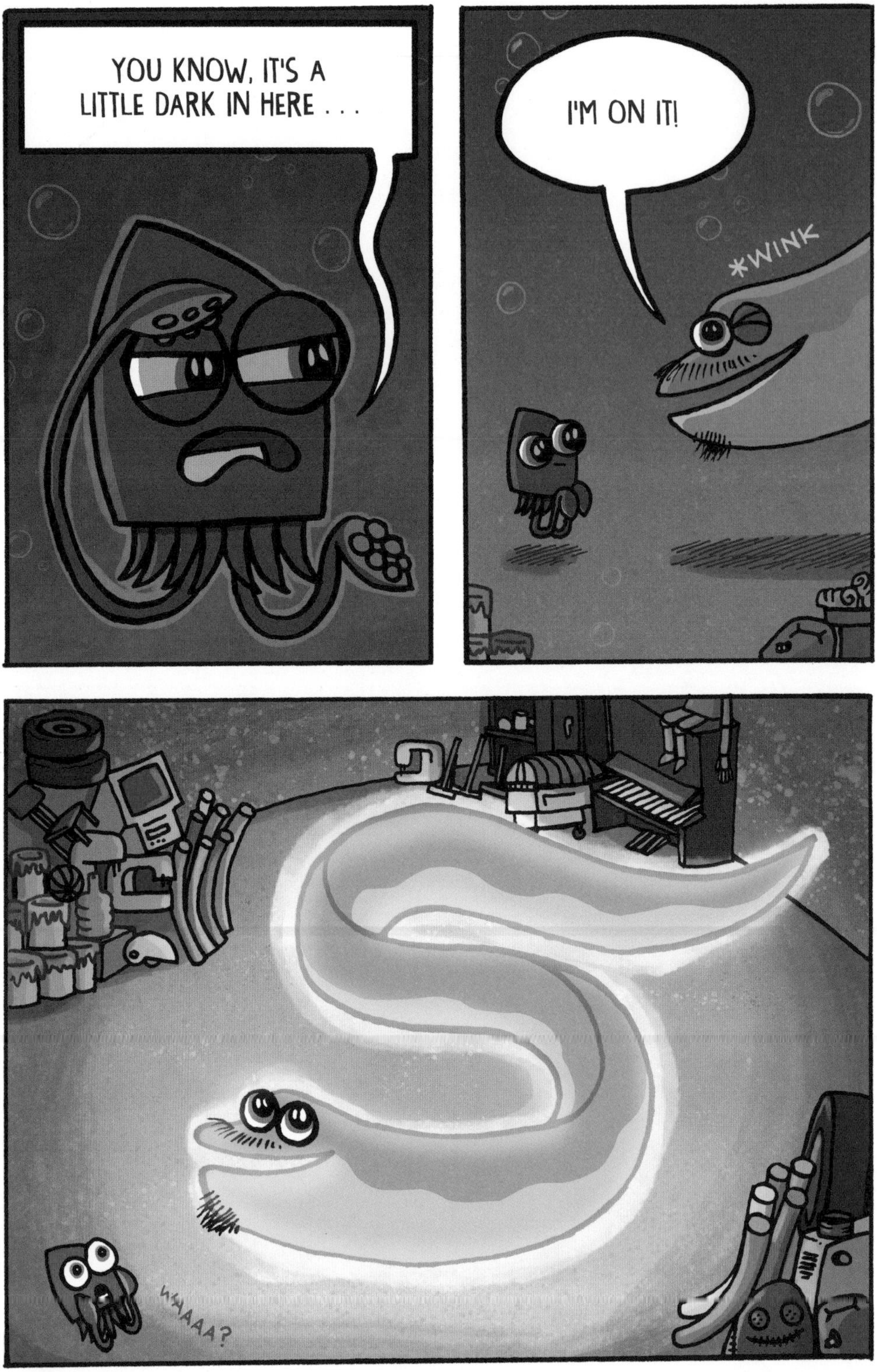
YOU KNOW, IT'S A LITTLE DARK IN HERE . . .
I'M ON IT!
*WINK
WHAAA?

ELECTRIC EELS ARE NOT REALLY EELS! THEY ARE MORE CLOSELY RELATED TO CATFISH. THEIR BODIES STORE ENERGY LIKE A BATTERY. THEY USE IT TO STUN THEIR PREY AND SCARE OFF PREDATORS.

THAT WAS **LEGIT** COOL!

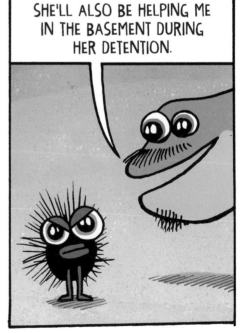

THANKS! NOW, SAY HI TO ANNIE. SHE'LL ALSO BE HELPING ME IN THE BASEMENT DURING HER DETENTION.

SO ... WHAT ARE YOU IN DETENTION FOR?

WELL, I'M A SEA URCHIN WITH KIND OF A PRICKLY PERSONALITY. SO I DON'T MAKE FRIENDS EASILY.

OUCH!

A BIG BULLY WAS PICKING ON THE ONE FRIEND I DO HAVE.

HEY, LITTLE JELLYFISH!

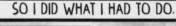

SO I DID WHAT I HAD TO DO.

YOU'RE TOAST!

I REGRET NOTHING.

NOW WE GOTTA CLEAR ALL THIS STUFF FROM THE ROOM. I'VE ALREADY COME UP WITH A SYSTEM.

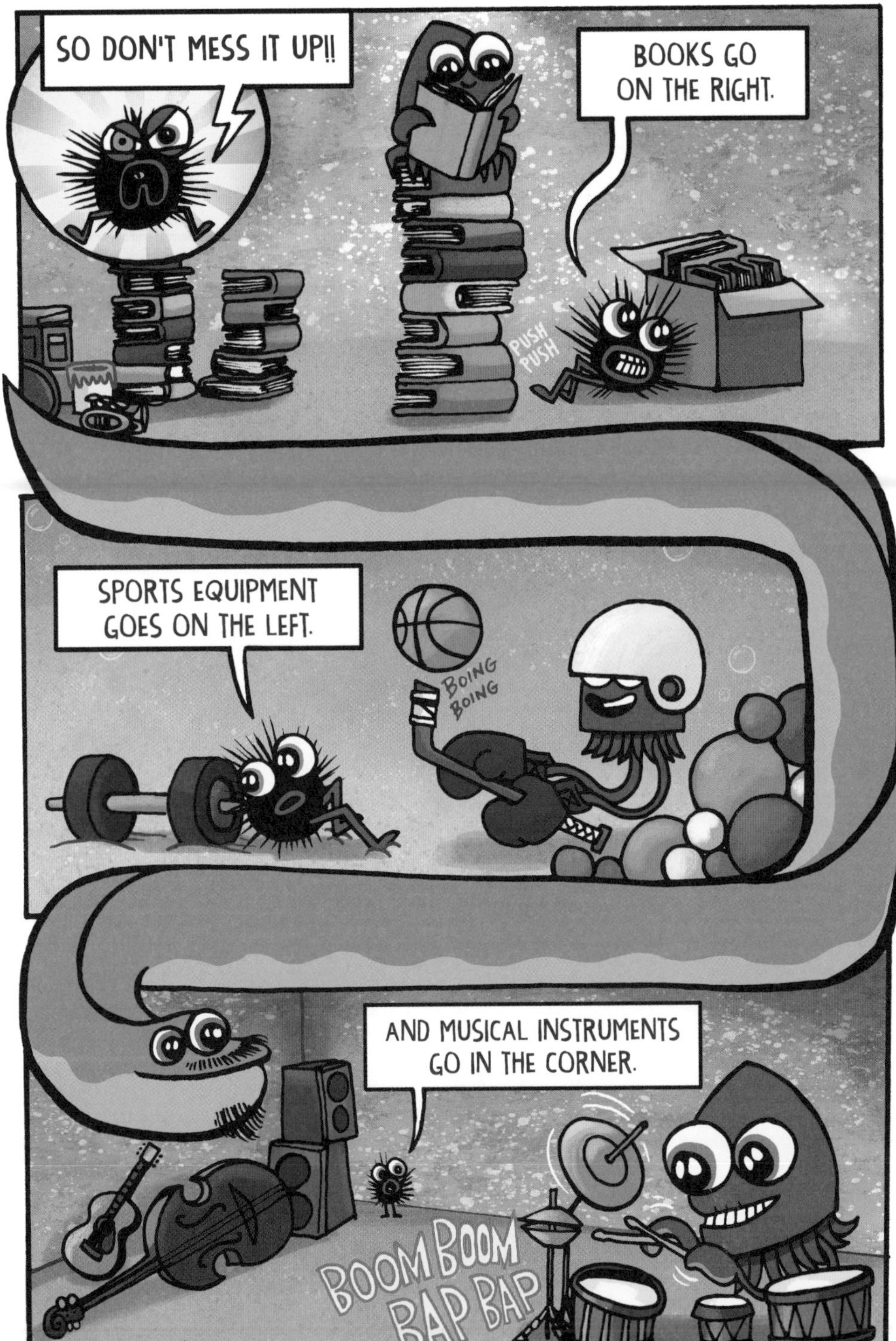
SO DON'T MESS IT UP!!
BOOKS GO ON THE RIGHT.
PUSH PUSH
SPORTS EQUIPMENT GOES ON THE LEFT.
BOING BOING
AND MUSICAL INSTRUMENTS GO IN THE CORNER.
BOOM BOOM BAP BAP

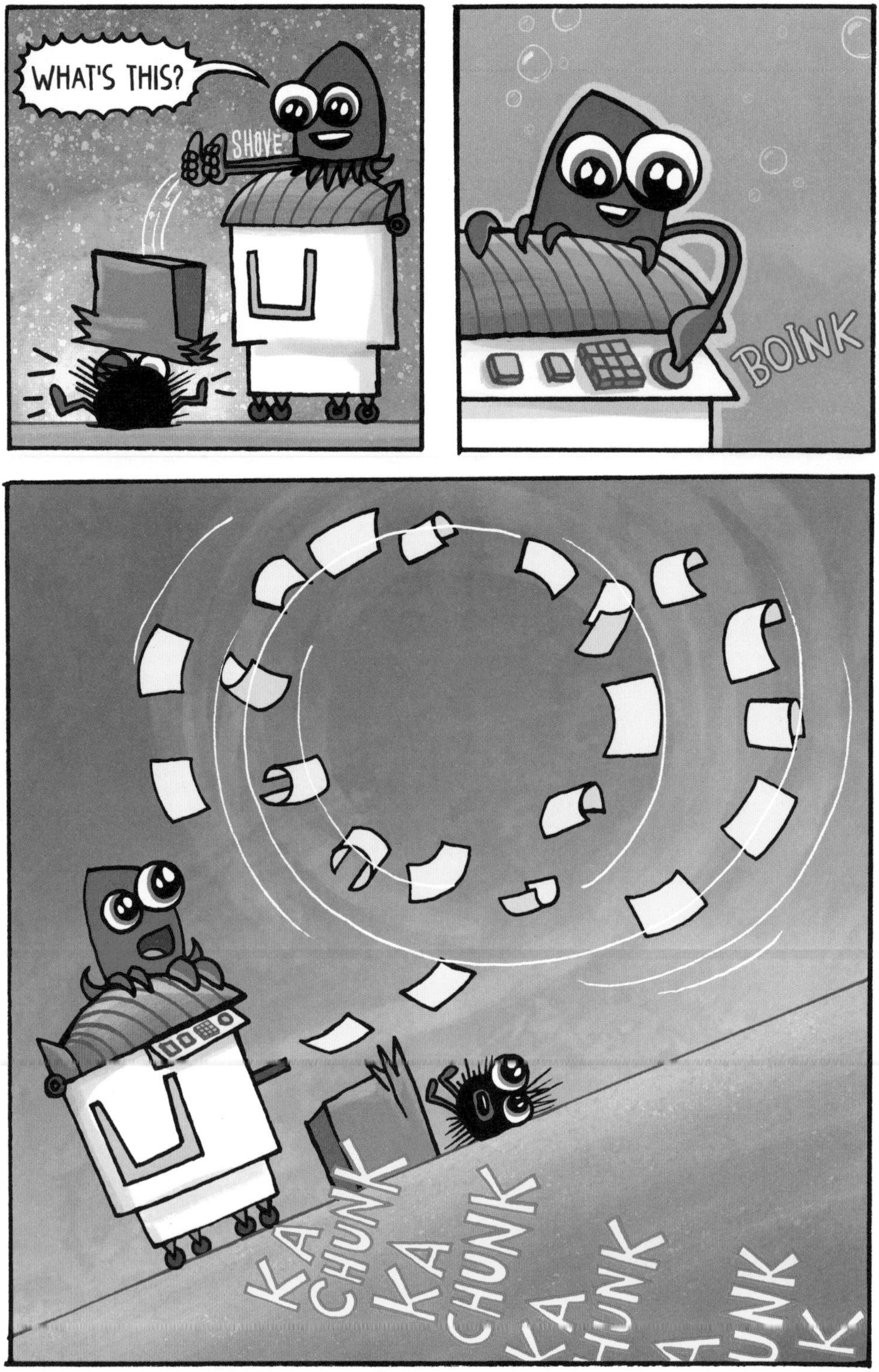
WHAT'S THIS?
SHOVE
BOINK
KA CHUNK KA CHUNK KA HUNK A UNK K

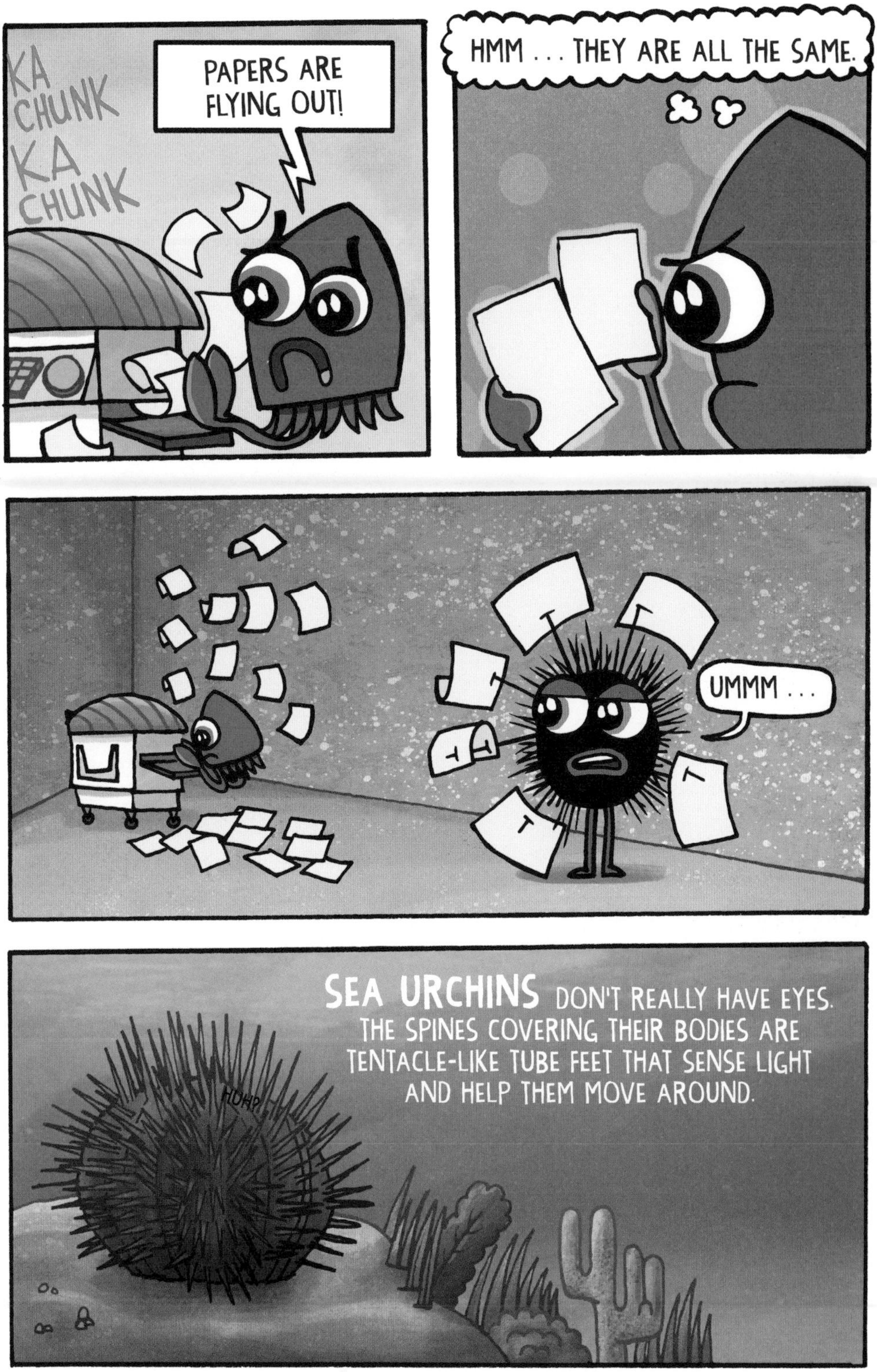

KA CHUNK KA CHUNK
PAPERS ARE FLYING OUT!
HMM . . . THEY ARE ALL THE SAME.
UMMM . . .
SEA URCHINS DON'T REALLY HAVE EYES. THE SPINES COVERING THEIR BODIES ARE TENTACLE-LIKE TUBE FEET THAT SENSE LIGHT AND HELP THEM MOVE AROUND.

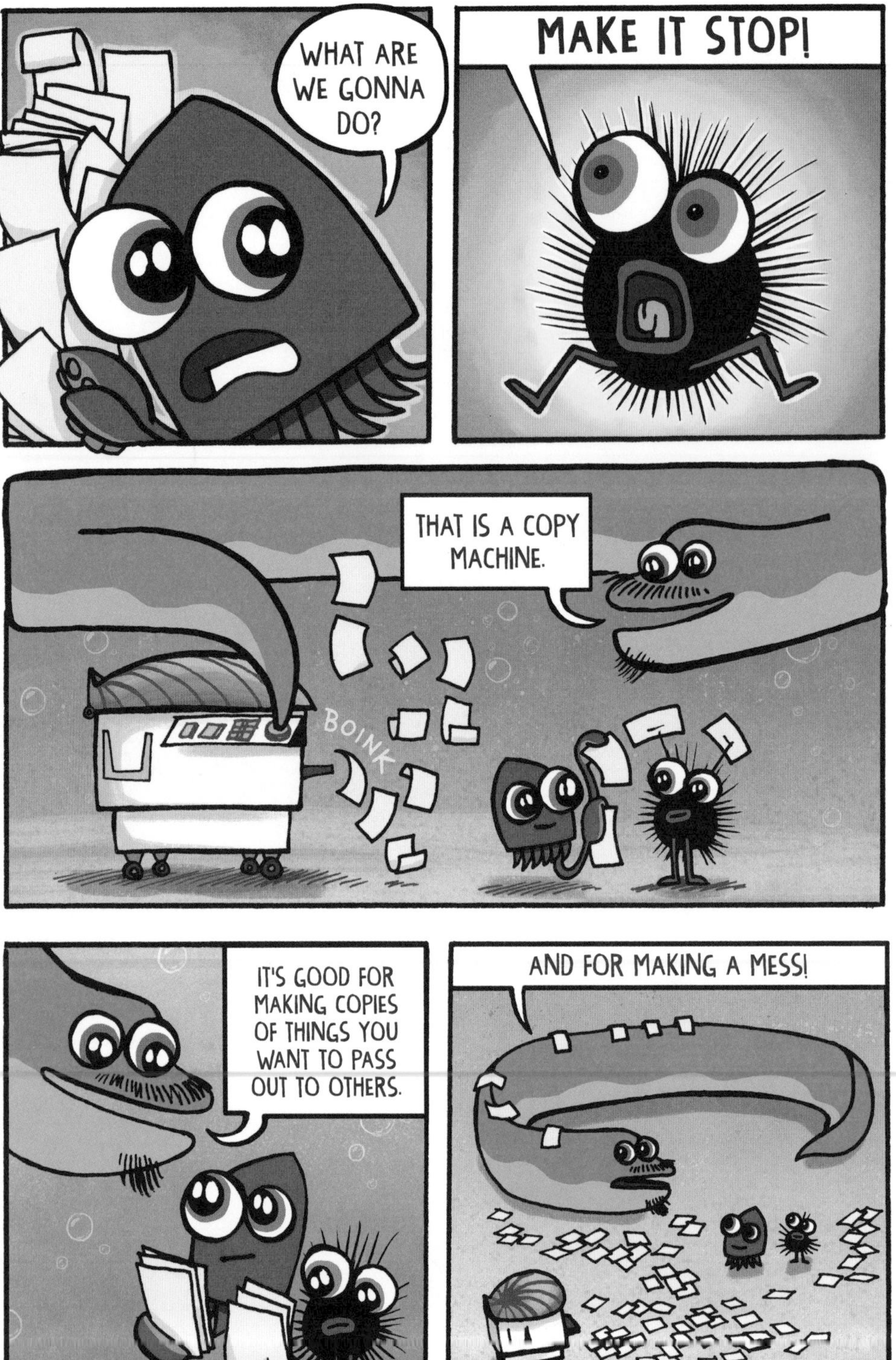
WHAT ARE WE GONNA DO?
MAKE IT STOP!
THAT IS A COPY MACHINE.
BOINK
IT'S GOOD FOR MAKING COPIES OF THINGS YOU WANT TO PASS OUT TO OTHERS.
AND FOR MAKING A MESS!

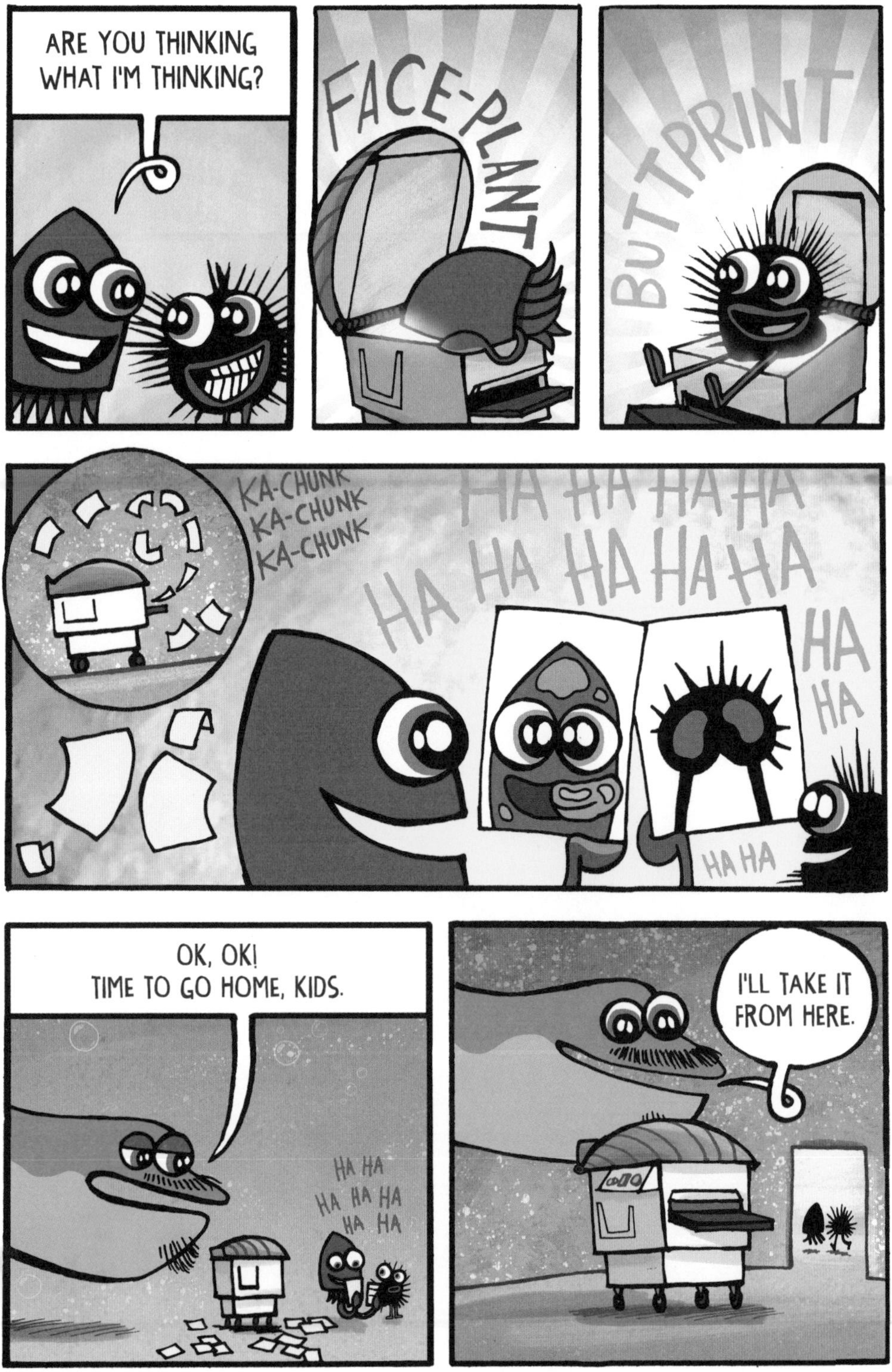
ARE YOU THINKING WHAT I'M THINKING?
FACE-PLANT
BUTTPRINT
KA-CHUNK
KA-CHUNK
KA-CHUNK
HA HA HA HA
HA HA HA HA HA
HA
HA
HA HA
OK, OK!
TIME TO GO HOME, KIDS.
HA HA
HA HA HA
HA HA
I'LL TAKE IT FROM HERE.

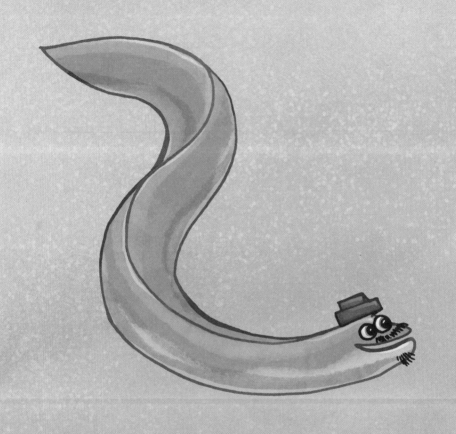

CHAPTER 4

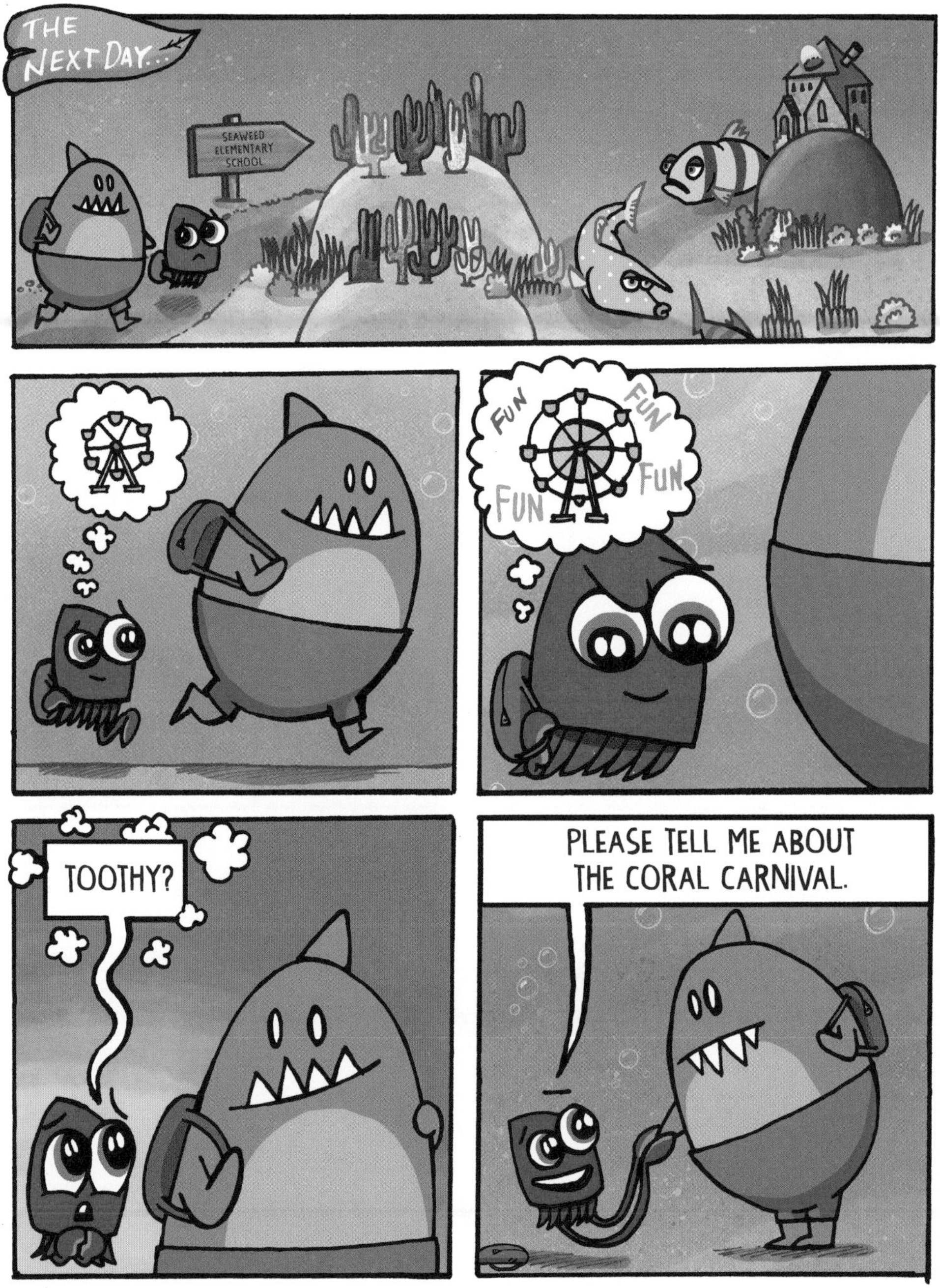
THE NEXT DAY...
SEAWEED ELEMENTARY SCHOOL
FUN
FUN
FUN
FUN
TOOTHY?
PLEASE TELL ME ABOUT THE CORAL CARNIVAL.

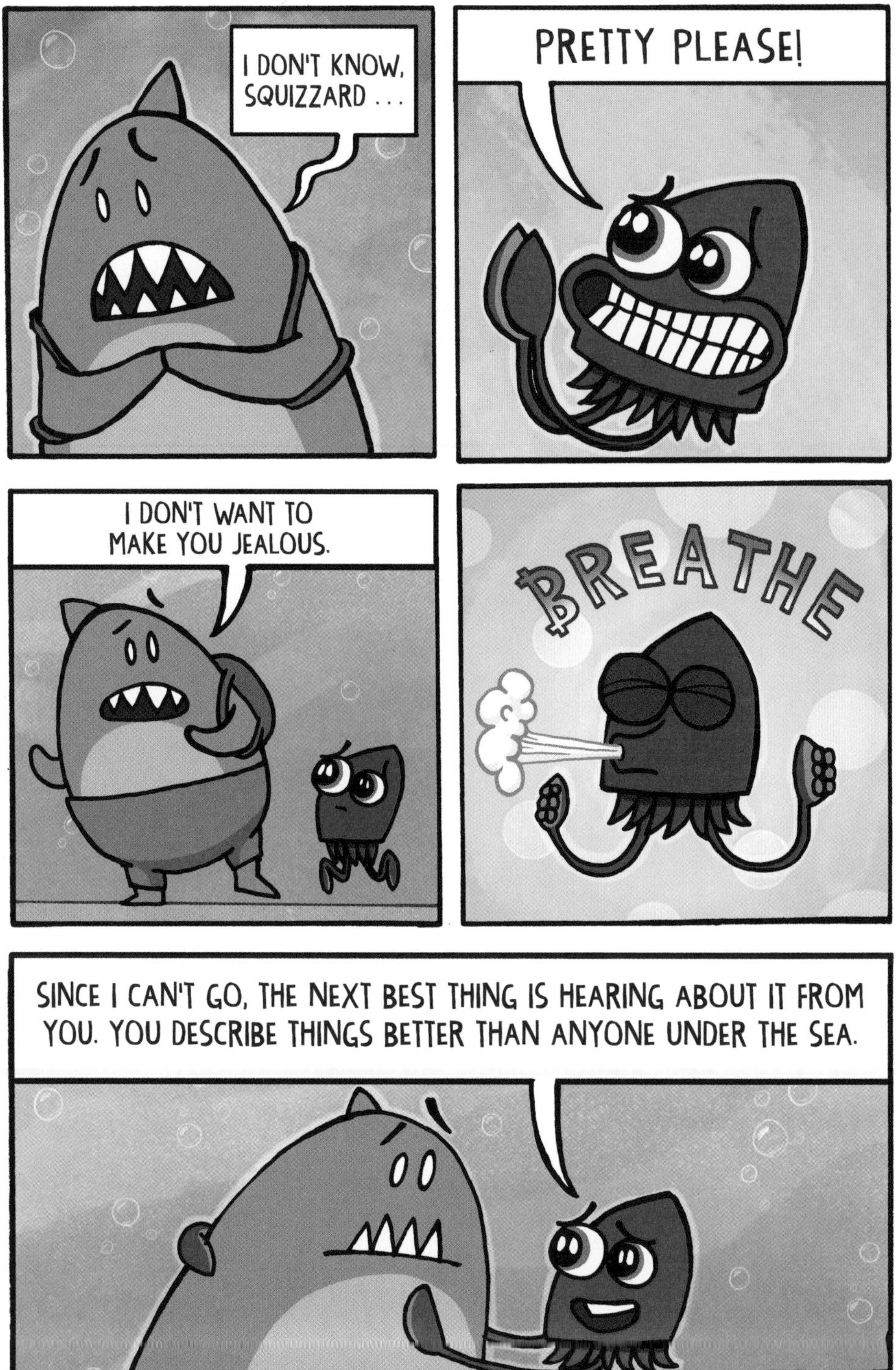
I DON'T KNOW, SQUIZZARD . . .
PRETTY PLEASE!
I DON'T WANT TO MAKE YOU JEALOUS.
BREATHE
SINCE I CAN'T GO, THE NEXT BEST THING IS HEARING ABOUT IT FROM YOU. YOU DESCRIBE THINGS BETTER THAN ANYONE UNDER THE SEA.

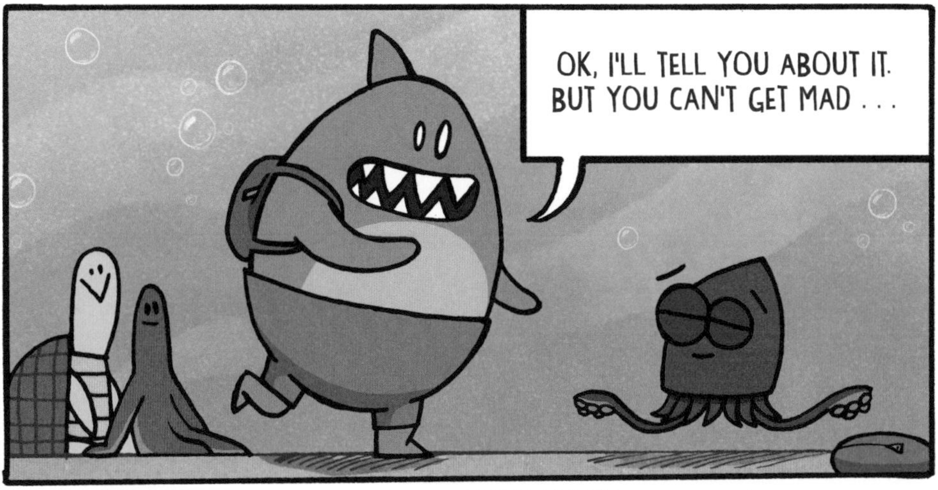
OK, I'LL TELL YOU ABOUT IT. BUT YOU CAN'T GET MAD . . .

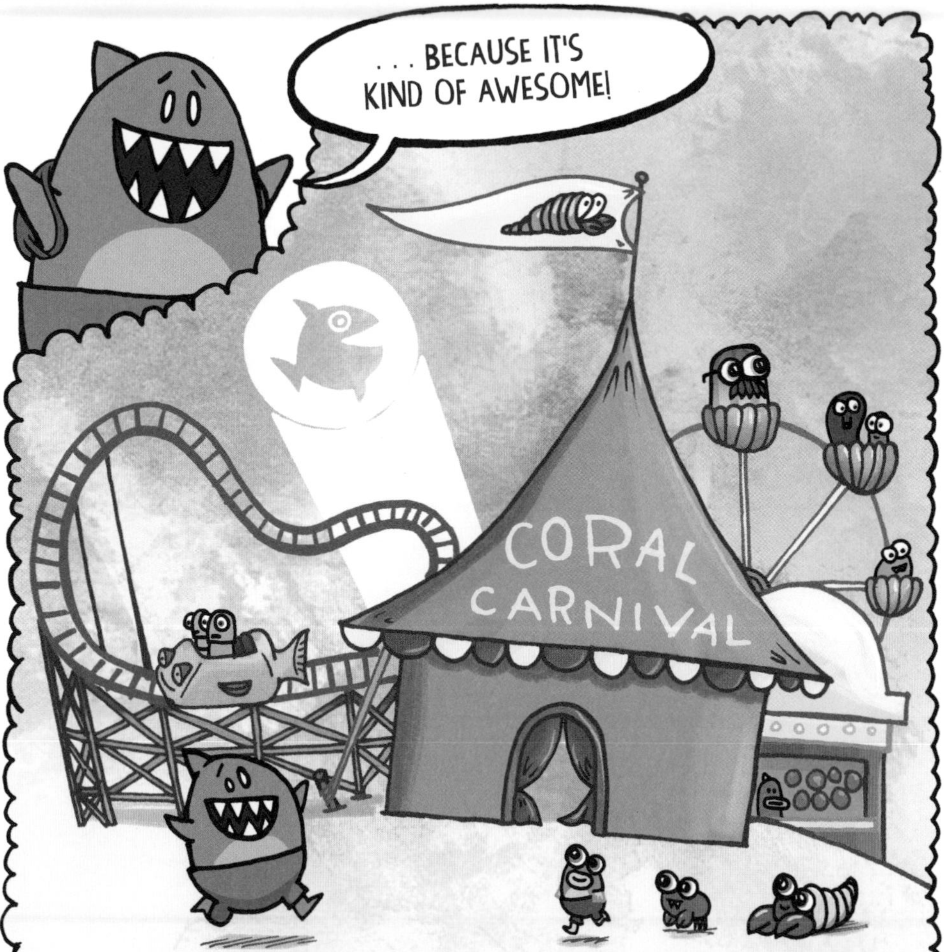
. . . BECAUSE IT'S KIND OF AWESOME!
CORAL CARNIVAL

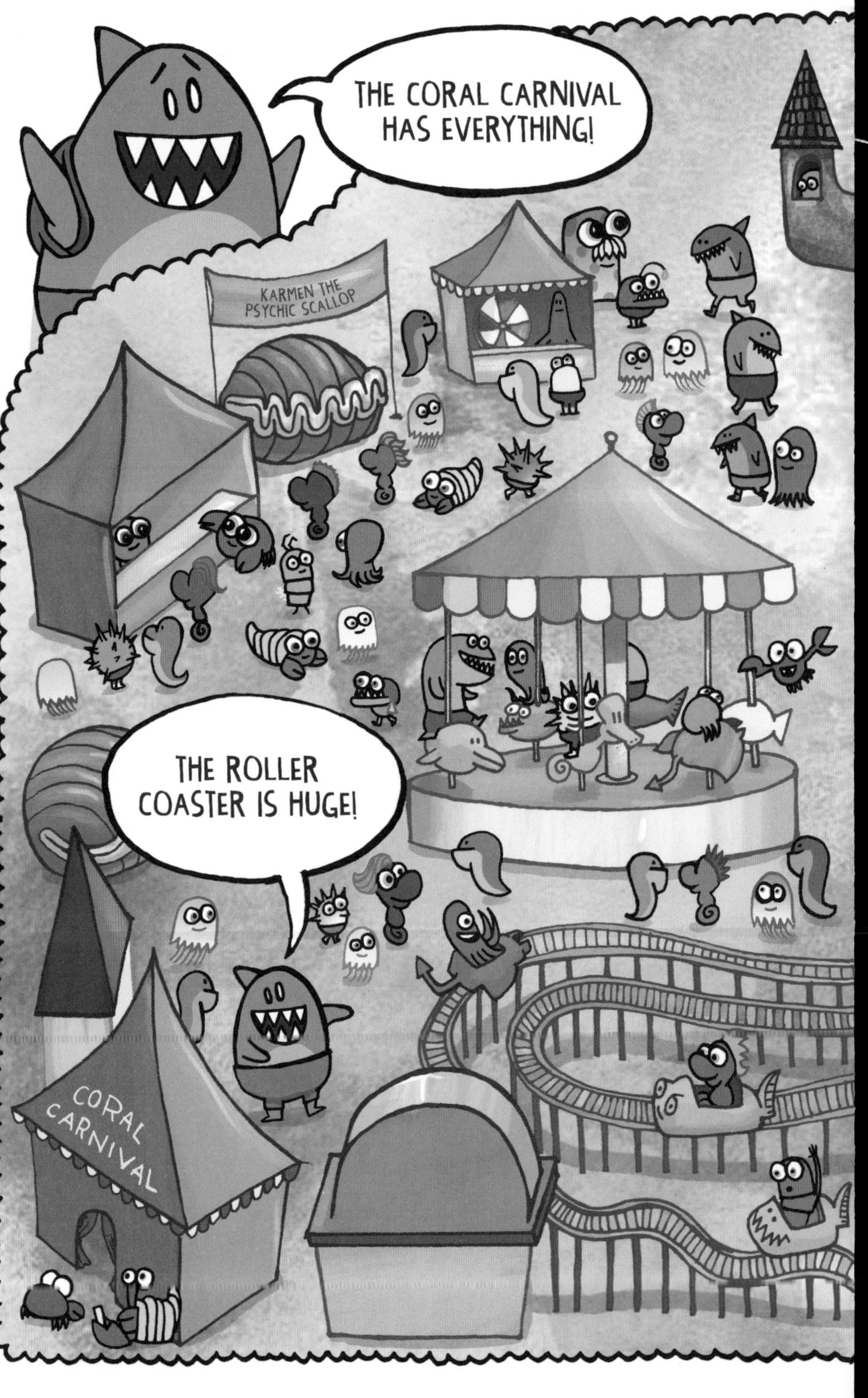
THE CORAL CARNIVAL HAS EVERYTHING!
KARMEN THE PSYCHIC SCALLOP
THE ROLLER COASTER IS HUGE!
CORAL CARNIVAL

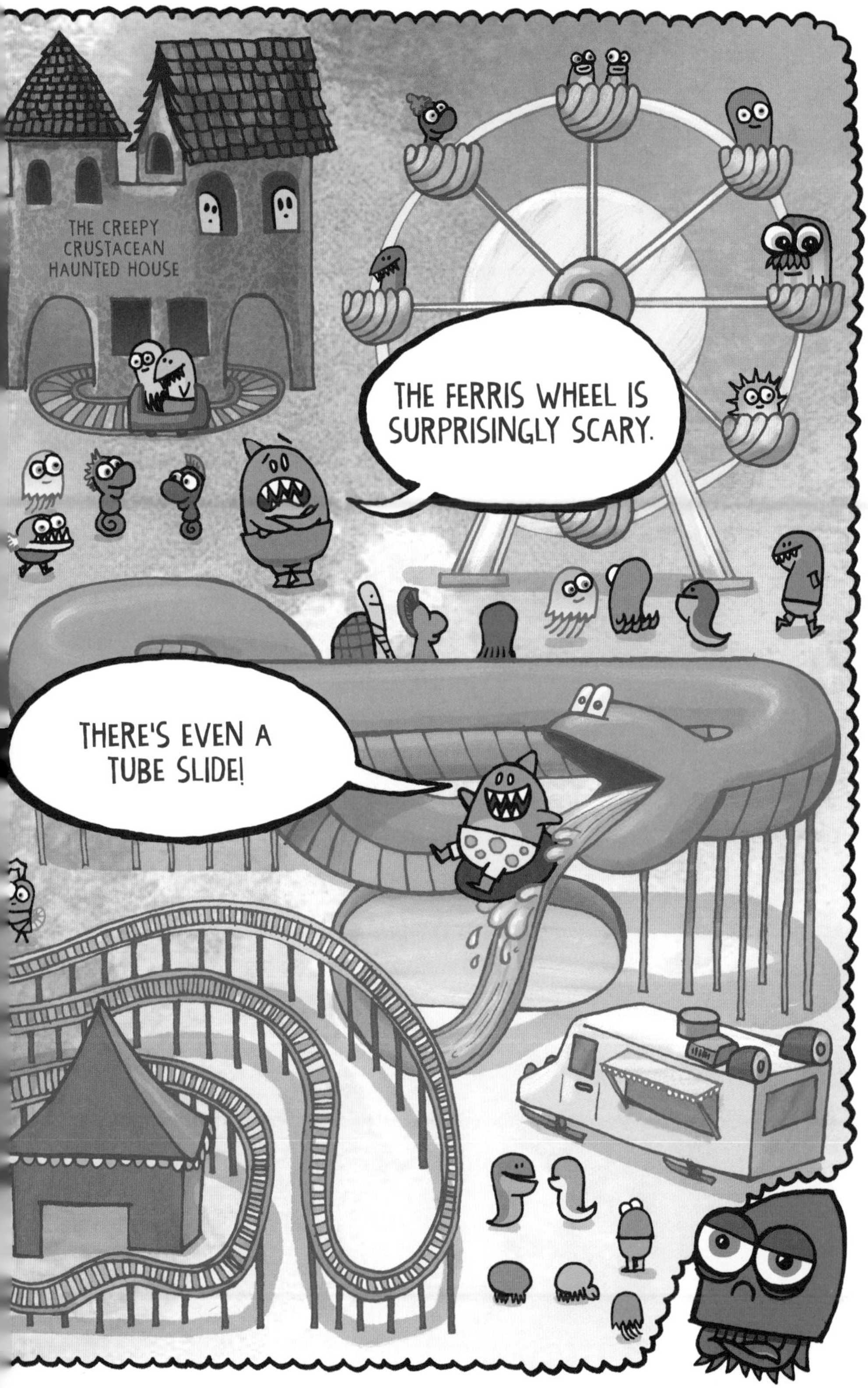
THE CREEPY CRUSTACEAN HAUNTED HOUSE
THE FERRIS WHEEL IS SURPRISINGLY SCARY.
THERE'S EVEN A TUBE SLIDE!

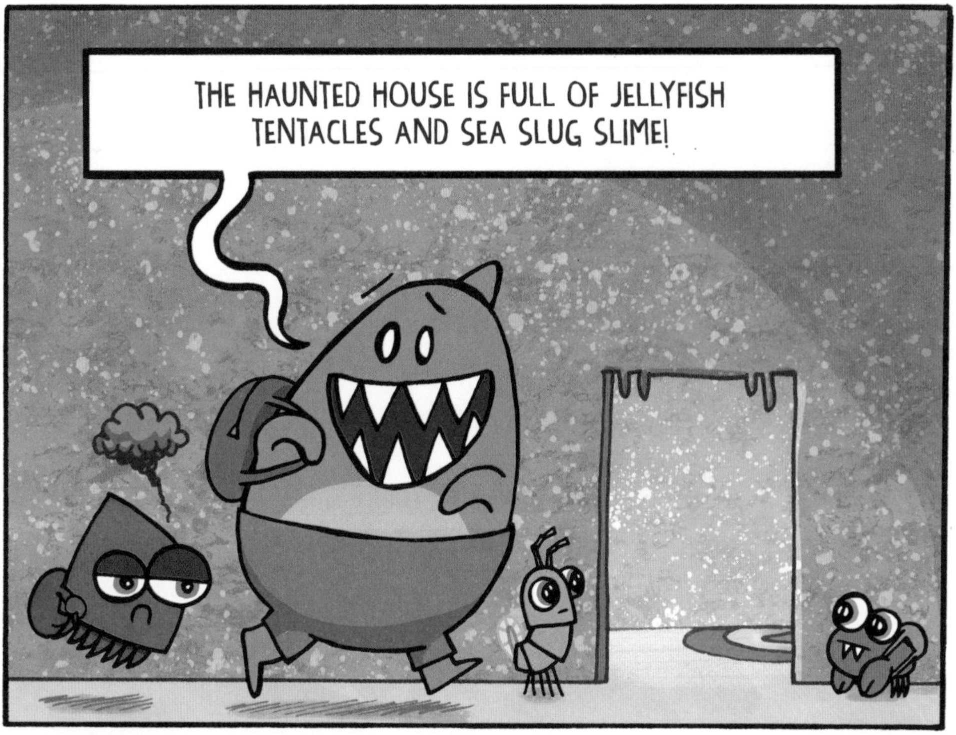
THE HAUNTED HOUSE IS FULL OF JELLYFISH TENTACLES AND SEA SLUG SLIME!

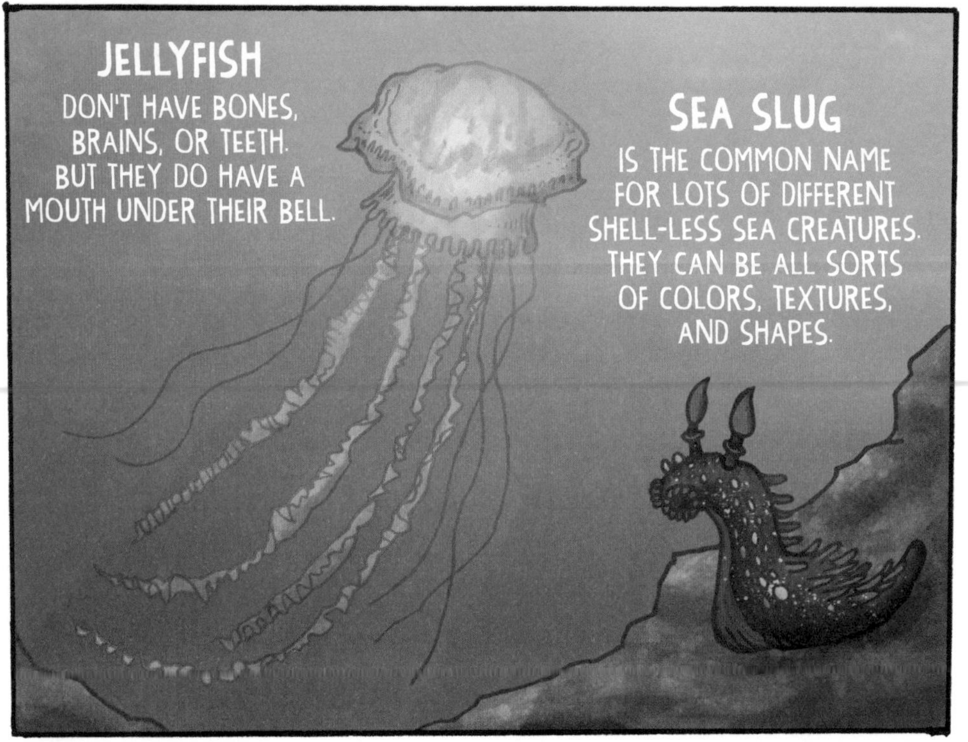
JELLYFISH
DON'T HAVE BONES, BRAINS, OR TEETH. BUT THEY DO HAVE A MOUTH UNDER THEIR BELL.
SEA SLUG
IS THE COMMON NAME FOR LOTS OF DIFFERENT SHELL-LESS SEA CREATURES. THEY CAN BE ALL SORTS OF COLORS, TEXTURES, AND SHAPES.

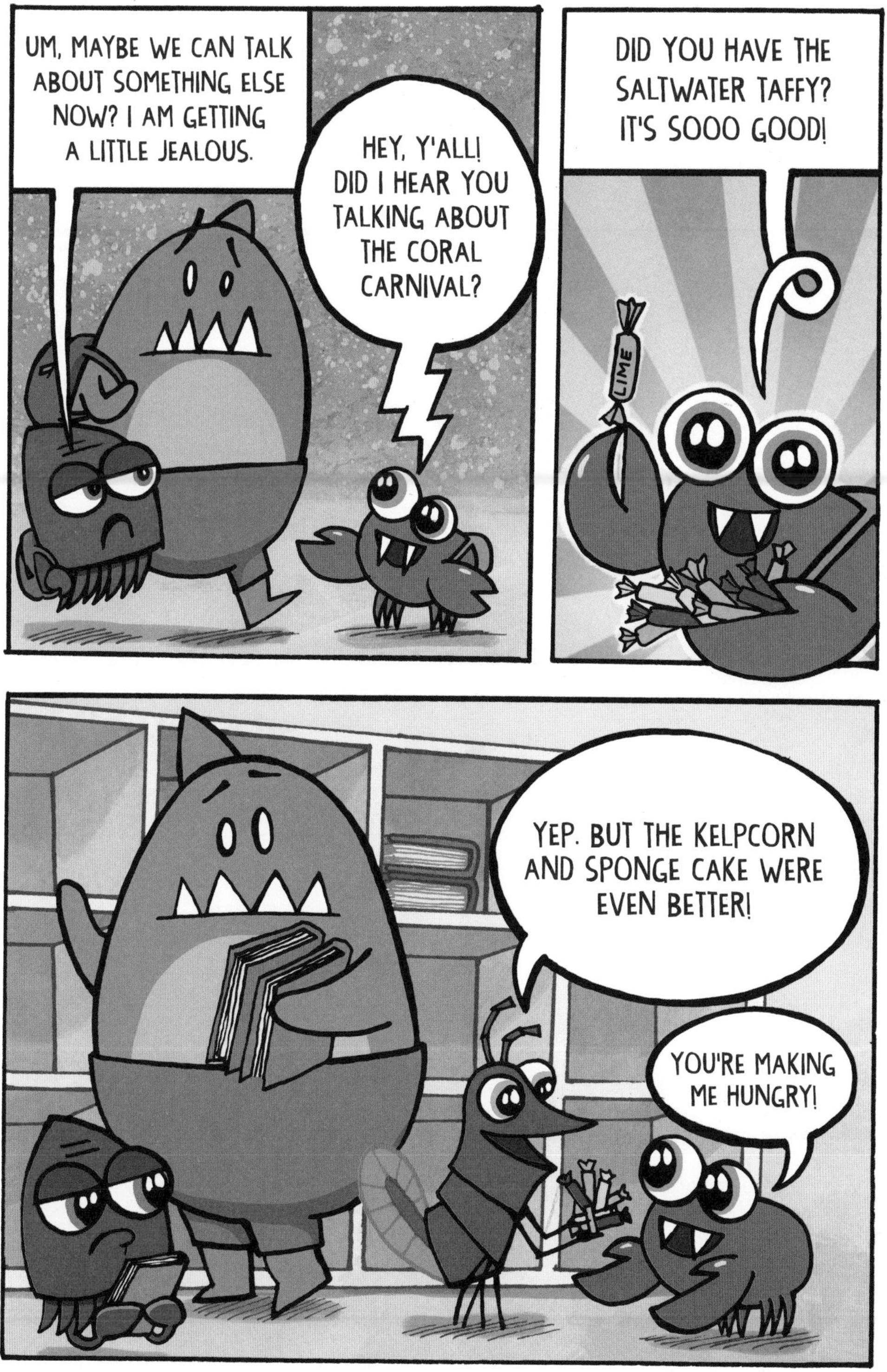
UM, MAYBE WE CAN TALK ABOUT SOMETHING ELSE NOW? I AM GETTING A LITTLE JEALOUS.
HEY, Y'ALL! DID I HEAR YOU TALKING ABOUT THE CORAL CARNIVAL?
DID YOU HAVE THE SALTWATER TAFFY? IT'S SOOO GOOD!
LIME
YEP. BUT THE KELPCORN AND SPONGE CAKE WERE EVEN BETTER!
YOU'RE MAKING ME HUNGRY!

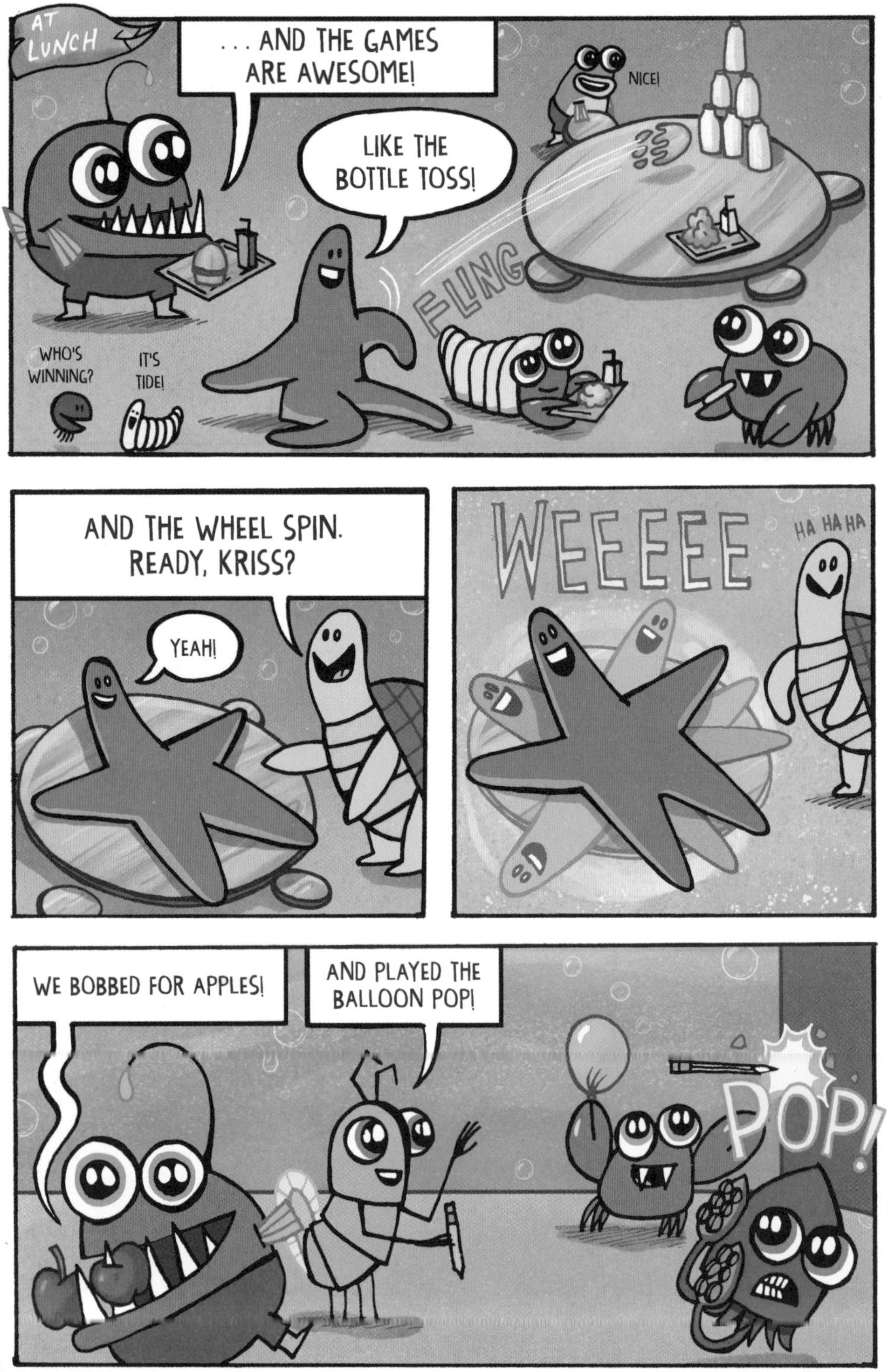
AT LUNCH
. . . AND THE GAMES ARE AWESOME!
LIKE THE BOTTLE TOSS!
NICE!
FLING
WHO'S WINNING?
IT'S TIDE!
AND THE WHEEL SPIN. READY, KRISS?
YEAH!
WEEEEE
HA HA HA
WE BOBBED FOR APPLES!
AND PLAYED THE BALLOON POP!
POP!

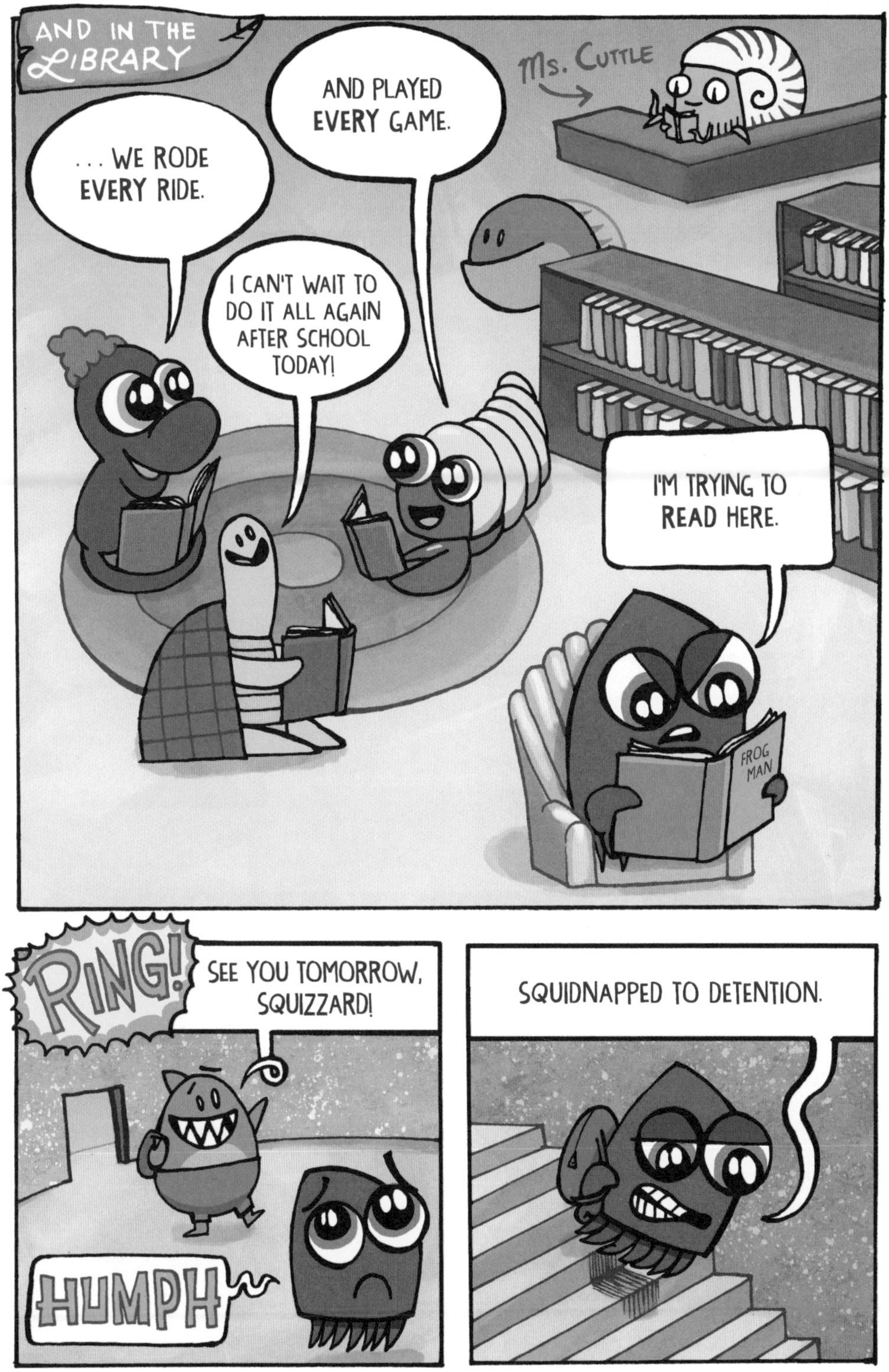
AND IN THE LIBRARY
MS. CUTTLE
. . . WE RODE EVERY RIDE.
AND PLAYED EVERY GAME.
I CAN'T WAIT TO DO IT ALL AGAIN AFTER SCHOOL TODAY!
I'M TRYING TO READ HERE.
FROG MAN
RING!
SEE YOU TOMORROW, SQUIZZARD!
HUMPH
SQUIDNAPPED TO DETENTION.

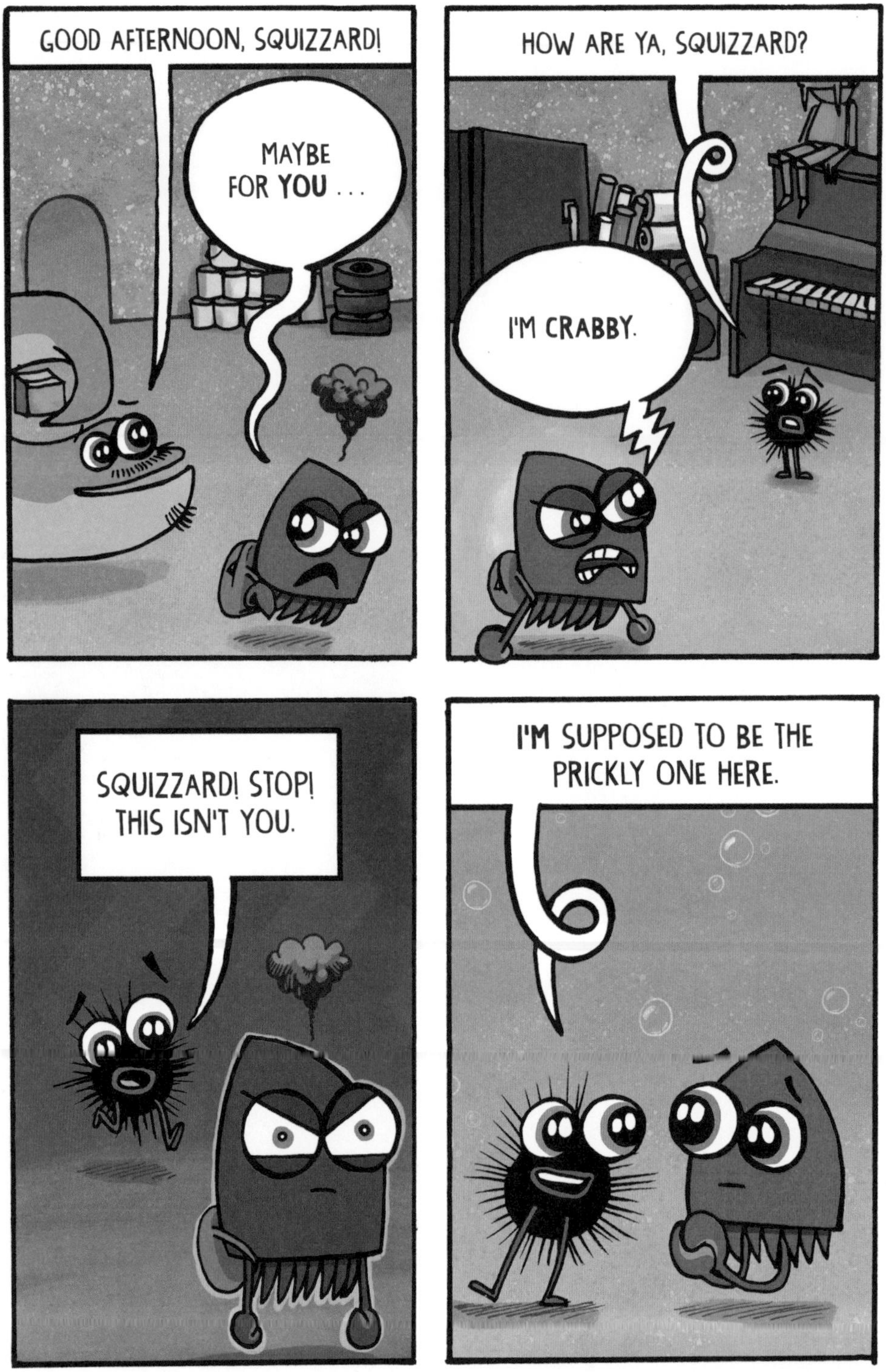
GOOD AFTERNOON, SQUIZZARD!
MAYBE FOR YOU . . .
HOW ARE YA, SQUIZZARD?
I'M CRABBY.
SQUIZZARD! STOP! THIS ISN'T YOU.
I'M SUPPOSED TO BE THE PRICKLY ONE HERE.

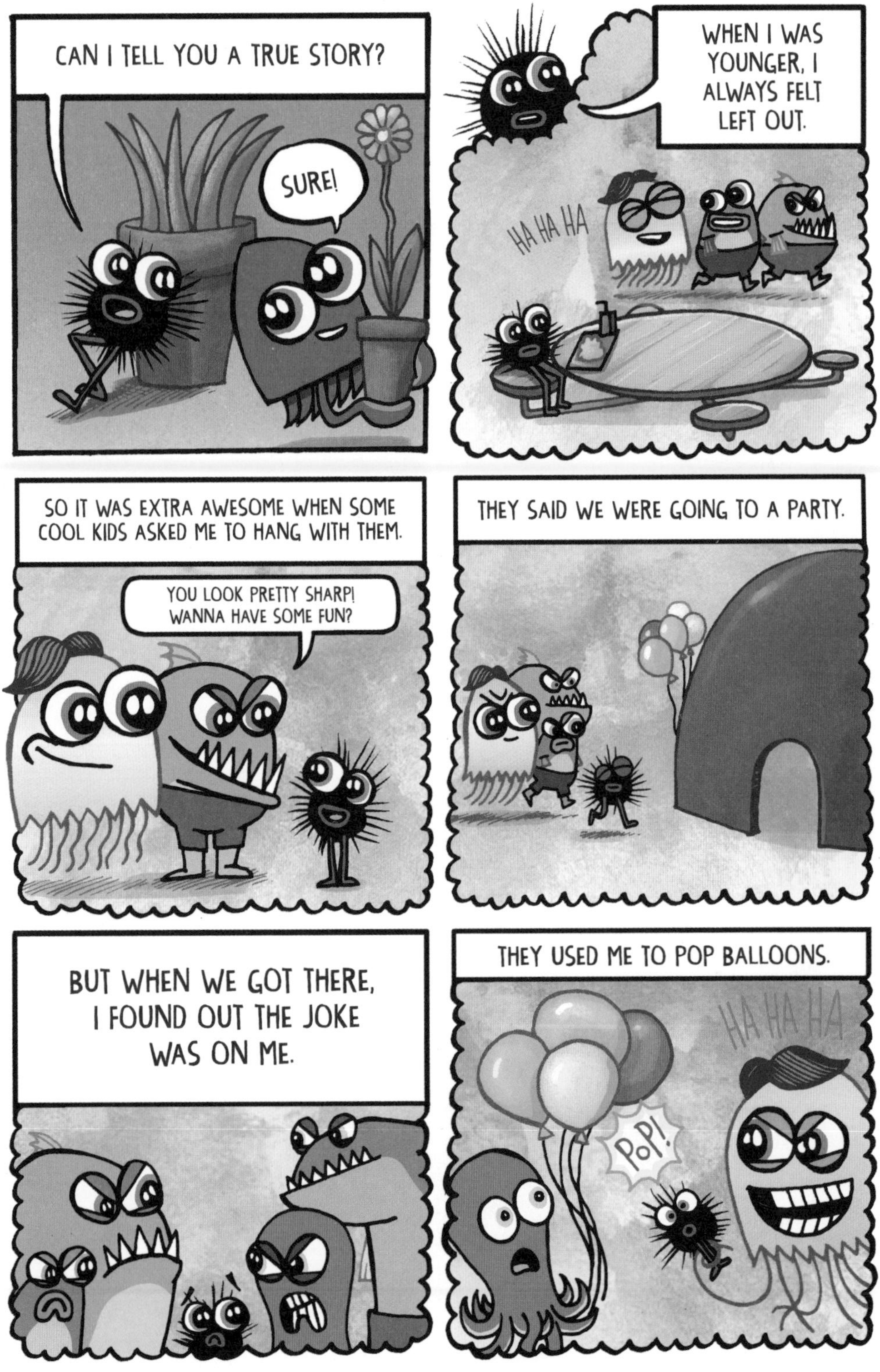
CAN I TELL YOU A TRUE STORY?
SURE!
WHEN I WAS YOUNGER, I ALWAYS FELT LEFT OUT.
HA HA HA
SO IT WAS EXTRA AWESOME WHEN SOME COOL KIDS ASKED ME TO HANG WITH THEM.
YOU LOOK PRETTY SHARP! WANNA HAVE SOME FUN?
THEY SAID WE WERE GOING TO A PARTY.
BUT WHEN WE GOT THERE, I FOUND OUT THE JOKE WAS ON ME.
THEY USED ME TO POP BALLOONS.
HA HA HA
POP!

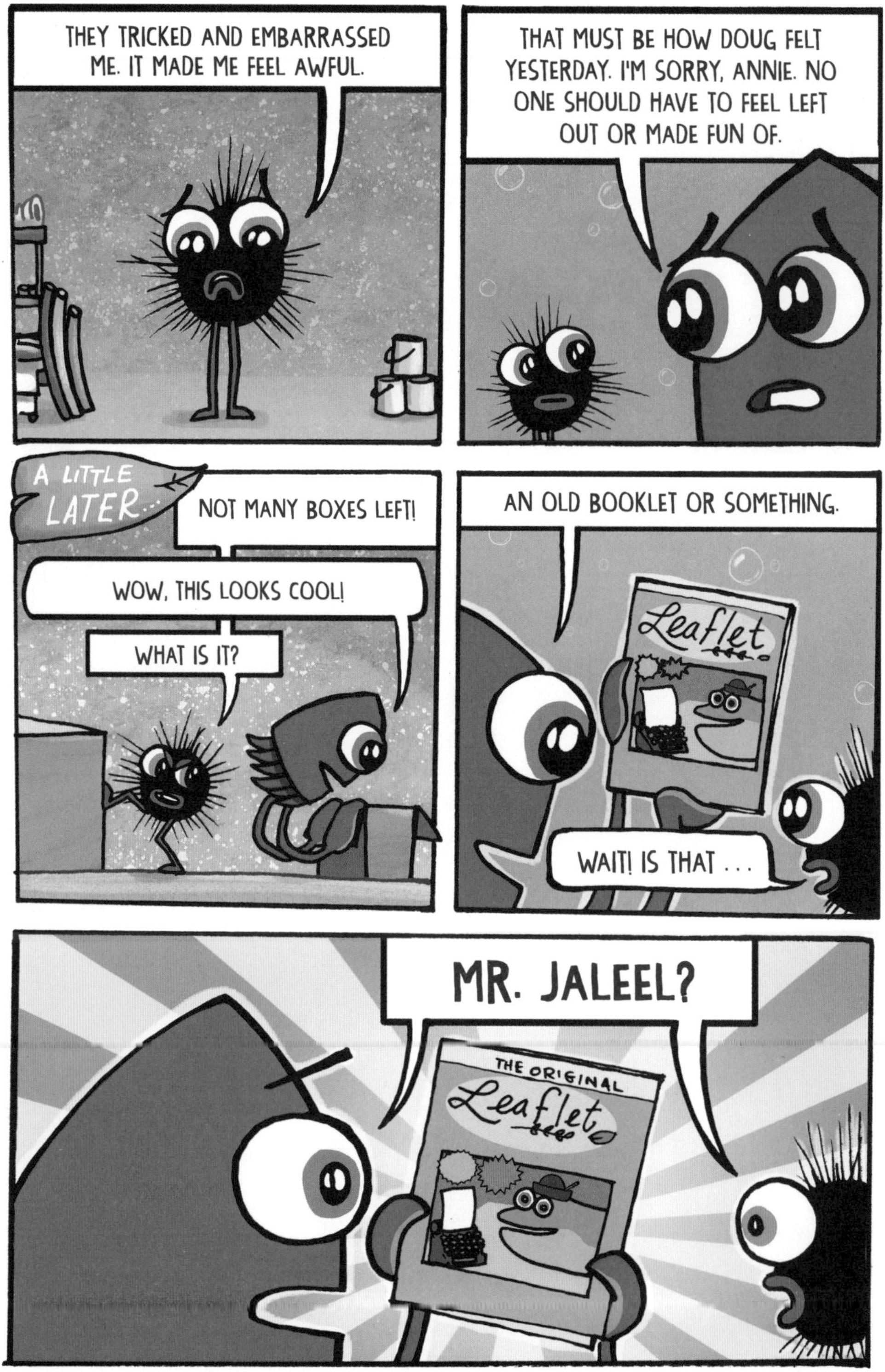
THEY TRICKED AND EMBARRASSED ME. IT MADE ME FEEL AWFUL.
THAT MUST BE HOW DOUG FELT YESTERDAY. I'M SORRY, ANNIE. NO ONE SHOULD HAVE TO FEEL LEFT OUT OR MADE FUN OF.
A LITTLE LATER...
NOT MANY BOXES LEFT!
WOW, THIS LOOKS COOL!
WHAT IS IT?
AN OLD BOOKLET OR SOMETHING.
Leaflet
WAIT! IS THAT . . .
MR. JALEEL?
THE ORIGINAL
Leaflet

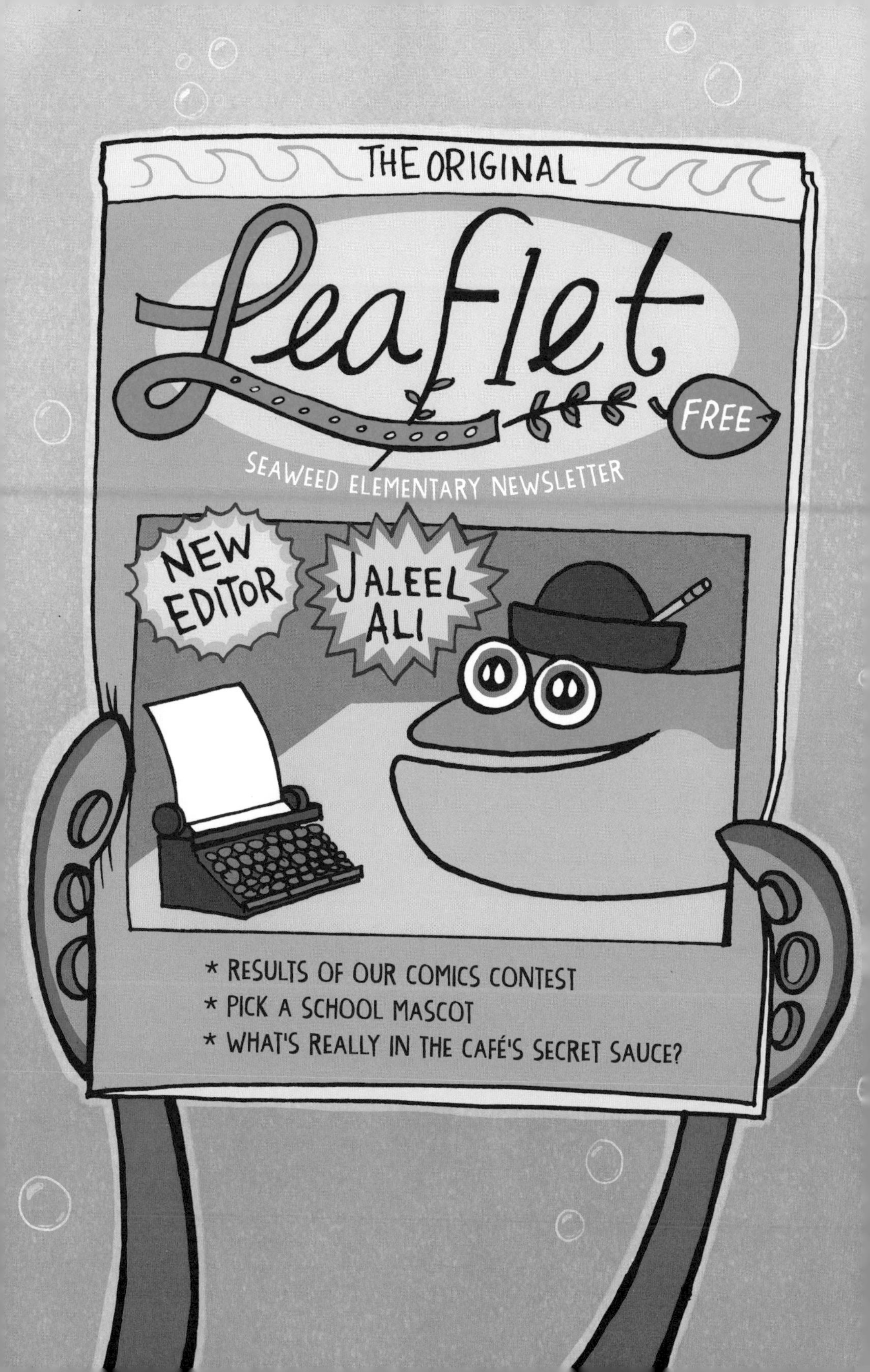
THE ORIGINAL
Leaflet
FREE
SEAWEED ELEMENTARY NEWSLETTER
NEW EDITOR
JALEEL ALI
* RESULTS OF OUR COMICS CONTEST
* PICK A SCHOOL MASCOT
* WHAT'S REALLY IN THE CAFÉ'S SECRET SAUCE?

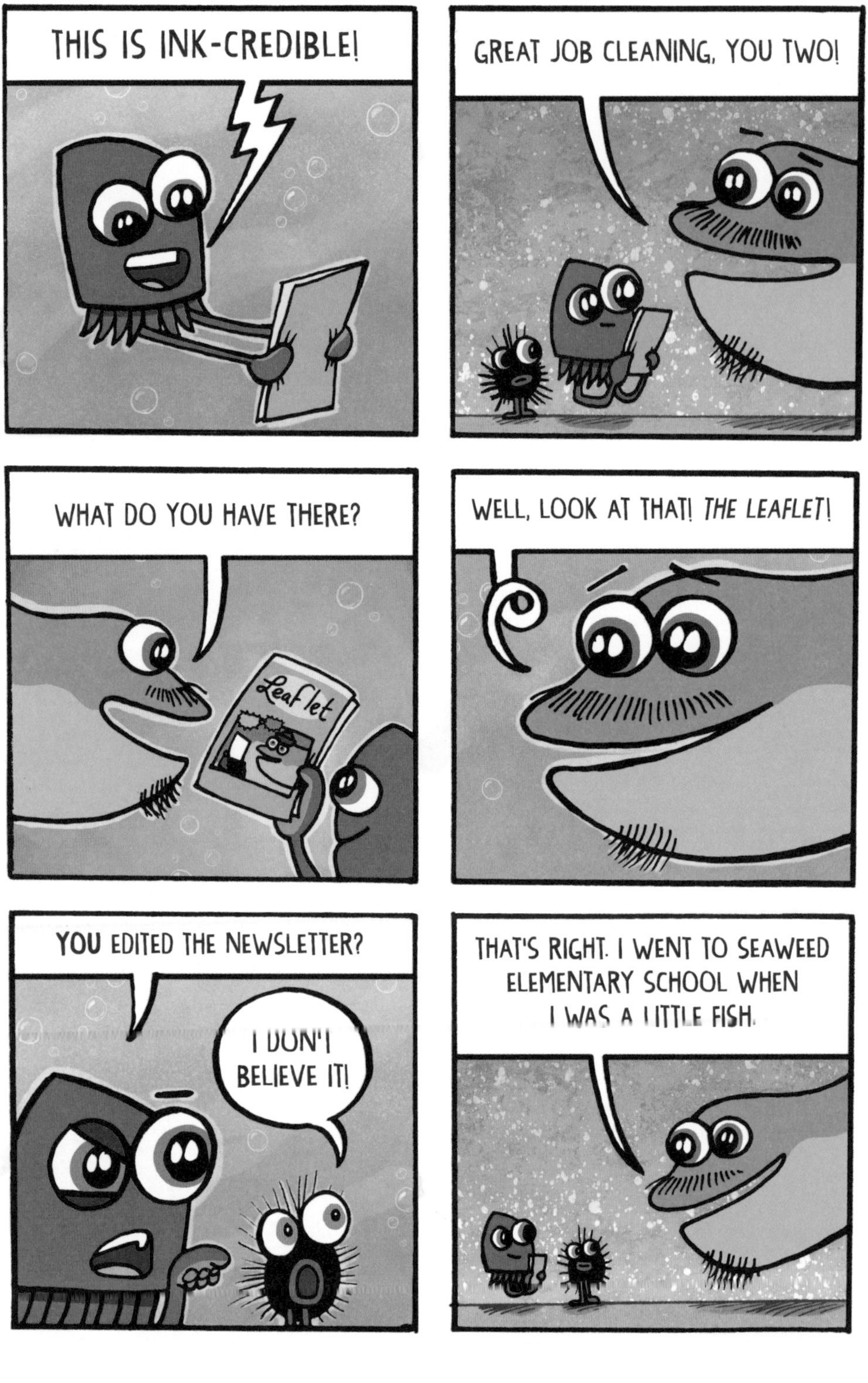
THIS IS INK-CREDIBLE!
GREAT JOB CLEANING, YOU TWO!
WHAT DO YOU HAVE THERE?
Leaflet
WELL, LOOK AT THAT! *THE LEAFLET*!
YOU EDITED THE NEWSLETTER?
I DON'T BELIEVE IT!
THAT'S RIGHT. I WENT TO SEAWEED ELEMENTARY SCHOOL WHEN I WAS A LITTLE FISH.

BACK THEN, I HAD A LOT TO SAY. AND I WASN'T THE ONLY ONE . . .

SO MY FRIENDS AND I STARTED A NEWSLETTER.

SOME OF US WERE REPORTERS, AND SOME WROTE OPINIONS.

OTHERS TOOK PHOTOS AND DREW COMICS.

IN FACT, WE MADE THE NEWSLETTER ON THIS COPY MACHINE.

COOOOL!

WOW!

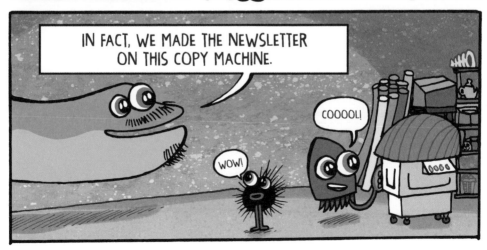

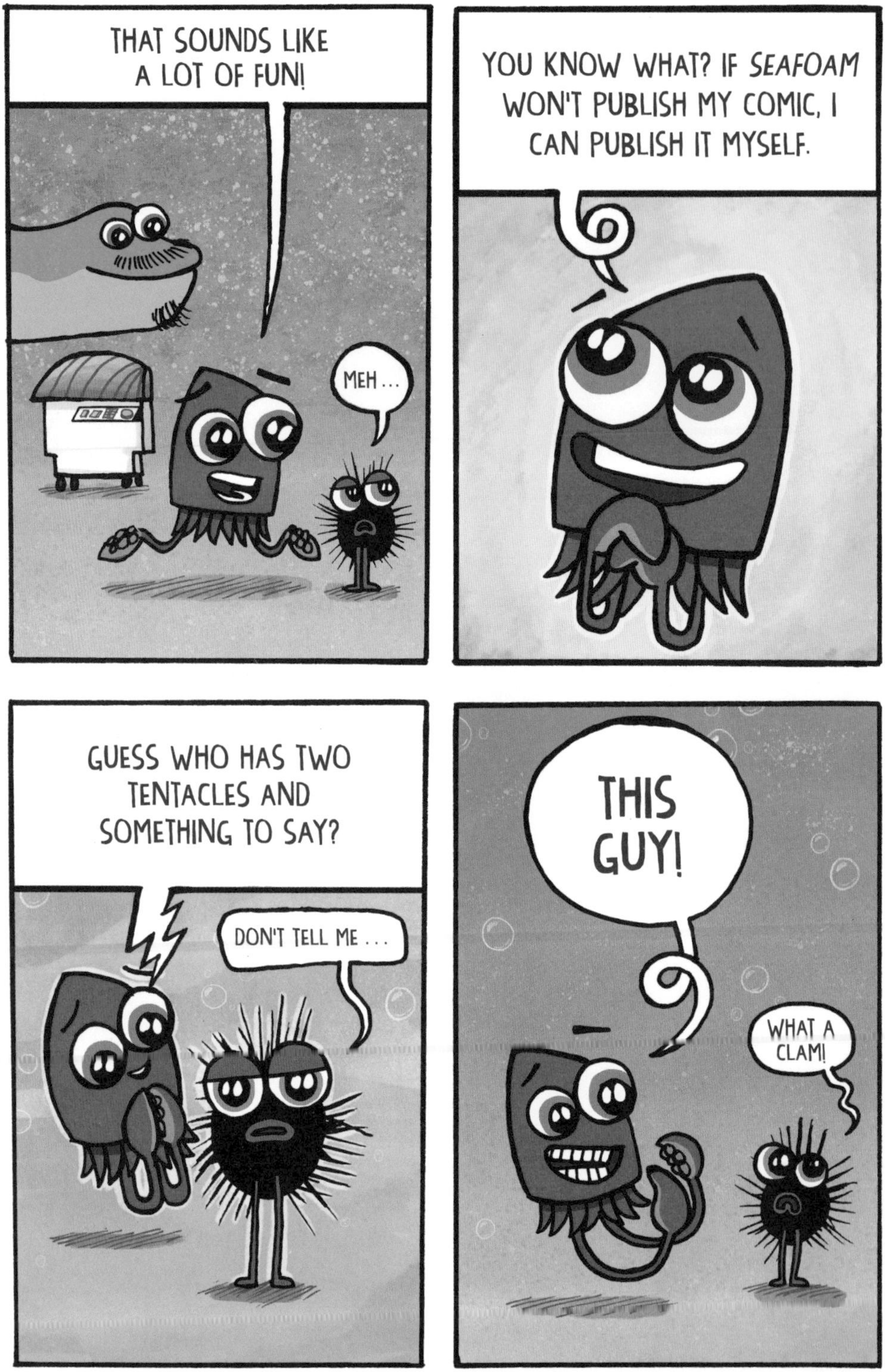
THAT SOUNDS LIKE A LOT OF FUN!
MEH . . .
YOU KNOW WHAT? IF *SEAFOAM* WON'T PUBLISH MY COMIC, I CAN PUBLISH IT MYSELF.
GUESS WHO HAS TWO TENTACLES AND SOMETHING TO SAY?
DON'T TELL ME . . .
THIS GUY!
WHAT A CLAM!

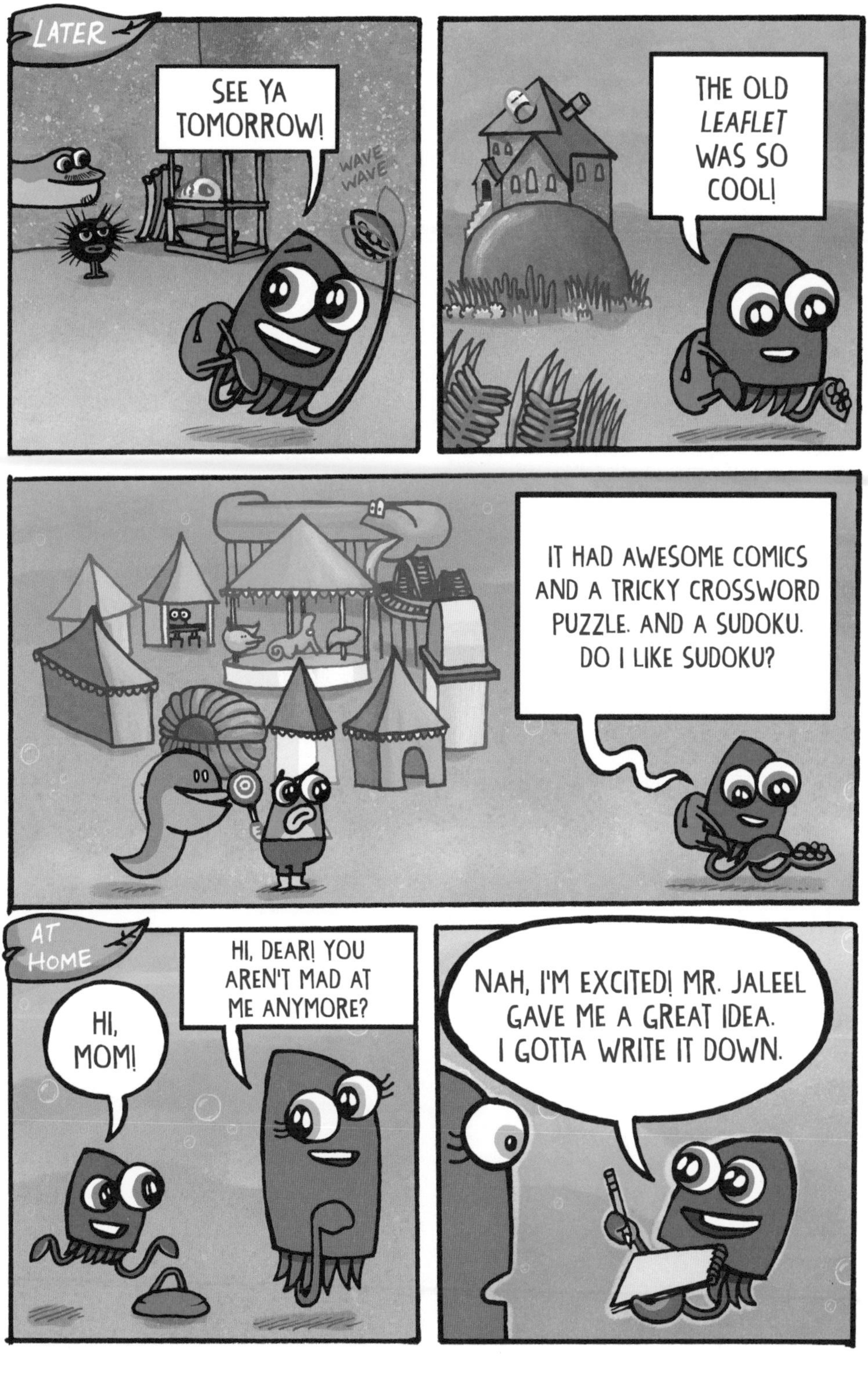
LATER
SEE YA TOMORROW!
WAVE WAVE
THE OLD *LEAFLET* WAS SO COOL!
IT HAD AWESOME COMICS AND A TRICKY CROSSWORD PUZZLE. AND A SUDOKU. DO I LIKE SUDOKU?
AT HOME
HI, MOM!
HI, DEAR! YOU AREN'T MAD AT ME ANYMORE?
NAH, I'M EXCITED! MR. JALEEL GAVE ME A GREAT IDEA. I GOTTA WRITE IT DOWN.

CHAPTER 5

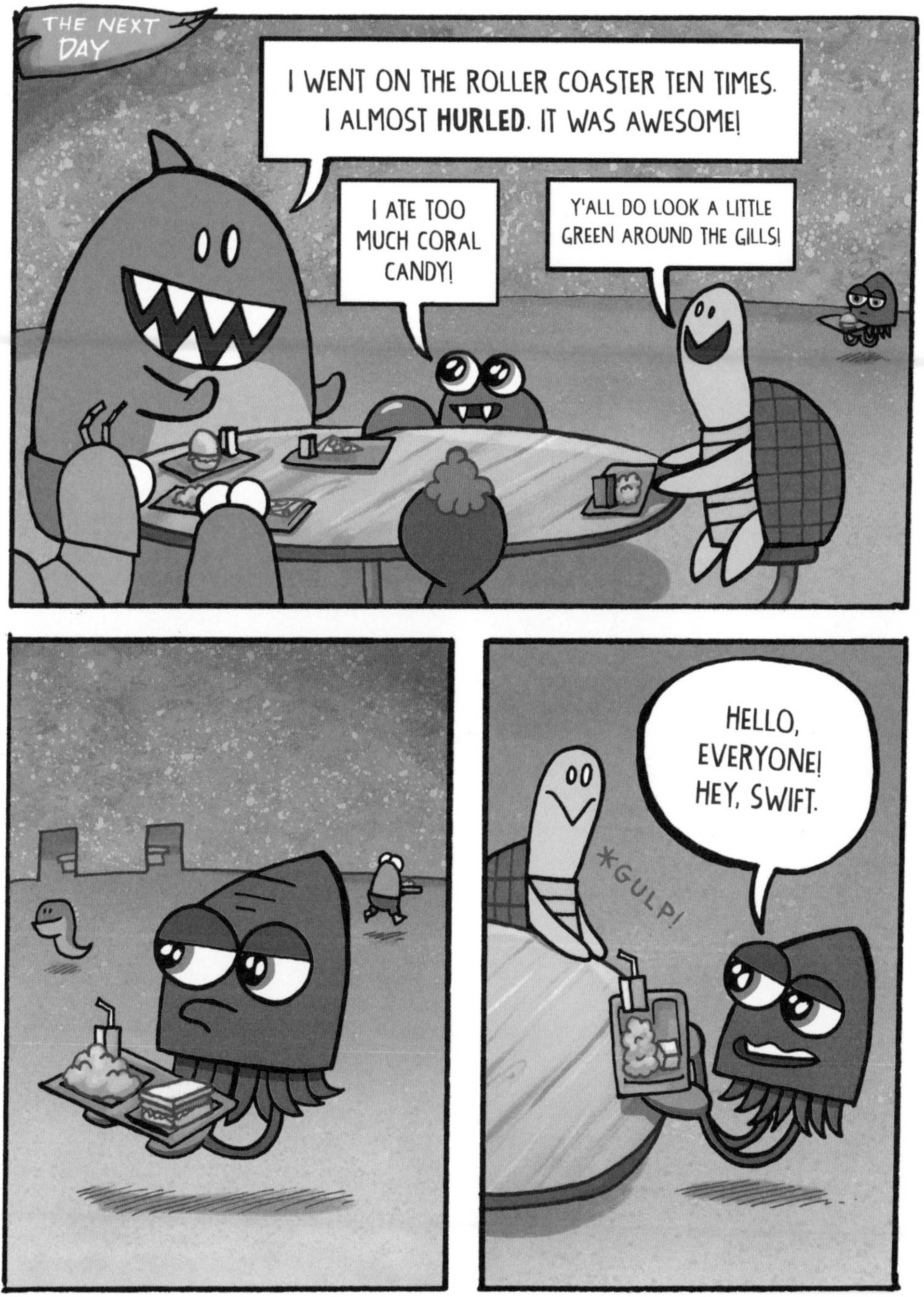
THE NEXT DAY
I WENT ON THE ROLLER COASTER TEN TIMES. I ALMOST **HURLED**. IT WAS AWESOME!
I ATE TOO MUCH CORAL CANDY!
Y'ALL DO LOOK A LITTLE GREEN AROUND THE GILLS!
HELLO, EVERYONE! HEY, SWIFT.
*GULP!

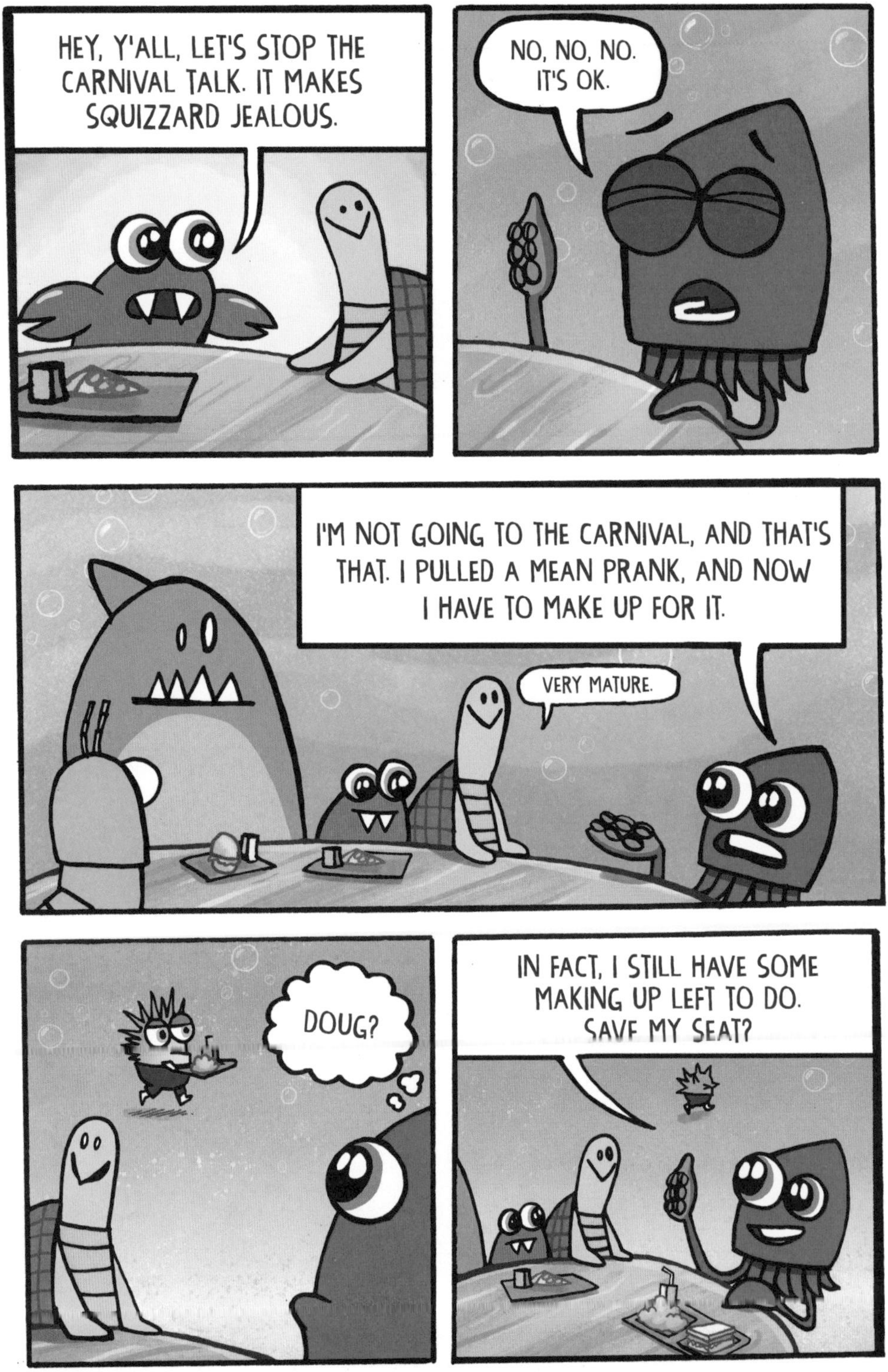
HEY, Y'ALL, LET'S STOP THE CARNIVAL TALK. IT MAKES SQUIZZARD JEALOUS.
NO, NO, NO. IT'S OK.
I'M NOT GOING TO THE CARNIVAL, AND THAT'S THAT. I PULLED A MEAN PRANK, AND NOW I HAVE TO MAKE UP FOR IT.
VERY MATURE.
DOUG?
IN FACT, I STILL HAVE SOME MAKING UP LEFT TO DO. SAVE MY SEAT?

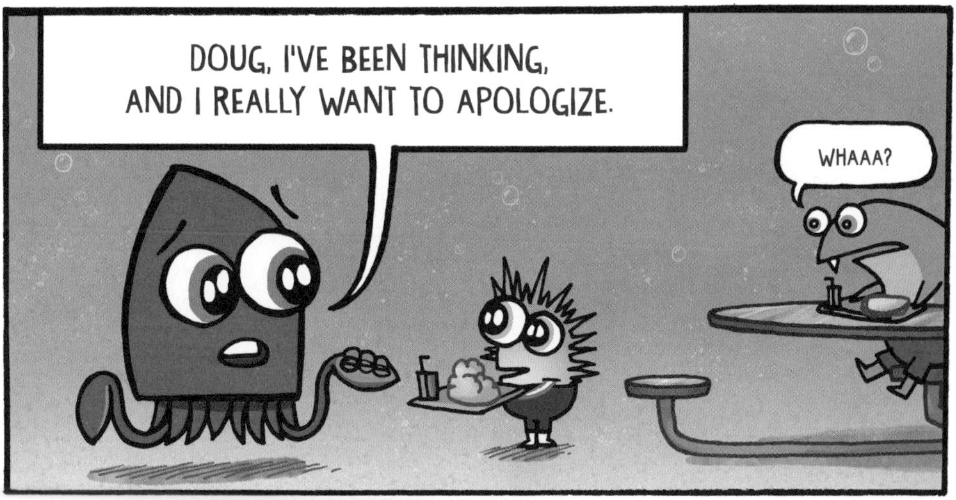
DOUG, I'VE BEEN THINKING, AND I REALLY WANT TO APOLOGIZE.
WHAAA?
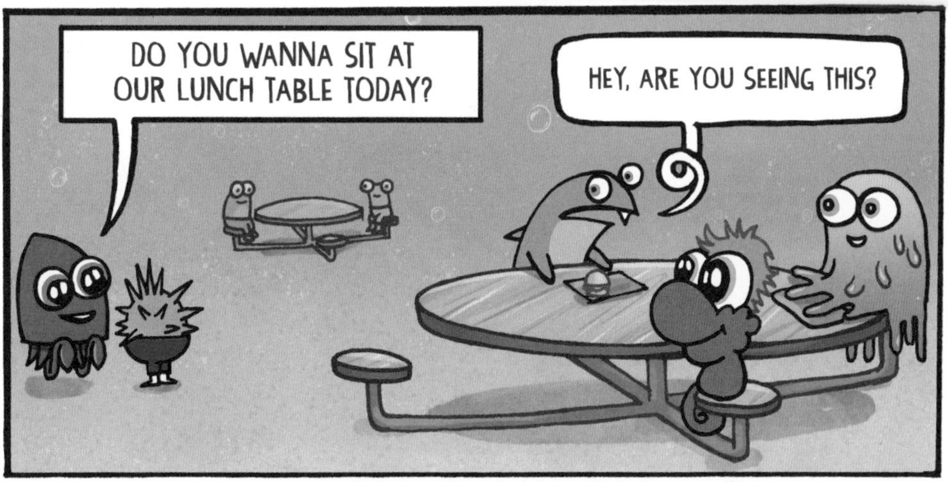
DO YOU WANNA SIT AT OUR LUNCH TABLE TODAY?
HEY, ARE YOU SEEING THIS?
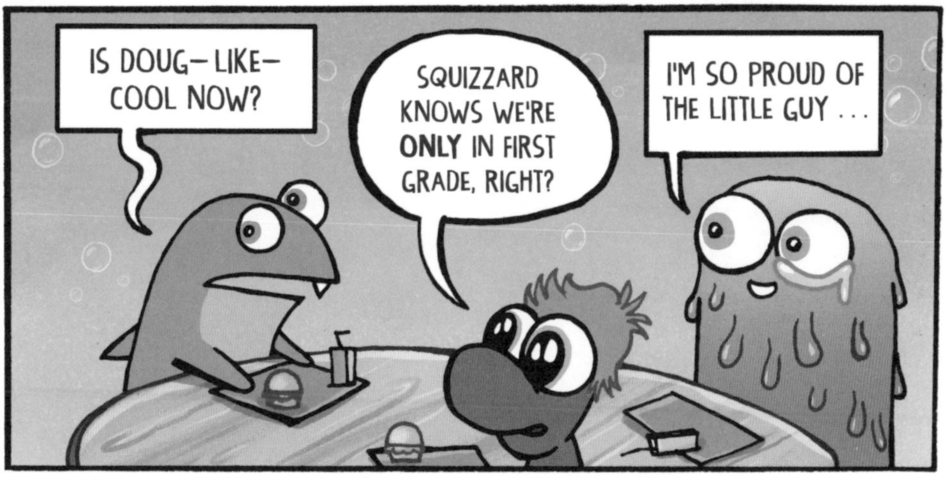
IS DOUG— LIKE— COOL NOW?
SQUIZZARD KNOWS WE'RE **ONLY** IN FIRST GRADE, RIGHT?
I'M SO PROUD OF THE LITTLE GUY . . .

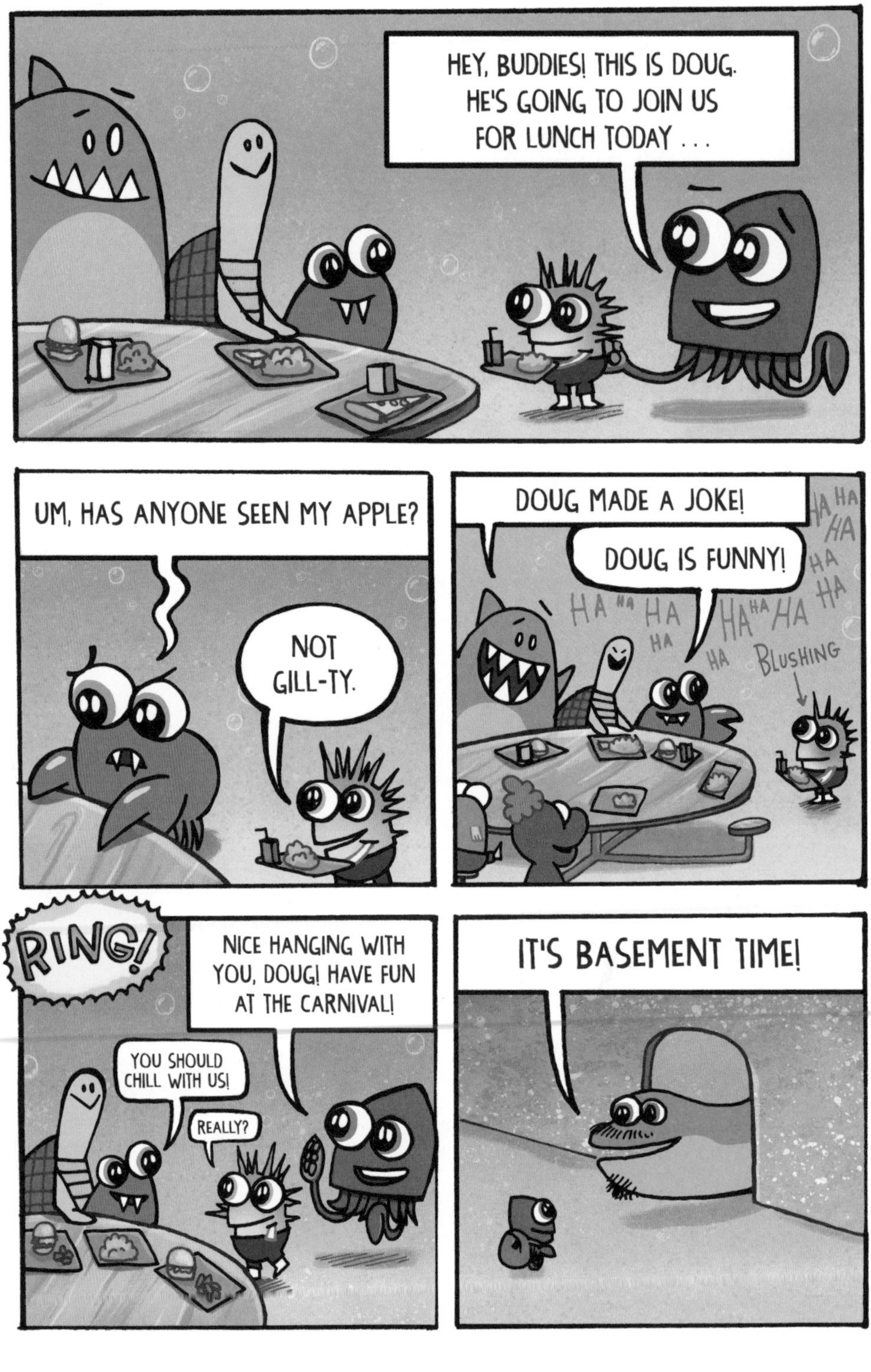

HEY, BUDDIES! THIS IS DOUG. HE'S GOING TO JOIN US FOR LUNCH TODAY . . .
UM, HAS ANYONE SEEN MY APPLE?
NOT GILL-TY.
DOUG MADE A JOKE!
DOUG IS FUNNY!
HA HA HA HA HA HA HA HA HA HA HA HA HA HA
BLUSHING
RING!
NICE HANGING WITH YOU, DOUG! HAVE FUN AT THE CARNIVAL!
YOU SHOULD CHILL WITH US!
REALLY?
IT'S BASEMENT TIME!

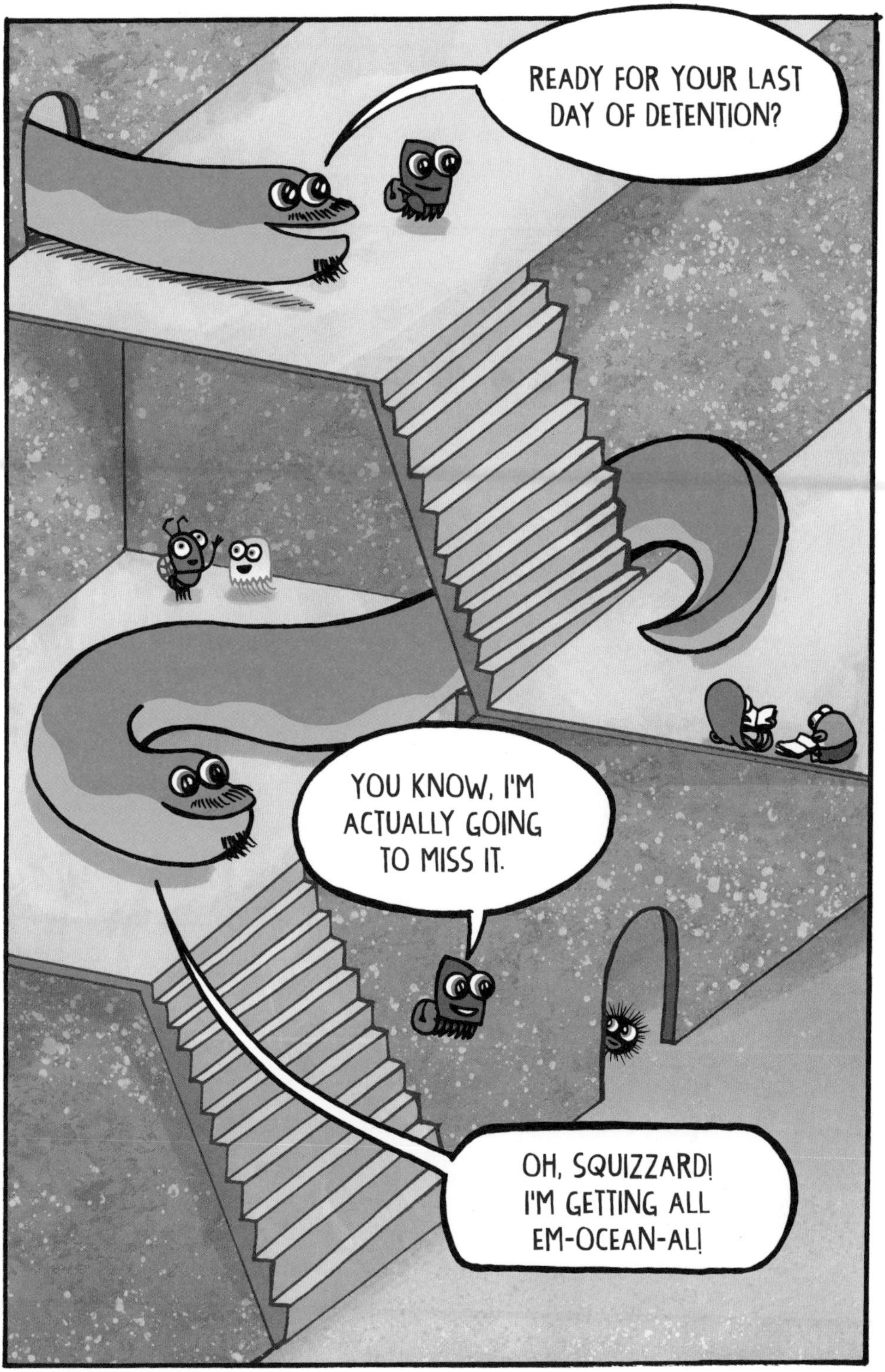
READY FOR YOUR LAST DAY OF DETENTION?
YOU KNOW, I'M ACTUALLY GOING TO MISS IT.
OH, SQUIZZARD! I'M GETTING ALL EM-OCEAN-AL!

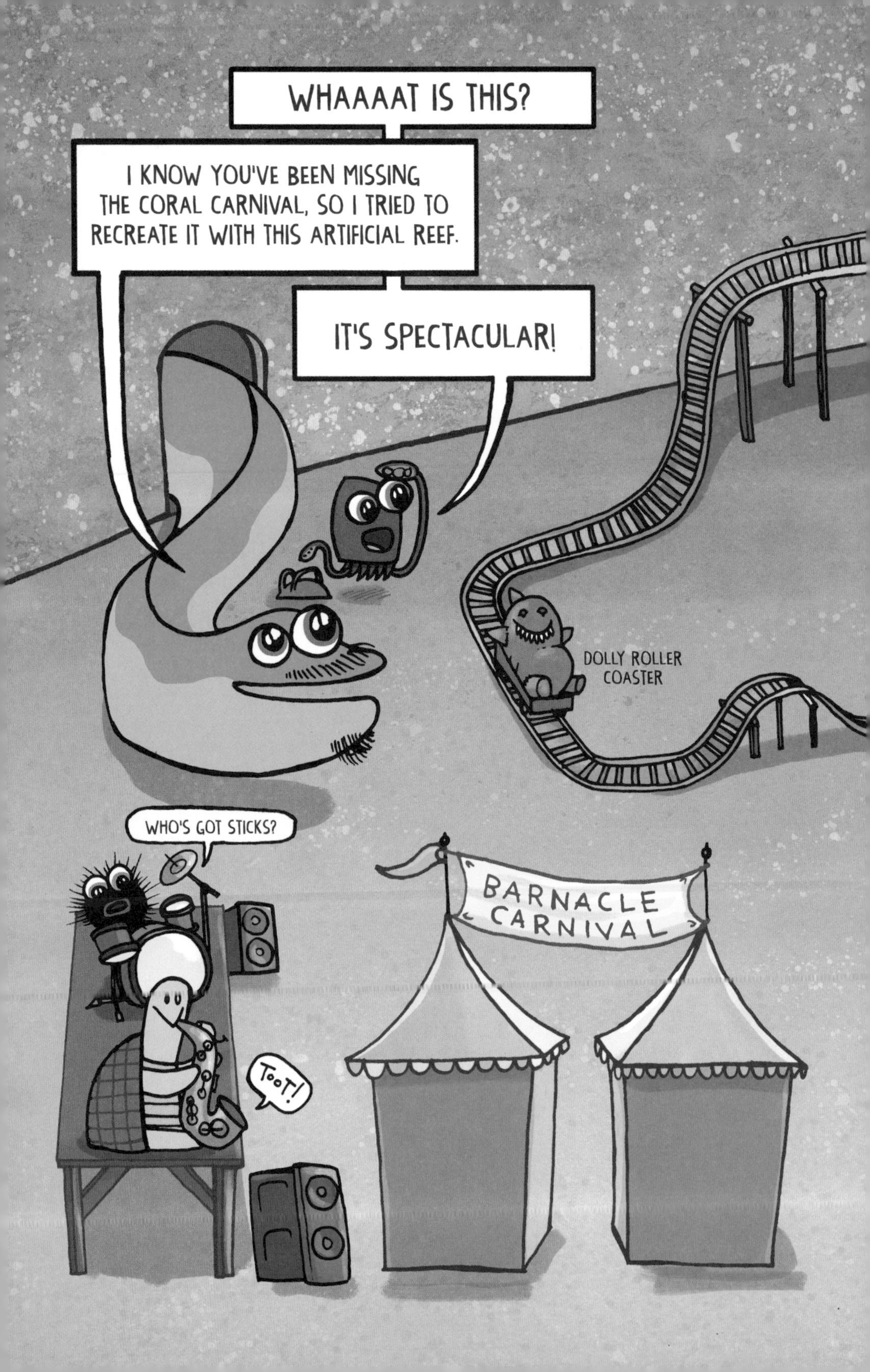
WHAAAAT IS THIS?
I KNOW YOU'VE BEEN MISSING THE CORAL CARNIVAL, SO I TRIED TO RECREATE IT WITH THIS ARTIFICIAL REEF.
IT'S SPECTACULAR!
DOLLY ROLLER COASTER
WHO'S GOT STICKS?
BARNACLE CARNIVAL
TOOT!

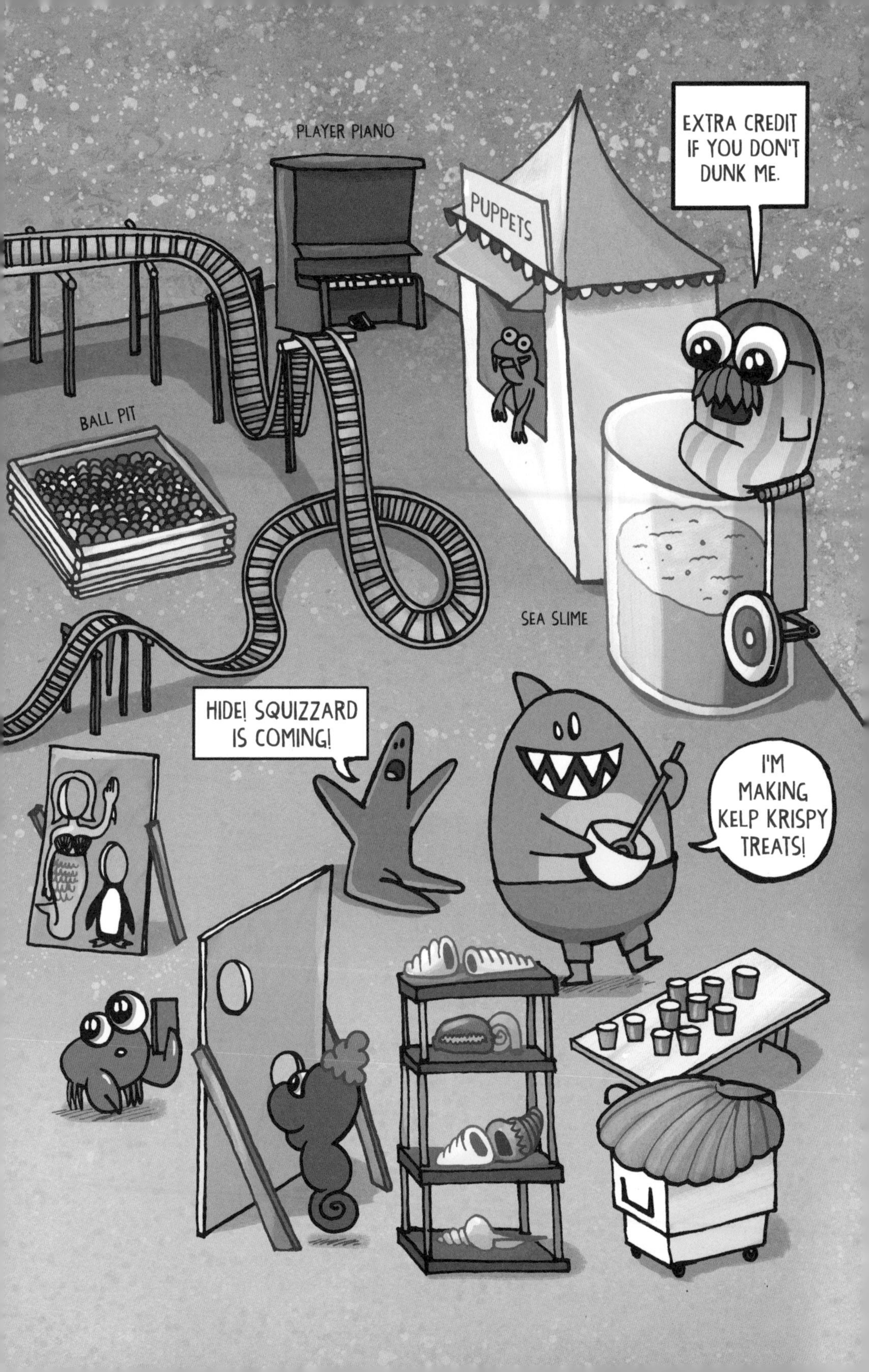
PLAYER PIANO
PUPPETS
EXTRA CREDIT IF YOU DON'T DUNK ME.
BALL PIT
SEA SLIME
HIDE! SQUIZZARD IS COMING!
I'M MAKING KELP KRISPY TREATS!

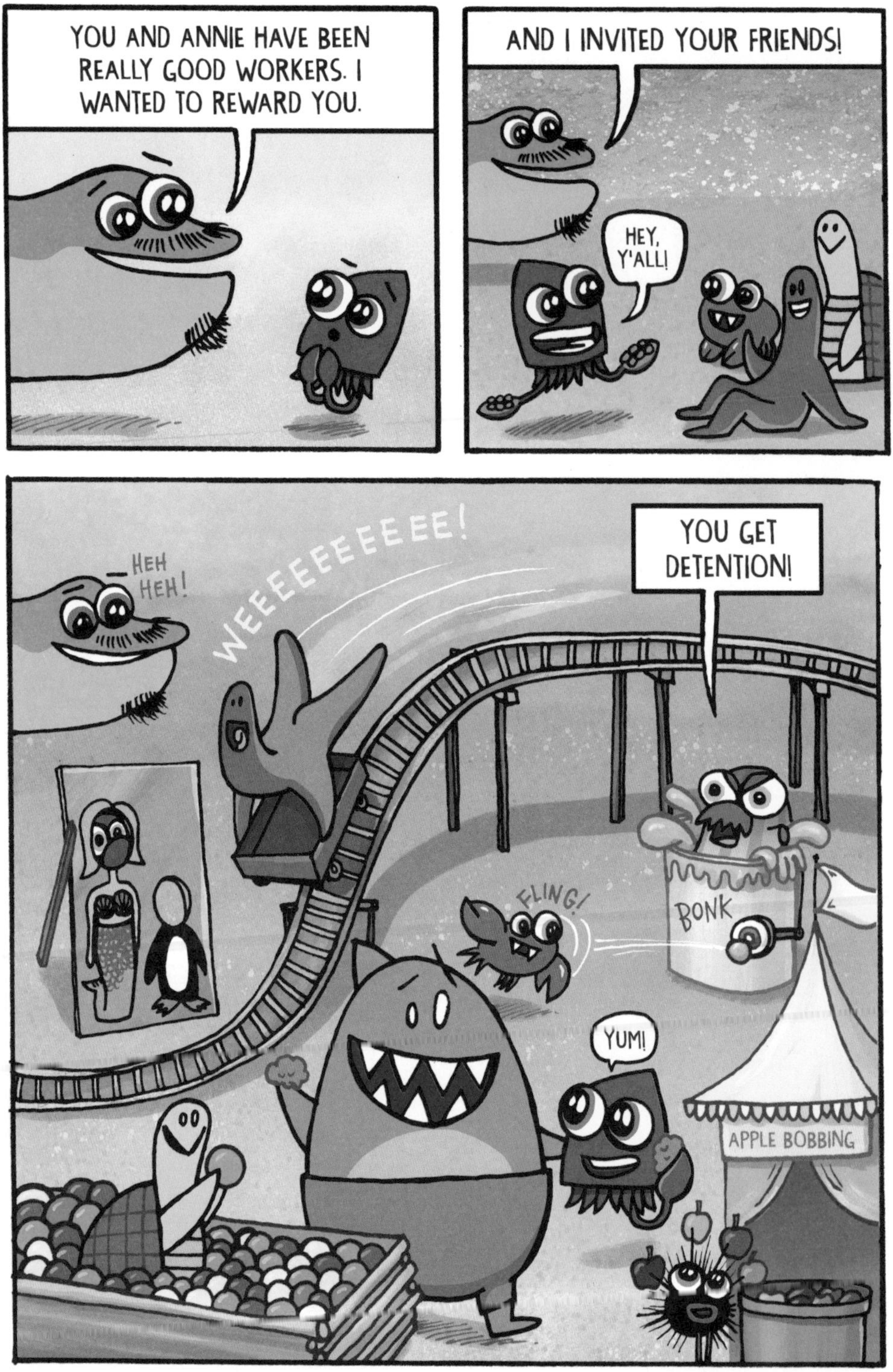

YOU AND ANNIE HAVE BEEN REALLY GOOD WORKERS. I WANTED TO REWARD YOU.
AND I INVITED YOUR FRIENDS!
HEY, Y'ALL!
HEH HEH!
WEEEEEEEEEEE!
YOU GET DETENTION!
FLING!
BONK
YUM!
APPLE BOBBING

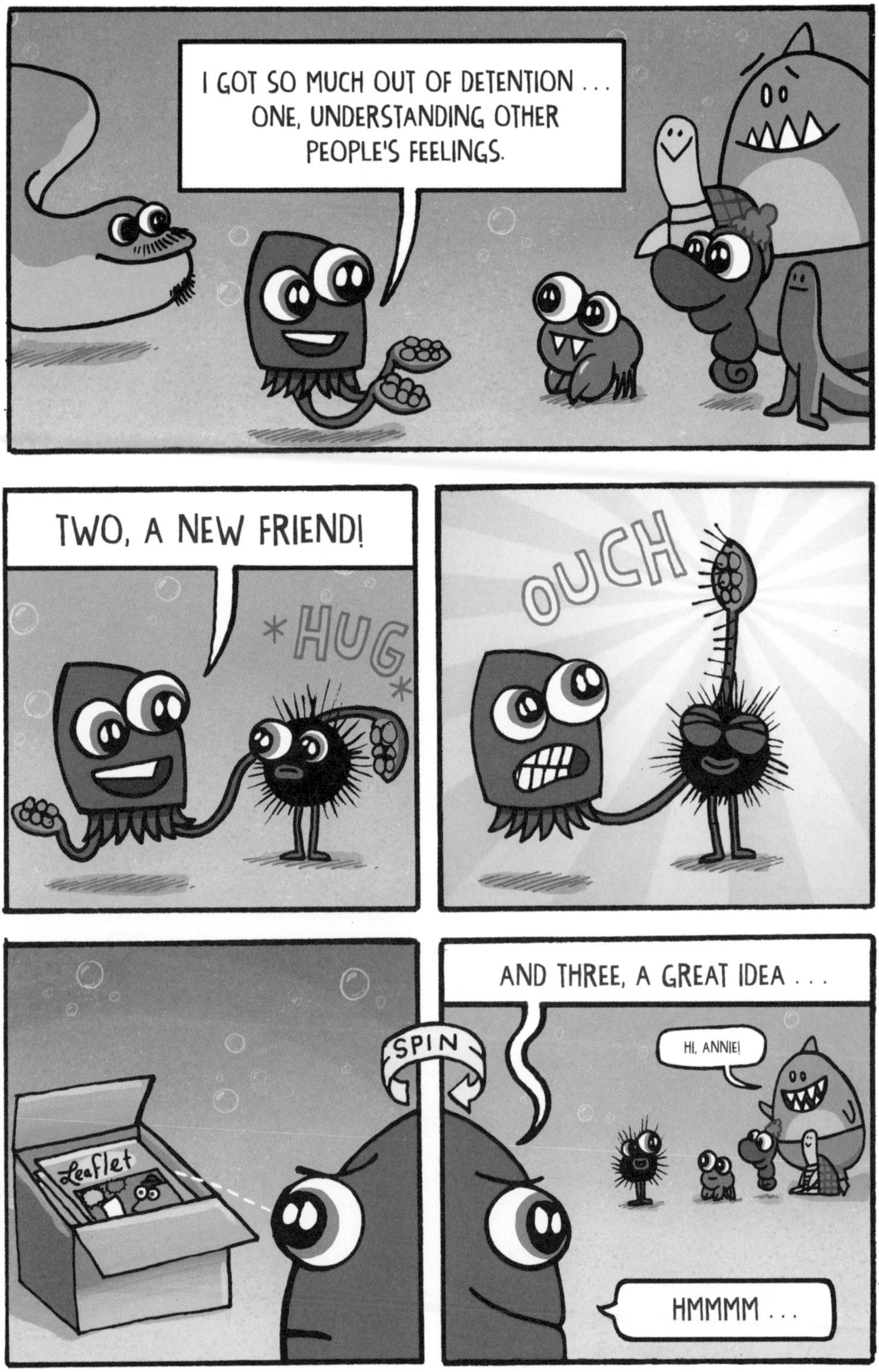
I GOT SO MUCH OUT OF DETENTION . . .
ONE, UNDERSTANDING OTHER PEOPLE'S FEELINGS.
TWO, A NEW FRIEND!
HUG
OUCH
SPIN
AND THREE, A GREAT IDEA . . .
HI, ANNIE!
HMMMM . . .

CHAPTER 6

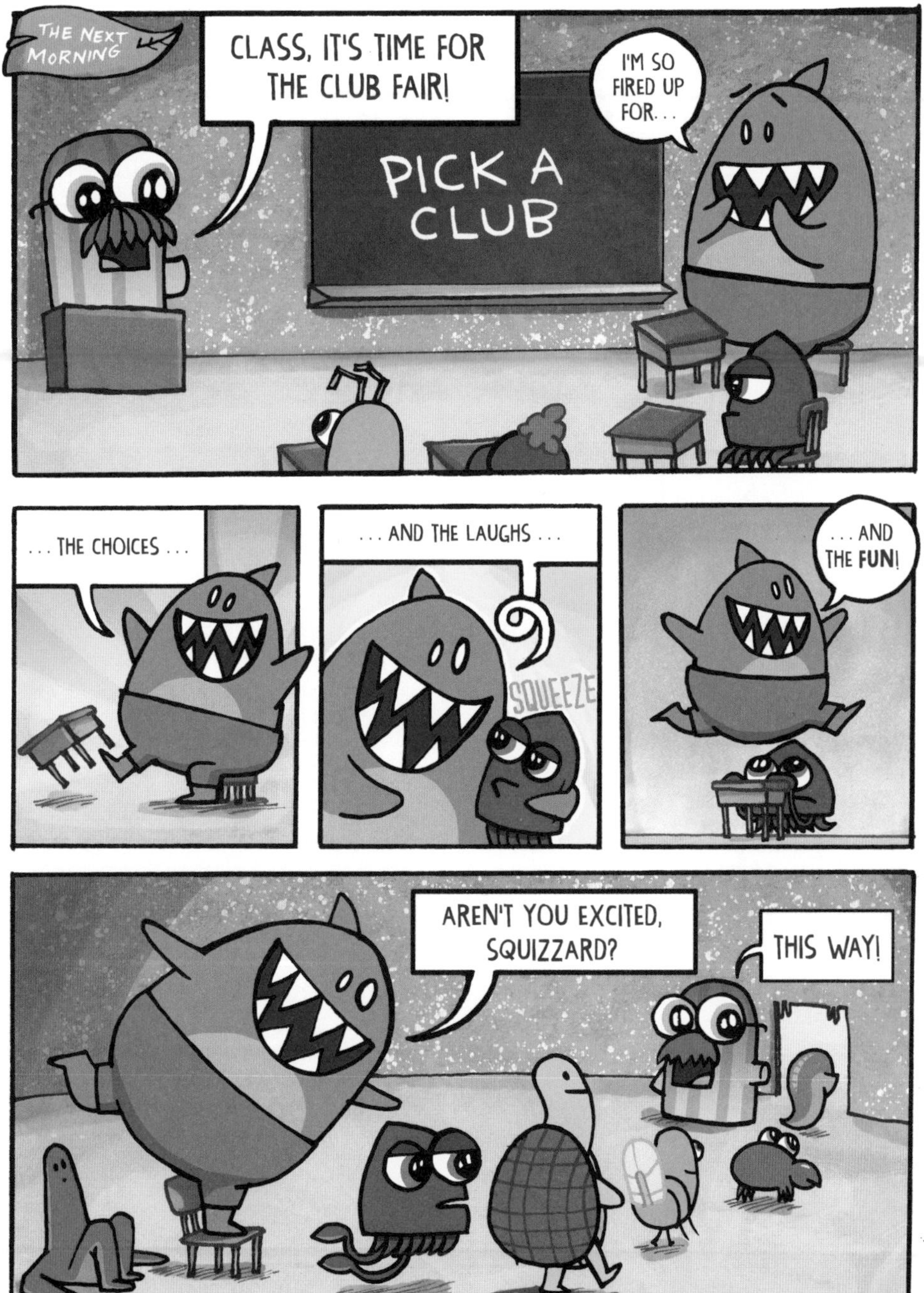

THE NEXT MORNING
CLASS, IT'S TIME FOR THE CLUB FAIR!
PICK A CLUB
I'M SO FIRED UP FOR...
...THE CHOICES...
...AND THE LAUGHS...
SQUEEZE
...AND THE FUN!
AREN'T YOU EXCITED, SQUIZZARD?
THIS WAY!

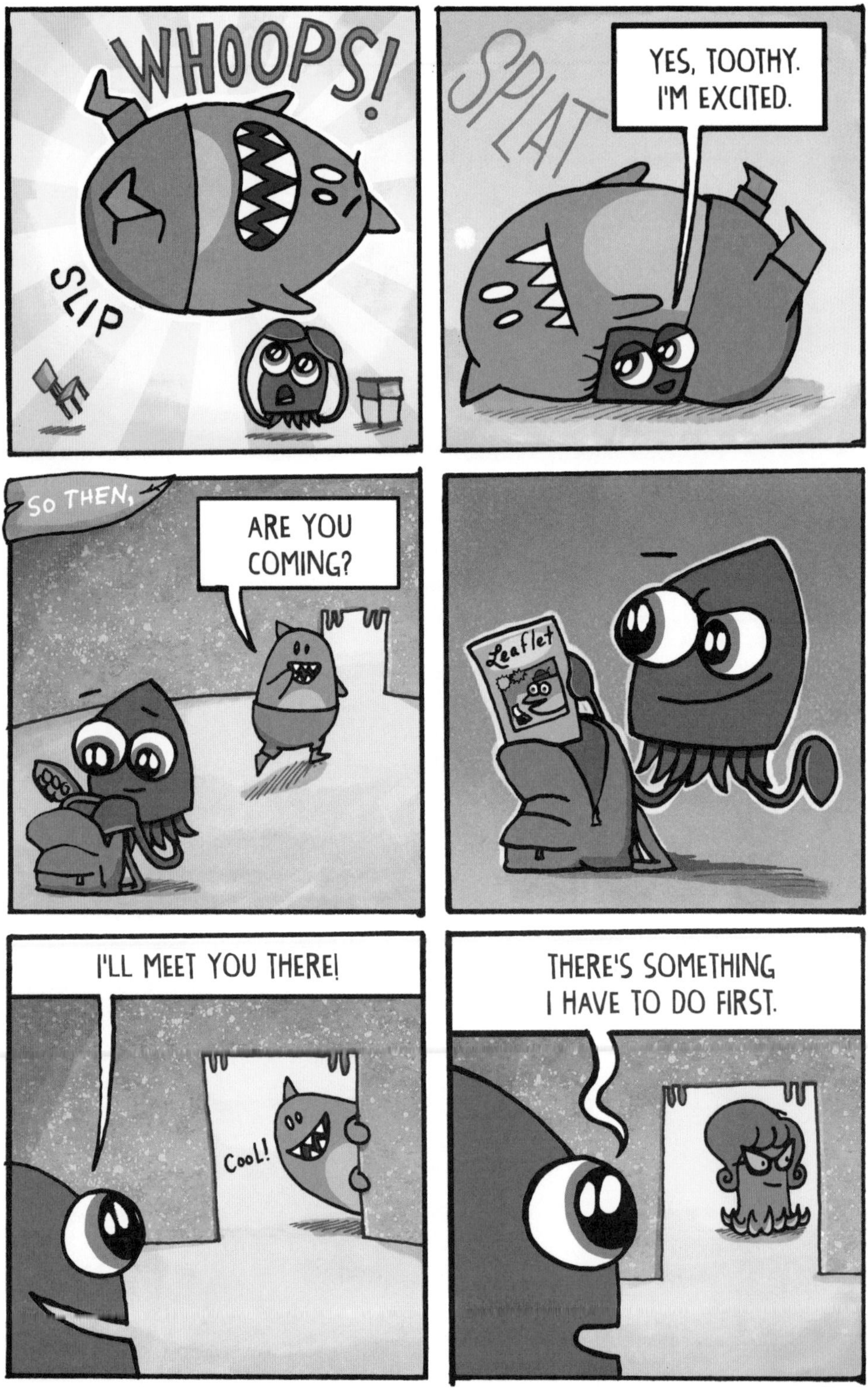
WHOOPS!
SLIP
SPLAT
YES, TOOTHY. I'M EXCITED.
SO THEN,
ARE YOU COMING?
Leaflet
I'LL MEET YOU THERE!
COOL!
THERE'S SOMETHING I HAVE TO DO FIRST.

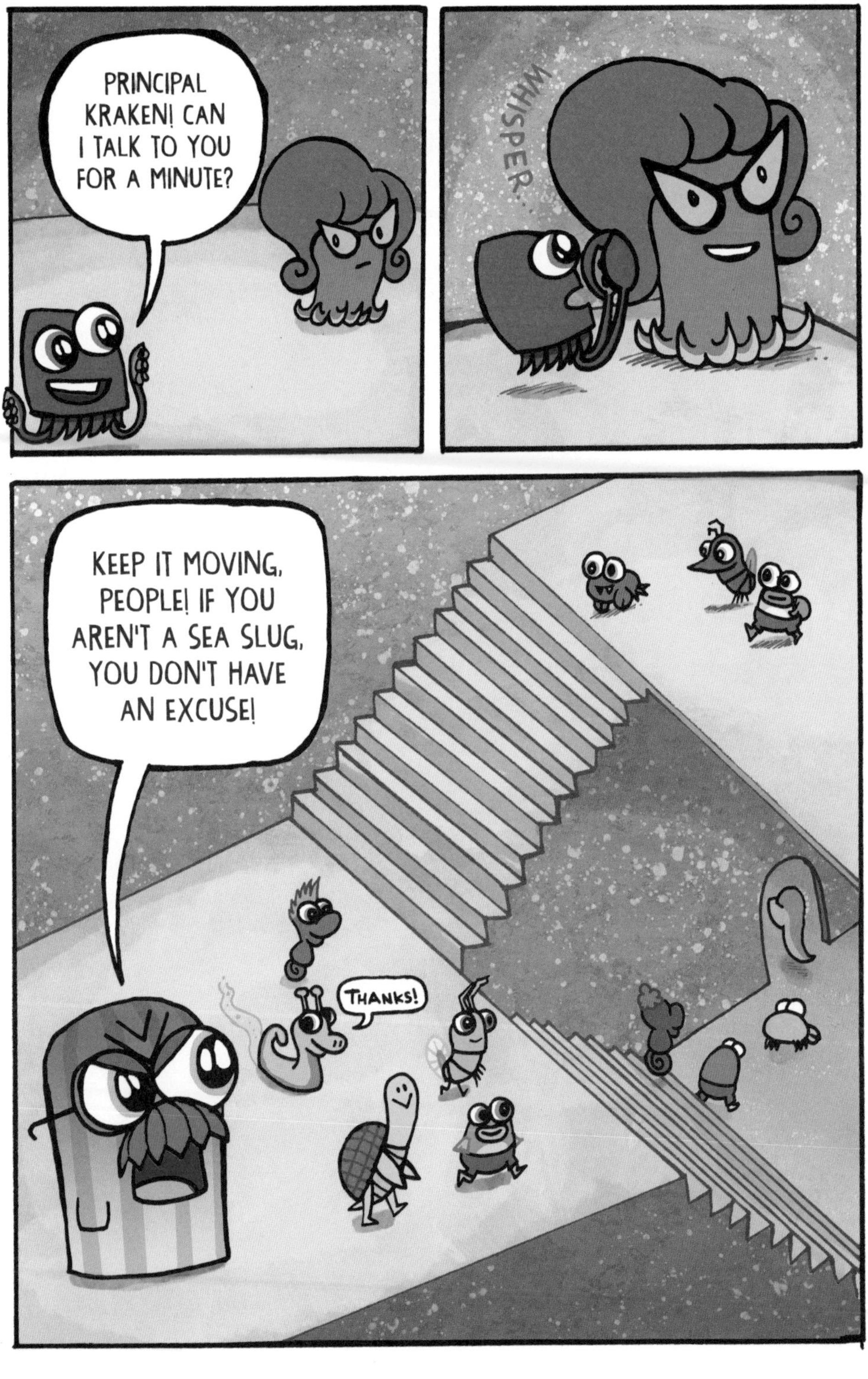
PRINCIPAL KRAKEN! CAN I TALK TO YOU FOR A MINUTE?
WHISPER...
KEEP IT MOVING, PEOPLE! IF YOU AREN'T A SEA SLUG, YOU DON'T HAVE AN EXCUSE!
THANKS!

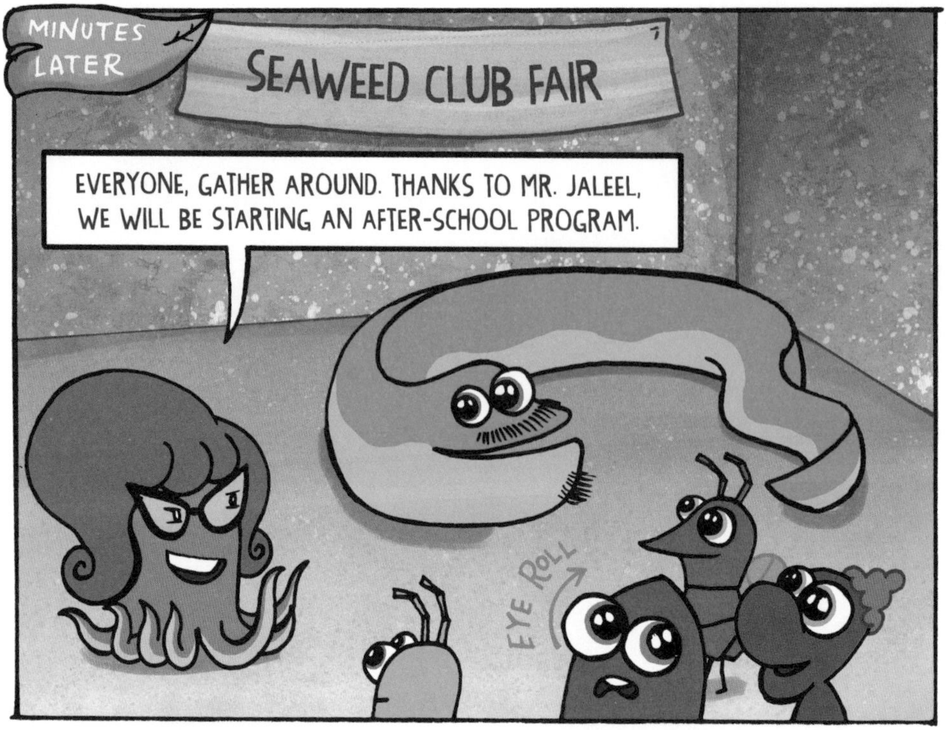
MINUTES LATER
SEAWEED CLUB FAIR
EVERYONE, GATHER AROUND. THANKS TO MR. JALEEL, WE WILL BE STARTING AN AFTER-SCHOOL PROGRAM.
EYE ROLL

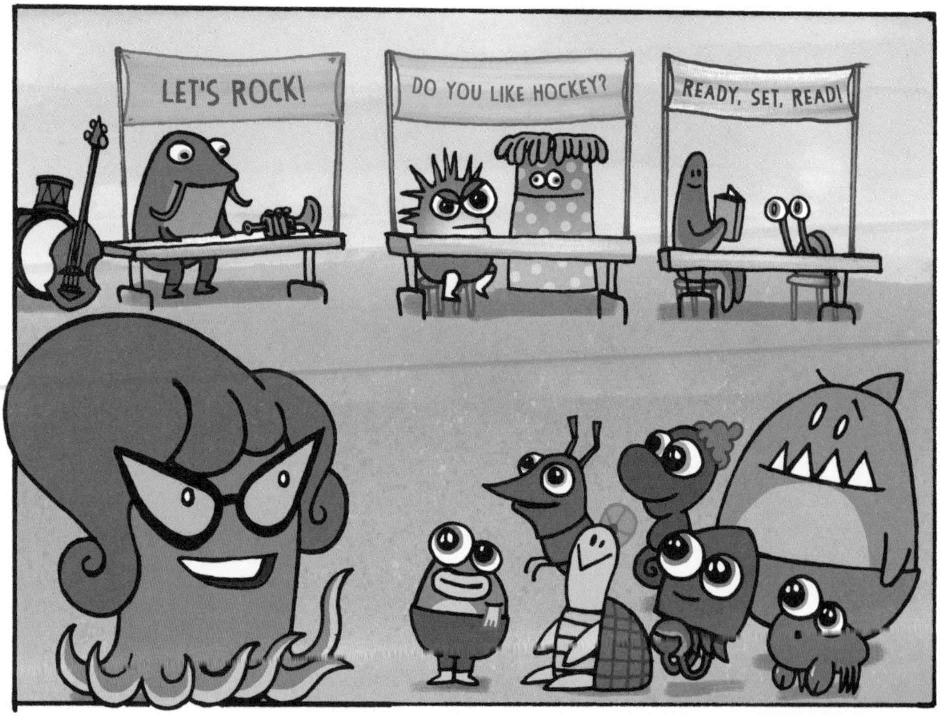
LET'S ROCK!
DO YOU LIKE HOCKEY?
READY, SET, READ!

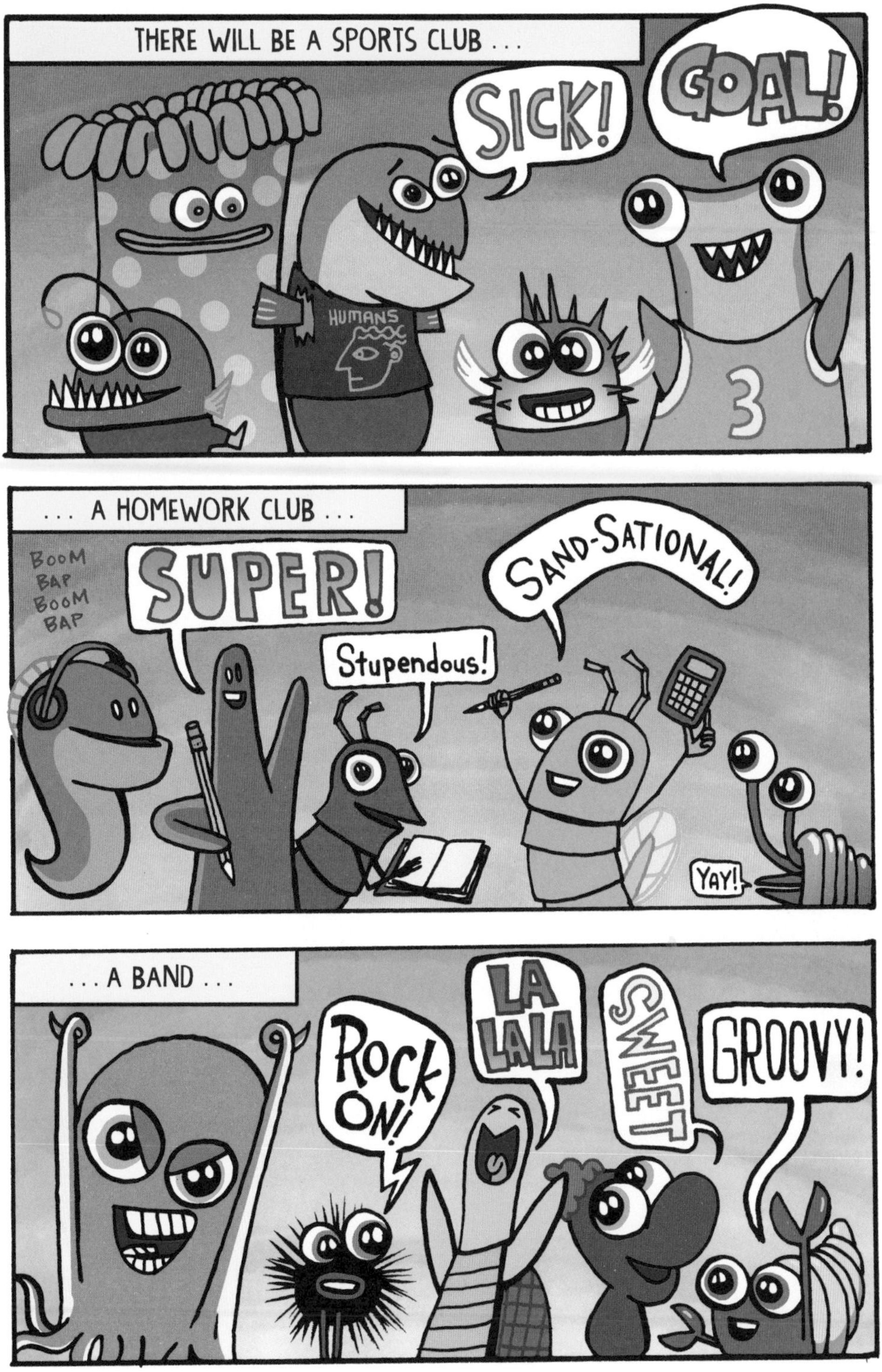
THERE WILL BE A SPORTS CLUB . . .
SICK!
GOAL!
HUMANS
3
. . . A HOMEWORK CLUB . . .
BOOM BAP BOOM BAP
SUPER!
Stupendous!
SAND-SATIONAL!
YAY!
. . . A BAND . . .
ROCK ON!
LA LALA
SWEET
GROOVY!

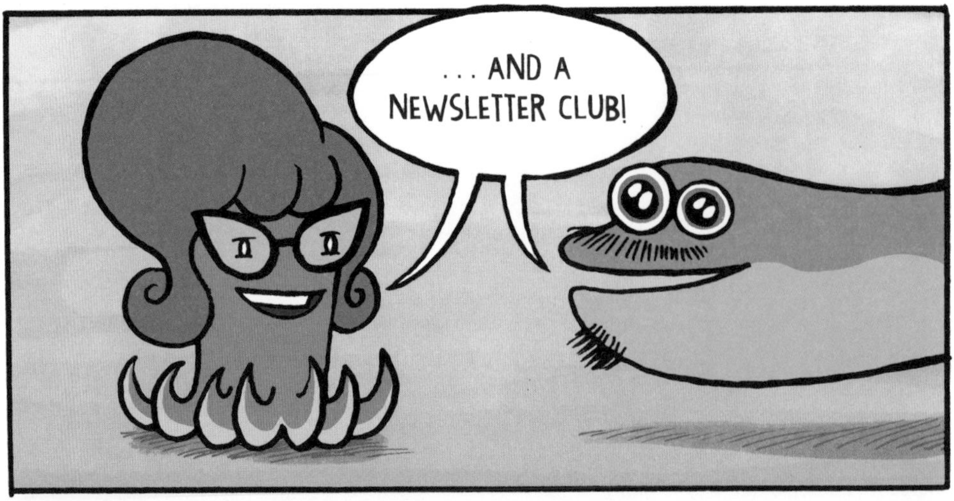
. . . AND A NEWSLETTER CLUB!

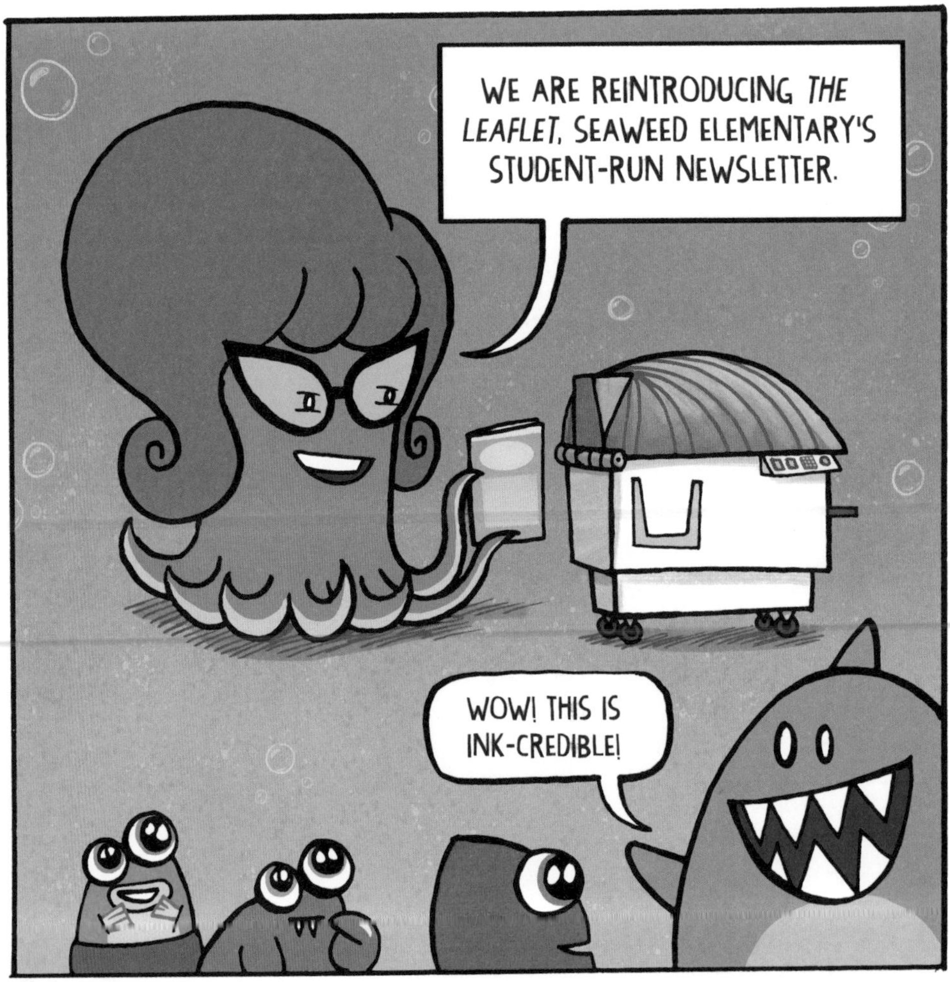
WE ARE REINTRODUCING *THE LEAFLET*, SEAWEED ELEMENTARY'S STUDENT-RUN NEWSLETTER.
WOW! THIS IS INK-CREDIBLE!

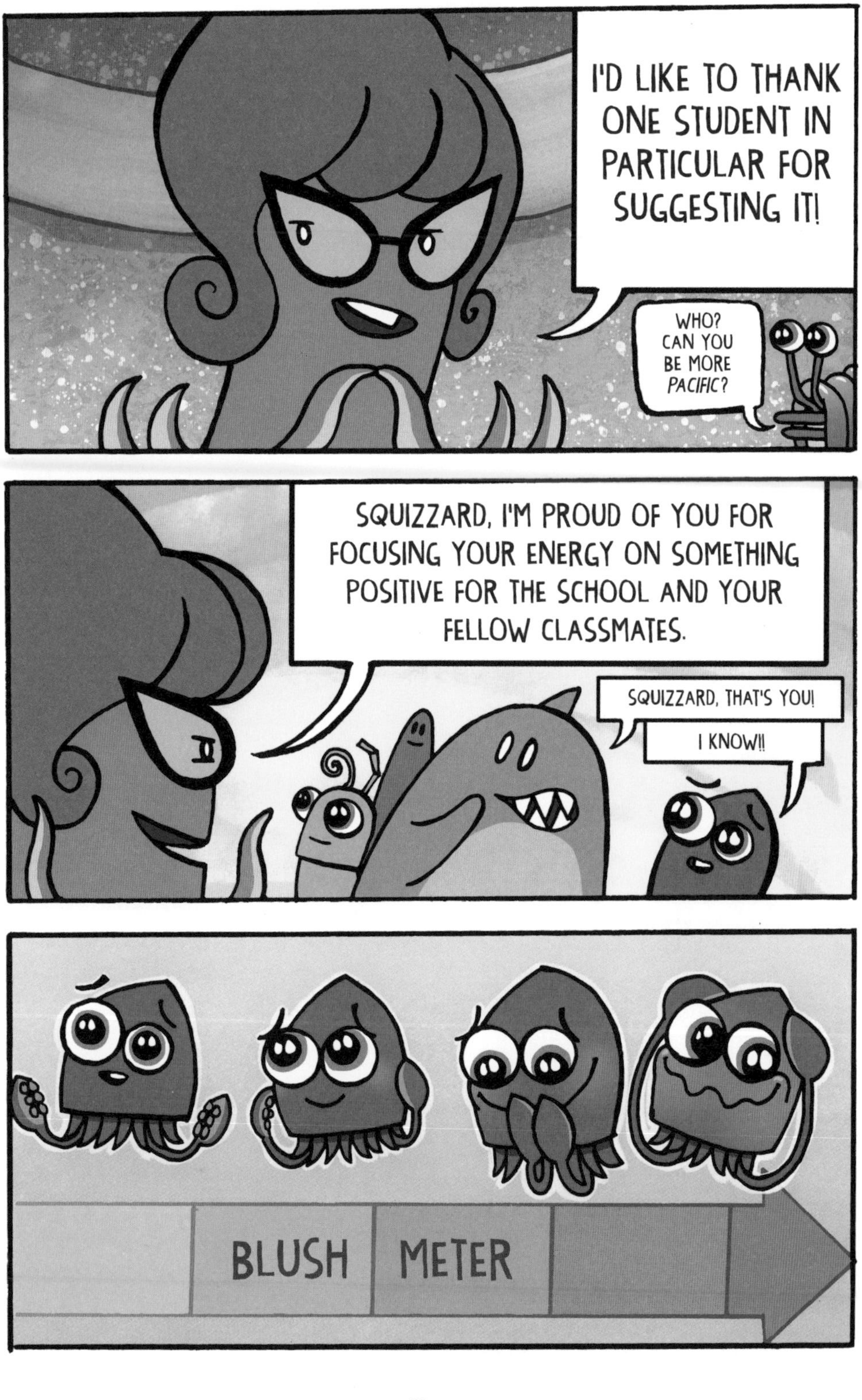

I'D LIKE TO THANK ONE STUDENT IN PARTICULAR FOR SUGGESTING IT!
WHO? CAN YOU BE MORE *PACIFIC*?
SQUIZZARD, I'M PROUD OF YOU FOR FOCUSING YOUR ENERGY ON SOMETHING POSITIVE FOR THE SCHOOL AND YOUR FELLOW CLASSMATES.
SQUIZZARD, THAT'S YOU!
I KNOW!!
BLUSH METER

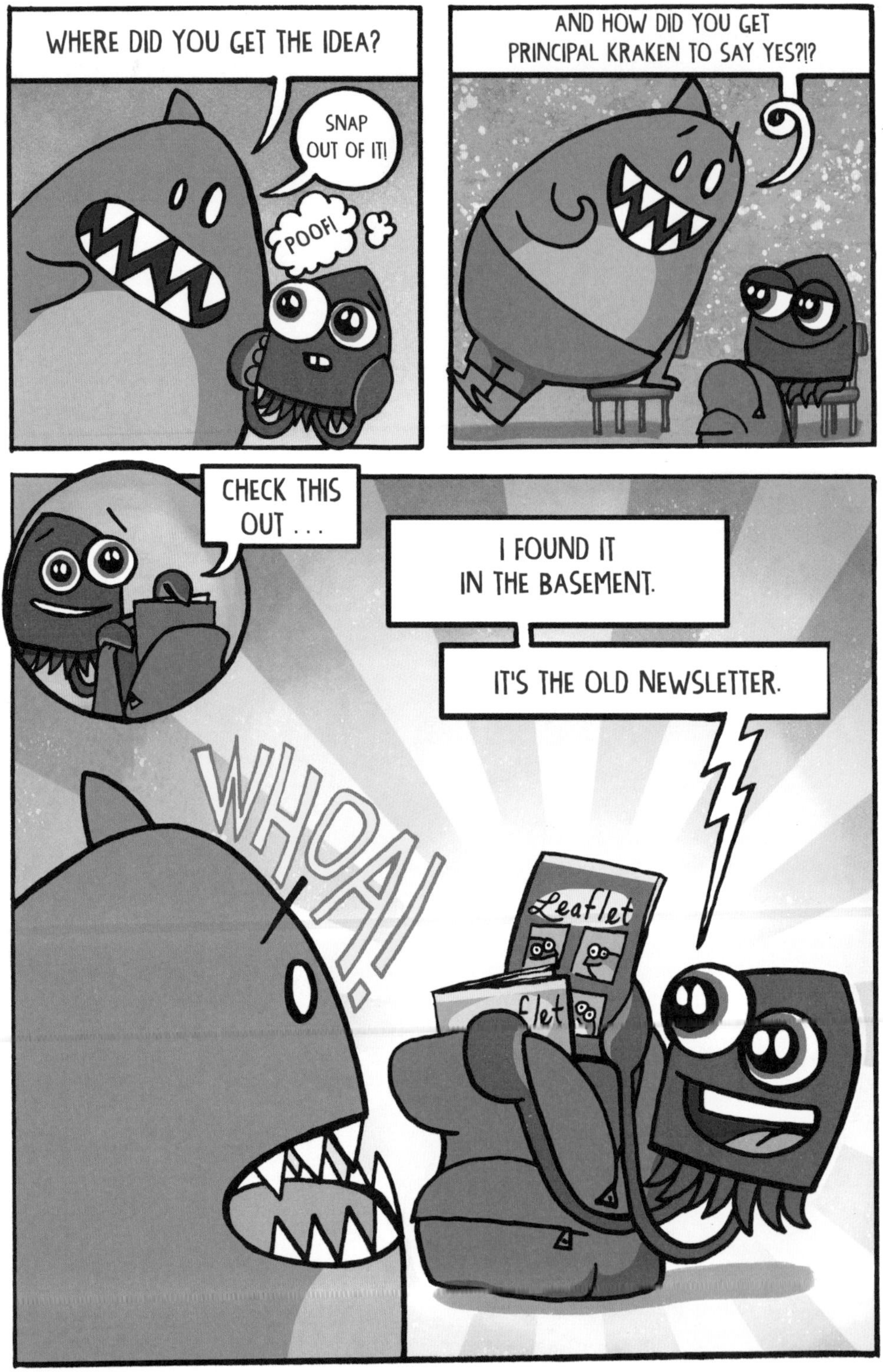

WHERE DID YOU GET THE IDEA?
SNAP OUT OF IT!
POOF!
AND HOW DID YOU GET PRINCIPAL KRAKEN TO SAY YES?!?
?
CHECK THIS OUT . . .
I FOUND IT IN THE BASEMENT.
IT'S THE OLD NEWSLETTER.
WHOA!
Leaflet
flet

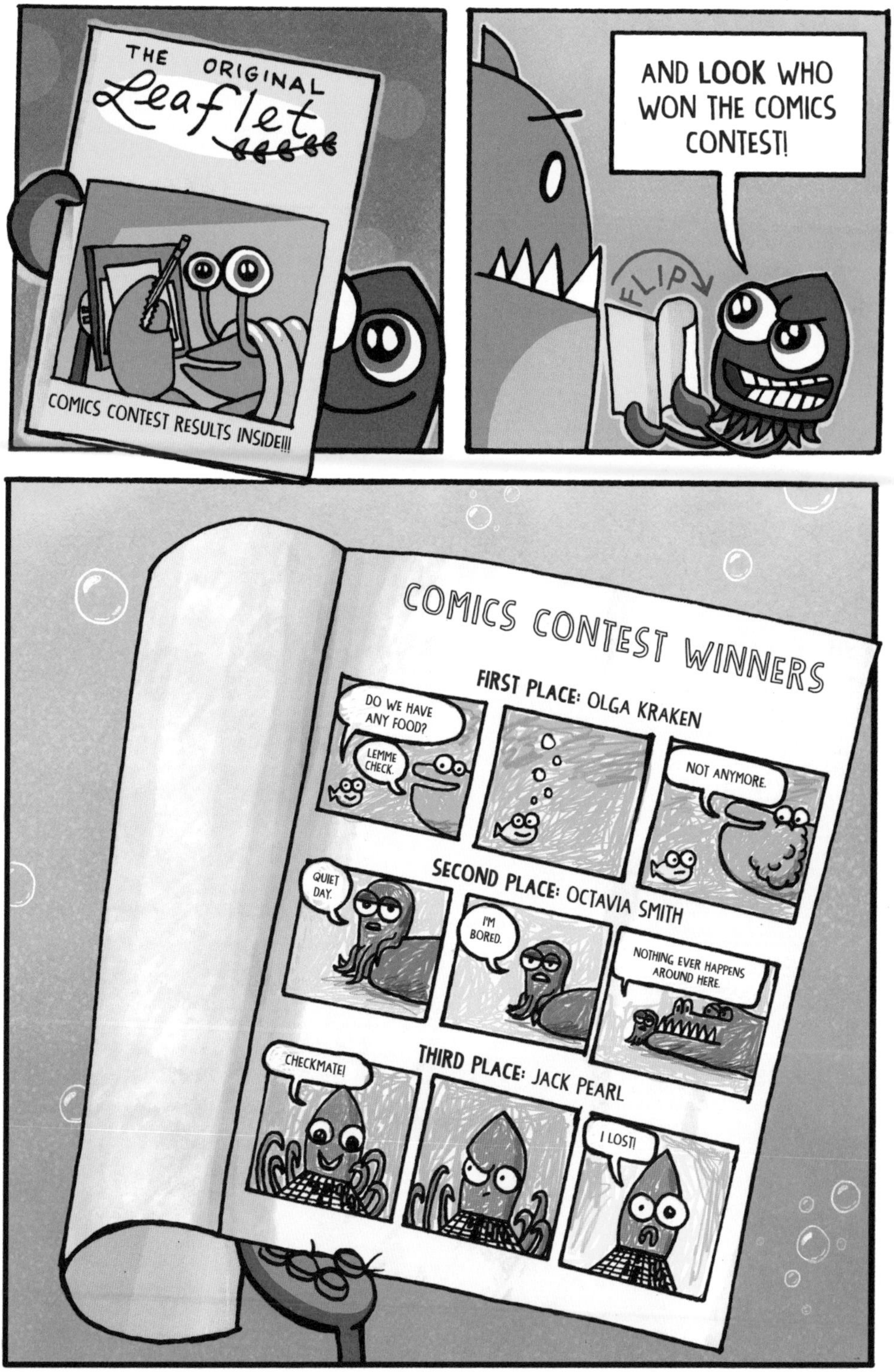
THE ORIGINAL Leaflet
COMICS CONTEST RESULTS INSIDE!!!
AND LOOK WHO WON THE COMICS CONTEST!
FLIP
COMICS CONTEST WINNERS
FIRST PLACE: OLGA KRAKEN
DO WE HAVE ANY FOOD?
LEMME CHECK.
NOT ANYMORE.
SECOND PLACE: OCTAVIA SMITH
QUIET DAY.
I'M BORED.
NOTHING EVER HAPPENS AROUND HERE.
THIRD PLACE: JACK PEARL
CHECKMATE!
I LOST!

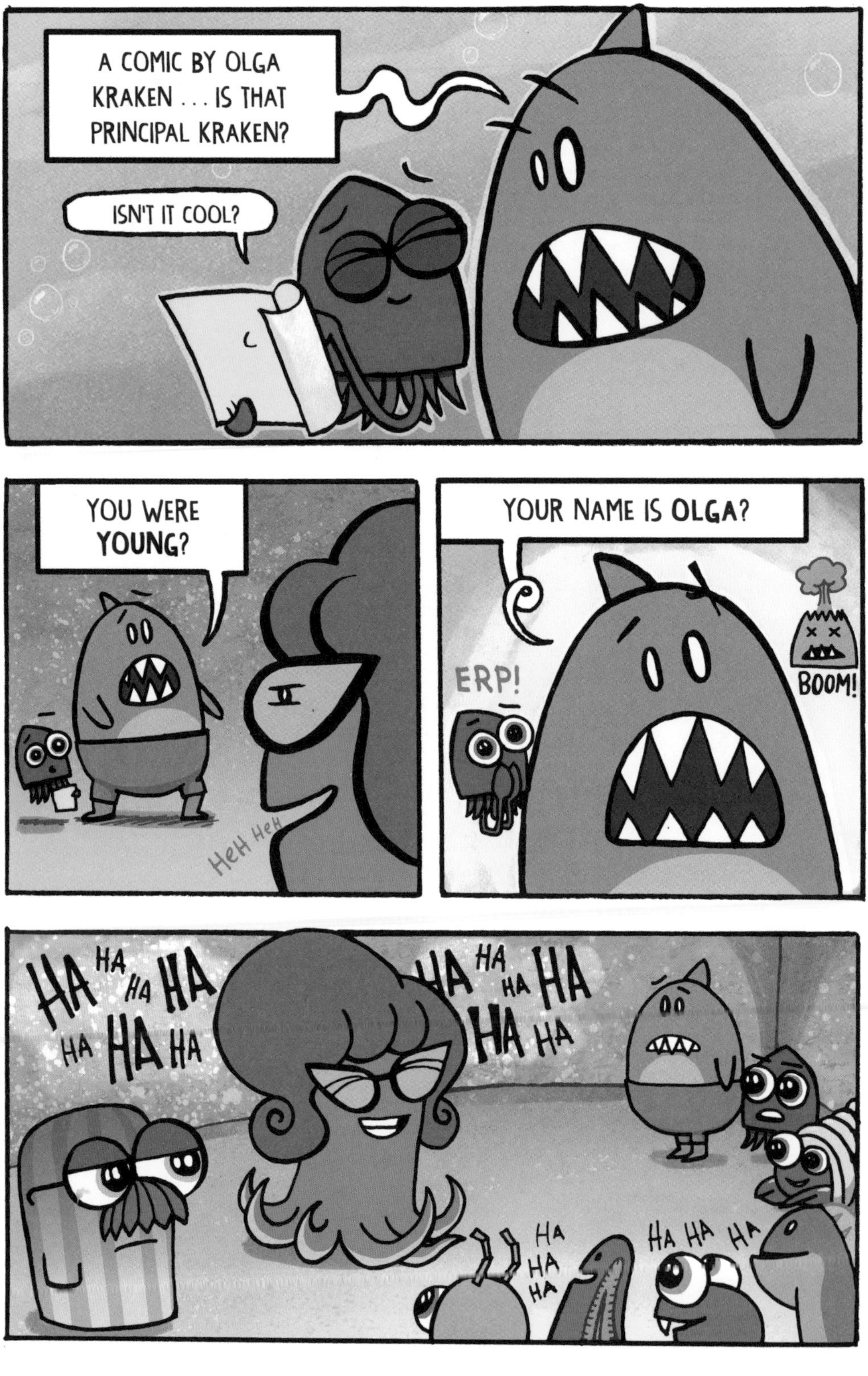
A COMIC BY OLGA KRAKEN . . . IS THAT PRINCIPAL KRAKEN?
ISN'T IT COOL?
YOU WERE YOUNG?
HEH HEH
YOUR NAME IS OLGA?
ERP!
BOOM!
HA HA HA HA HA HA HA
HA HA HA HA HA HA
HA HA HA
HA HA HA

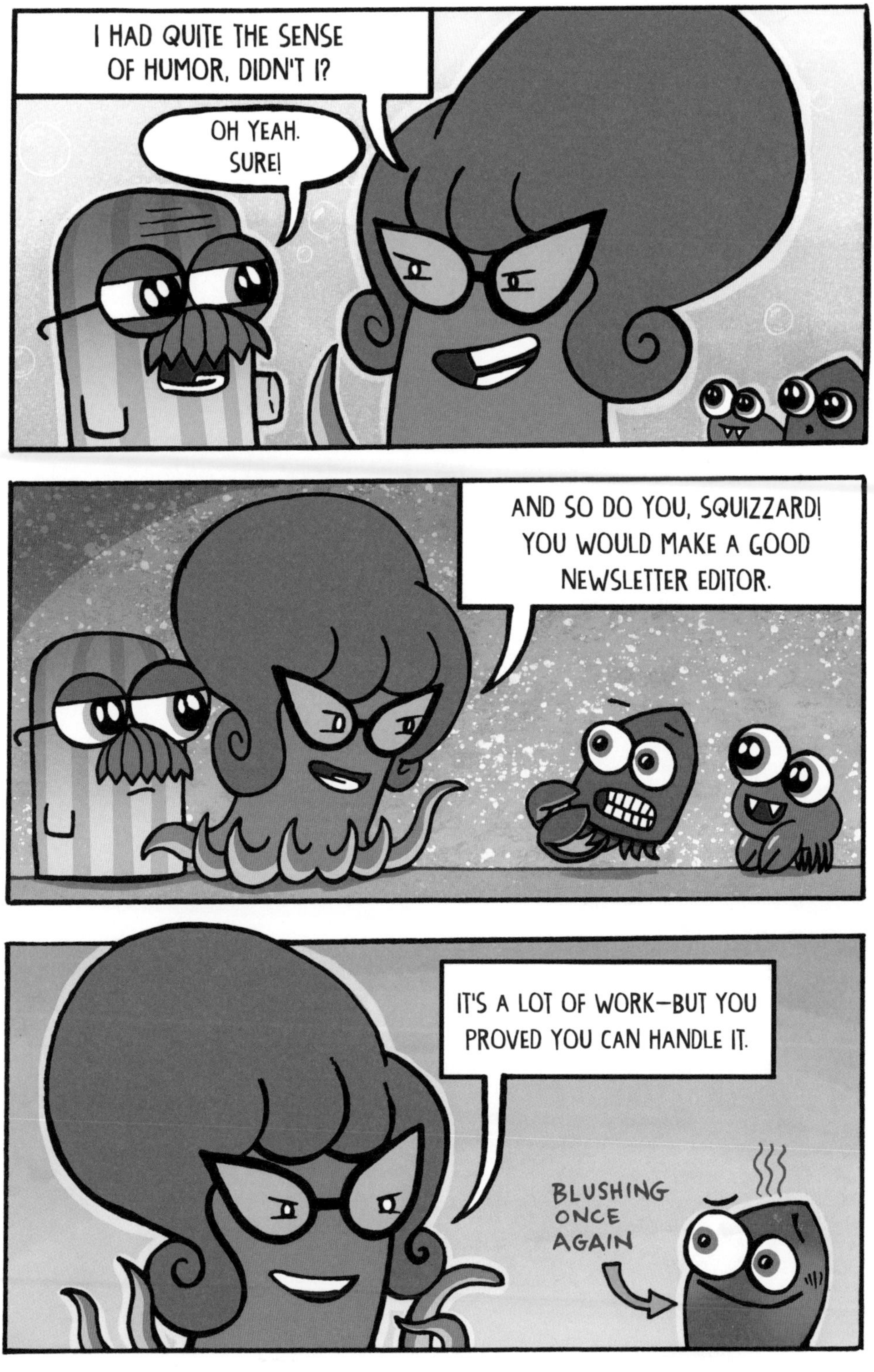
I HAD QUITE THE SENSE OF HUMOR, DIDN'T I?
OH YEAH. SURE!
AND SO DO YOU, SQUIZZARD! YOU WOULD MAKE A GOOD NEWSLETTER EDITOR.
IT'S A LOT OF WORK—BUT YOU PROVED YOU CAN HANDLE IT.
BLUSHING ONCE AGAIN

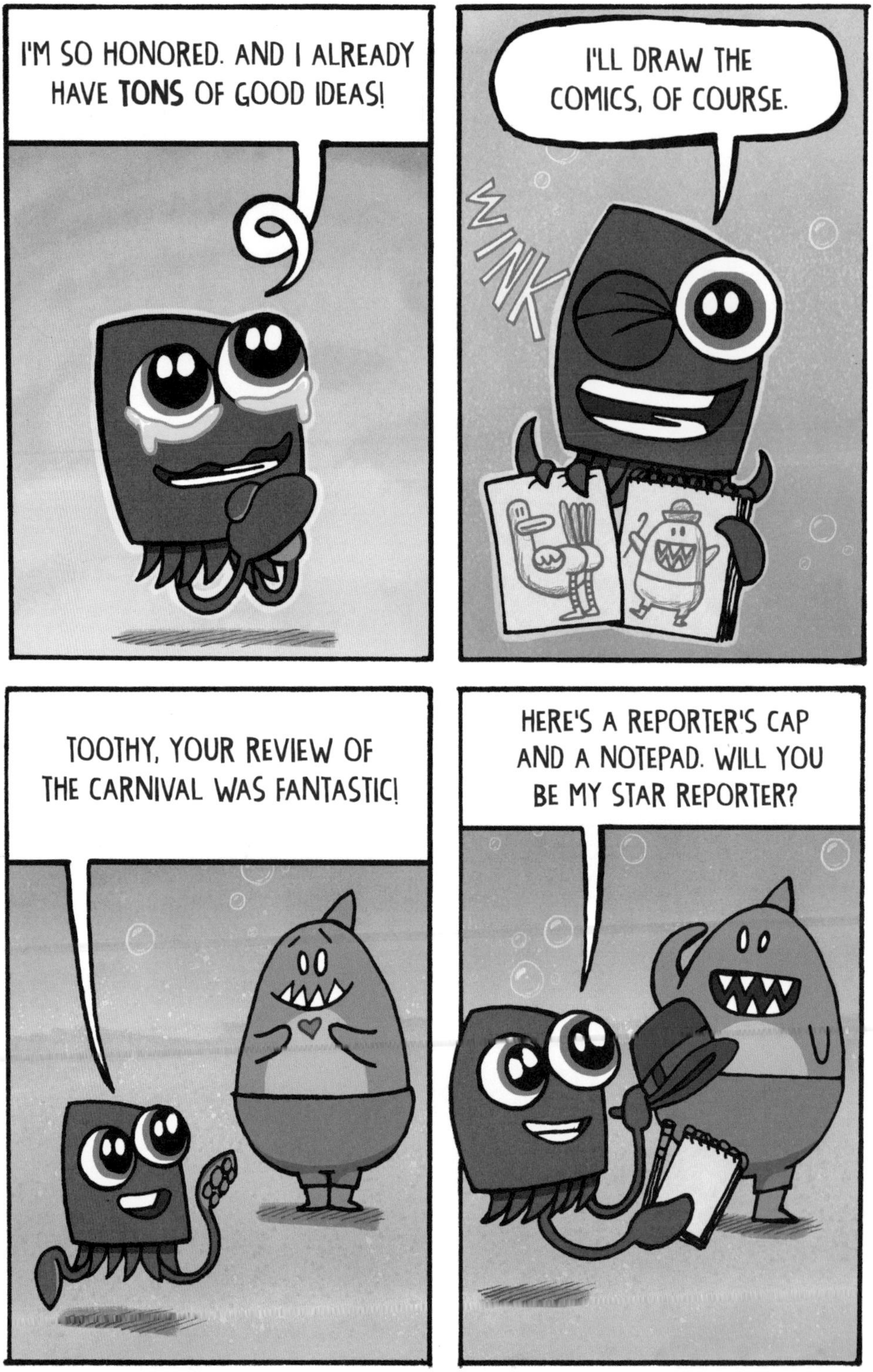
I'M SO HONORED. AND I ALREADY HAVE **TONS** OF GOOD IDEAS!
I'LL DRAW THE COMICS, OF COURSE.
WINK
TOOTHY, YOUR REVIEW OF THE CARNIVAL WAS FANTASTIC!
HERE'S A REPORTER'S CAP AND A NOTEPAD. WILL YOU BE MY STAR REPORTER?

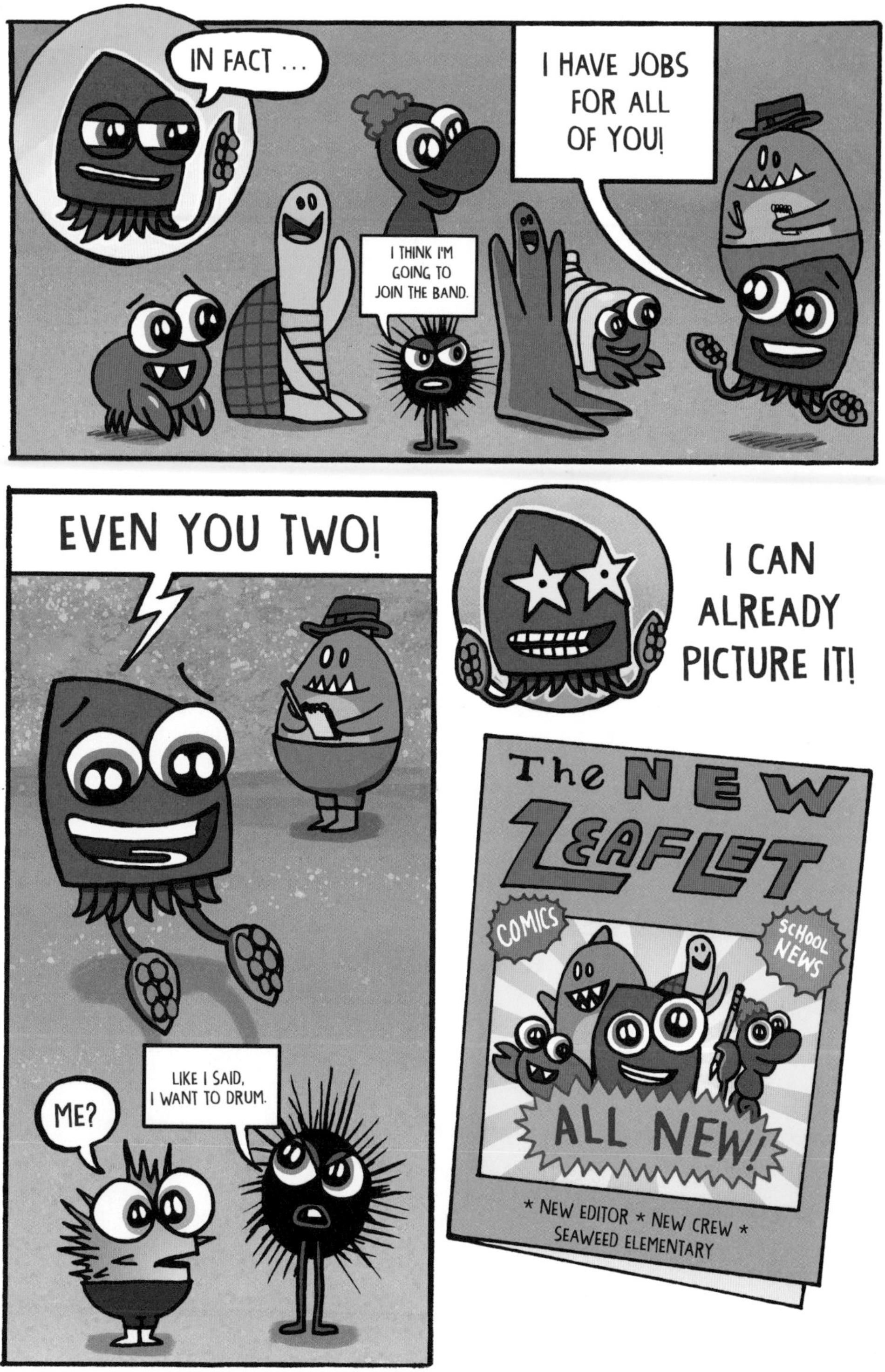
IN FACT . . .
I HAVE JOBS FOR ALL OF YOU!
I THINK I'M GOING TO JOIN THE BAND.
EVEN YOU TWO!
ME?
LIKE I SAID, I WANT TO DRUM.
I CAN ALREADY PICTURE IT!
The NEW LEAFLET
COMICS
SCHOOL NEWS
ALL NEW!
* NEW EDITOR * NEW CREW *
SEAWEED ELEMENTARY

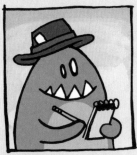

THE REAL SCOOP
BY TOOTHY

IT'S BEEN A BUSY WEEK IN THE DEEP REEF! THE TALENT SHOW IS IN JUST FIVE DAYS. I CAUGHT A PREVIEW OF NINA SEAL'S "SOMEWHERE UNDER A JET STREAM," AND IT DOESN'T DISAPPOINT!

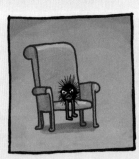

GENERAL COMPLAINTS
BY ANNIE

WHEN WILL BRINEY BITES RETURN TO THE CAFETERIA VENDING MACHINE? THEY'VE BEEN OUT OF STOCK FOR OVER TWO WEEKS. THAT'S LONGER THAN TOOTHY'S ORAL REPORTS!

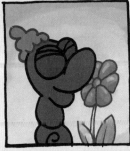

DEAR SHAY: ADVICE COLUMN

MY FRIEND IS MOVING AWAY AND I'M SAD. PLEASE HELP!
—KRISS

IT'S OK TO FEEL SAD. BUT JUST THINK: NOW YOU HAVE THE PERFECT PEN PAL AND A NEW PLACE TO VISIT!

TEN-TICKLES: A COMIC BY SQUIZZARD

CHOMP
CHOMP
CHOMP
CHOMP
CHOMP
CHOMP
CHIPS
CHOMP
CHIPS

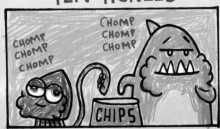

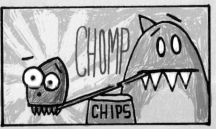

GUPPY GOALS
BY DOUG

FIRST GRADE IS A WHIRLWIND! WRITING COMPLETE
SENTENCES? KIND OF HARD. READING OUT LOUD?
NERVE-RACKING! AND TELLING TIME? WHAT AM I,
A SCIENTIST? BUT SCHOOL MEANS FRIENDS, SO I LOVE IT.

FIZZ'S TABLE

BREAKFAST IS IMPORTANT! SO I RECOMMEND THE
CAFETERIA'S MORNING SMOOTHIE. MADE FROM
BANANAS, APPLES, KELP, AND A DASH OF LOVE,
THIS SWEET JUICE IS UNBE-REEF-ABLY GOOD!

INTERVIEW WITH PRINCIPAL OLGA KRAKEN BY TOOTHY

TOOTHY: WHY START AN AFTER-SCHOOL PROGRAM?
P. OK: SO MANY OF OUR STUDENTS ARE TALENTED.
CLUBS ARE GREAT PLACES TO SHARE THOSE GIFTS.

PHOTOS
BY SWIFT

FACULTY ADVISER:
JALEEL ALI

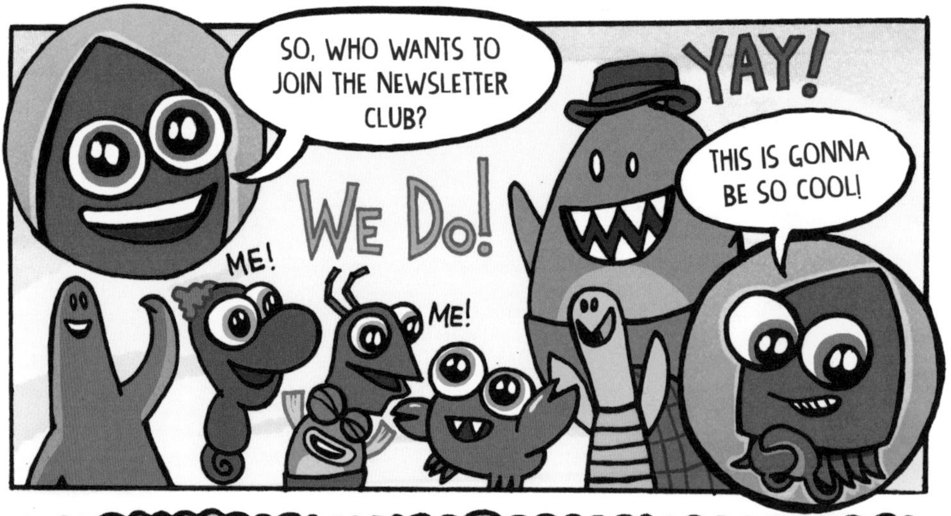
SO, WHO WANTS TO JOIN THE NEWSLETTER CLUB?
YAY!
THIS IS GONNA BE SO COOL!
WE DO!
ME!
ME!

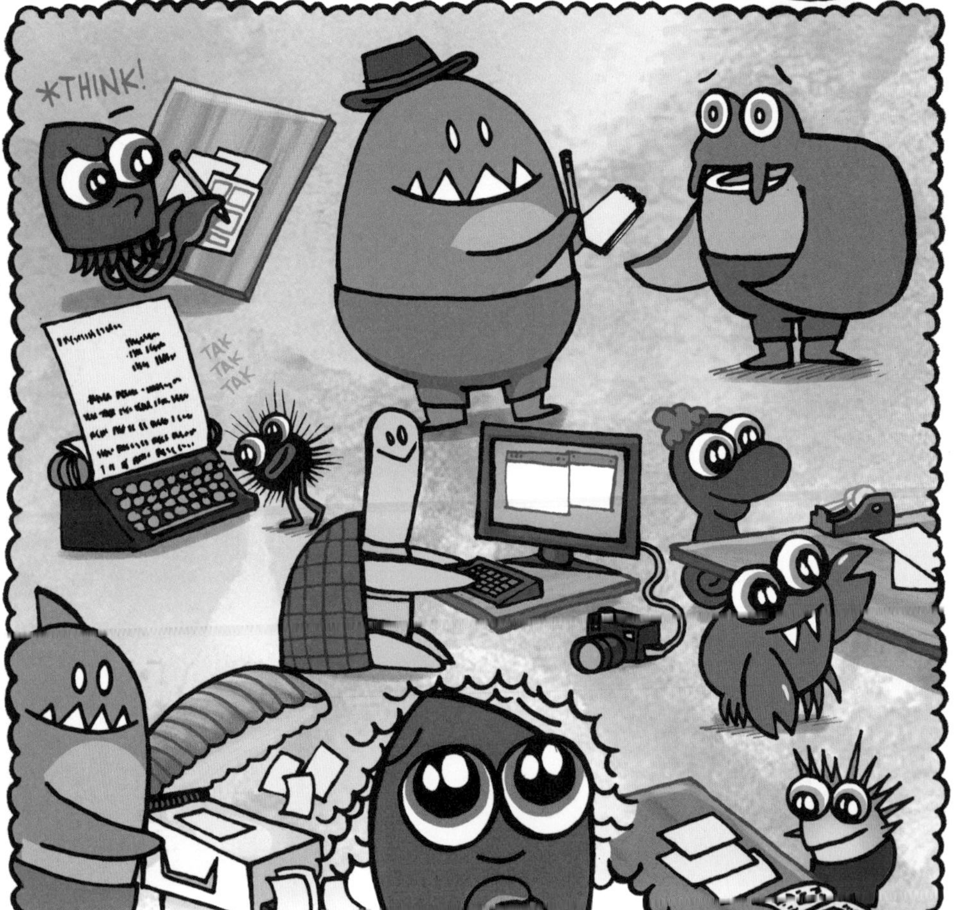
*THINK!
TAK TAK TAK

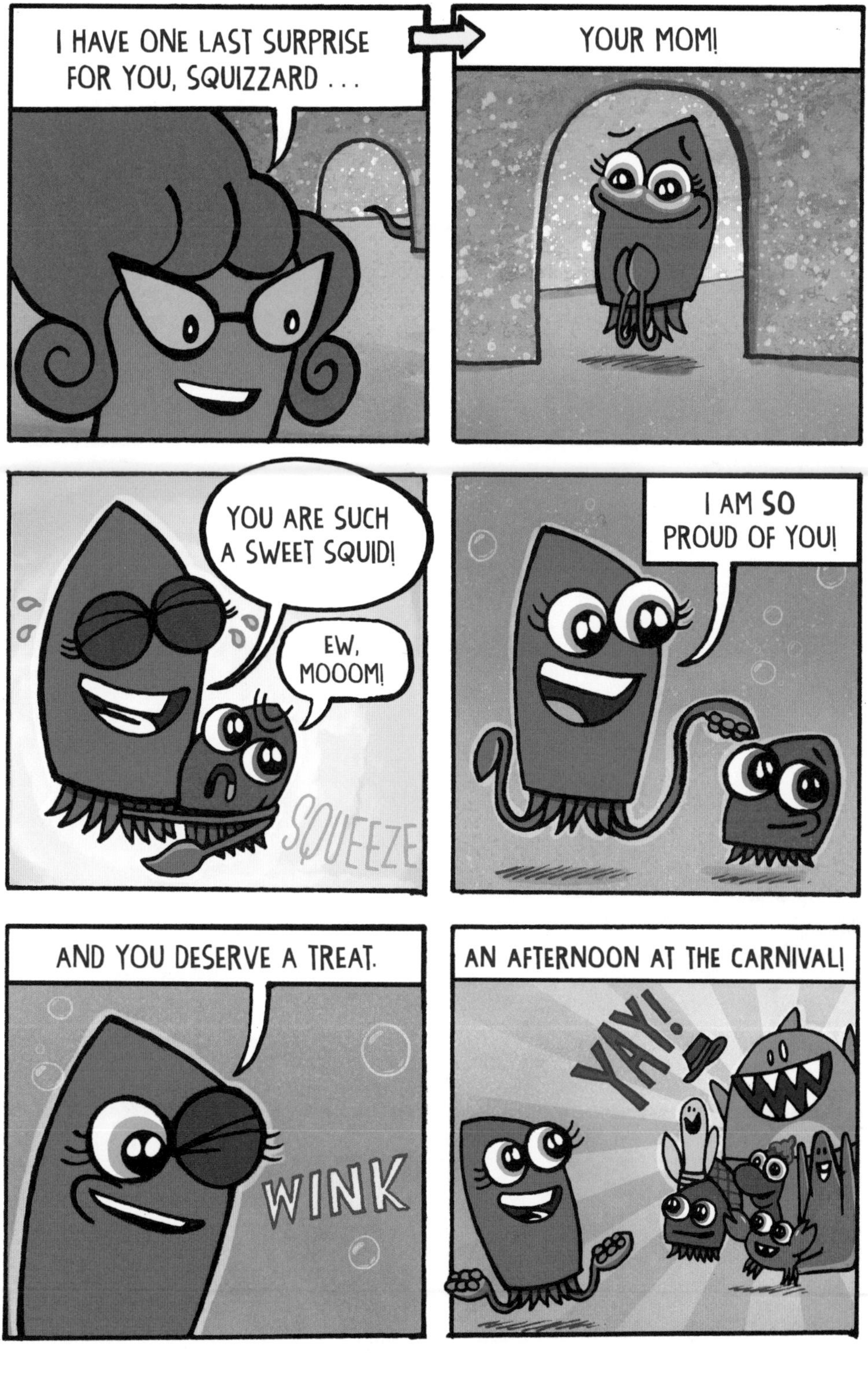
I HAVE ONE LAST SURPRISE FOR YOU, SQUIZZARD . . .
YOUR MOM!
YOU ARE SUCH A SWEET SQUID!
EW, MOOOM!
SQUEEZE
I AM SO PROUD OF YOU!
AND YOU DESERVE A TREAT.
WINK
AN AFTERNOON AT THE CARNIVAL!
YAY!

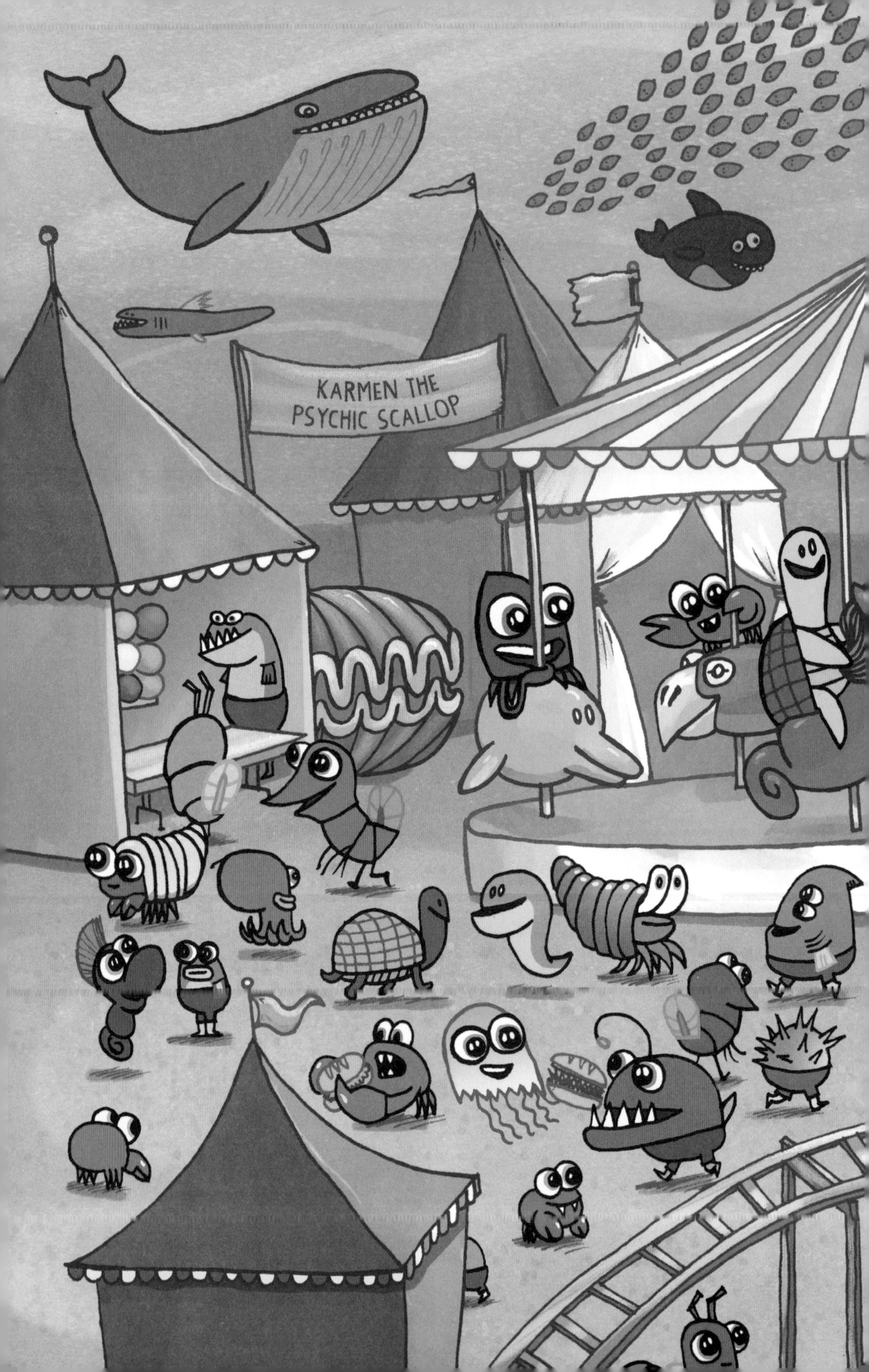
KARMEN THE
PSYCHIC SCALLOP

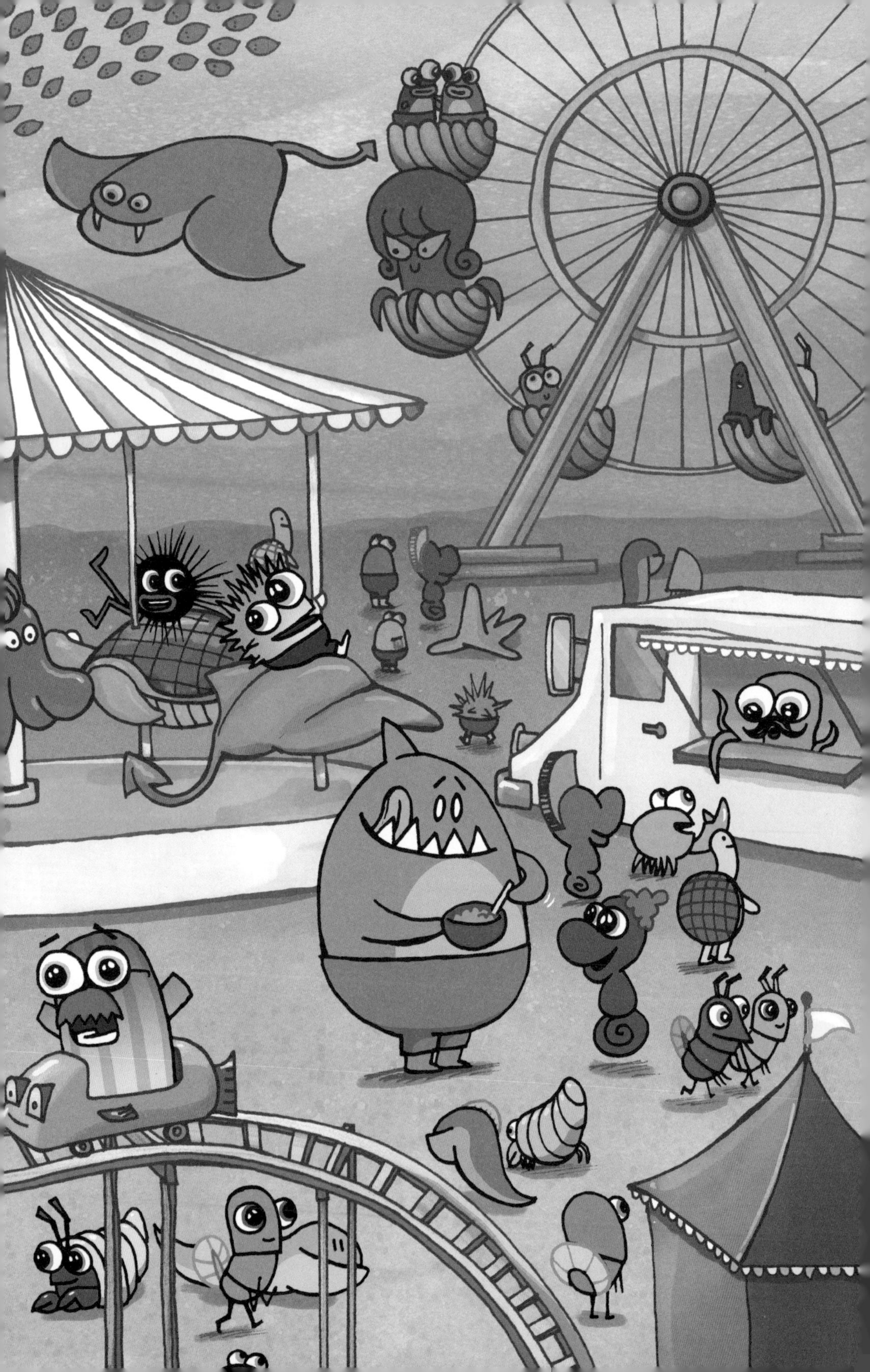

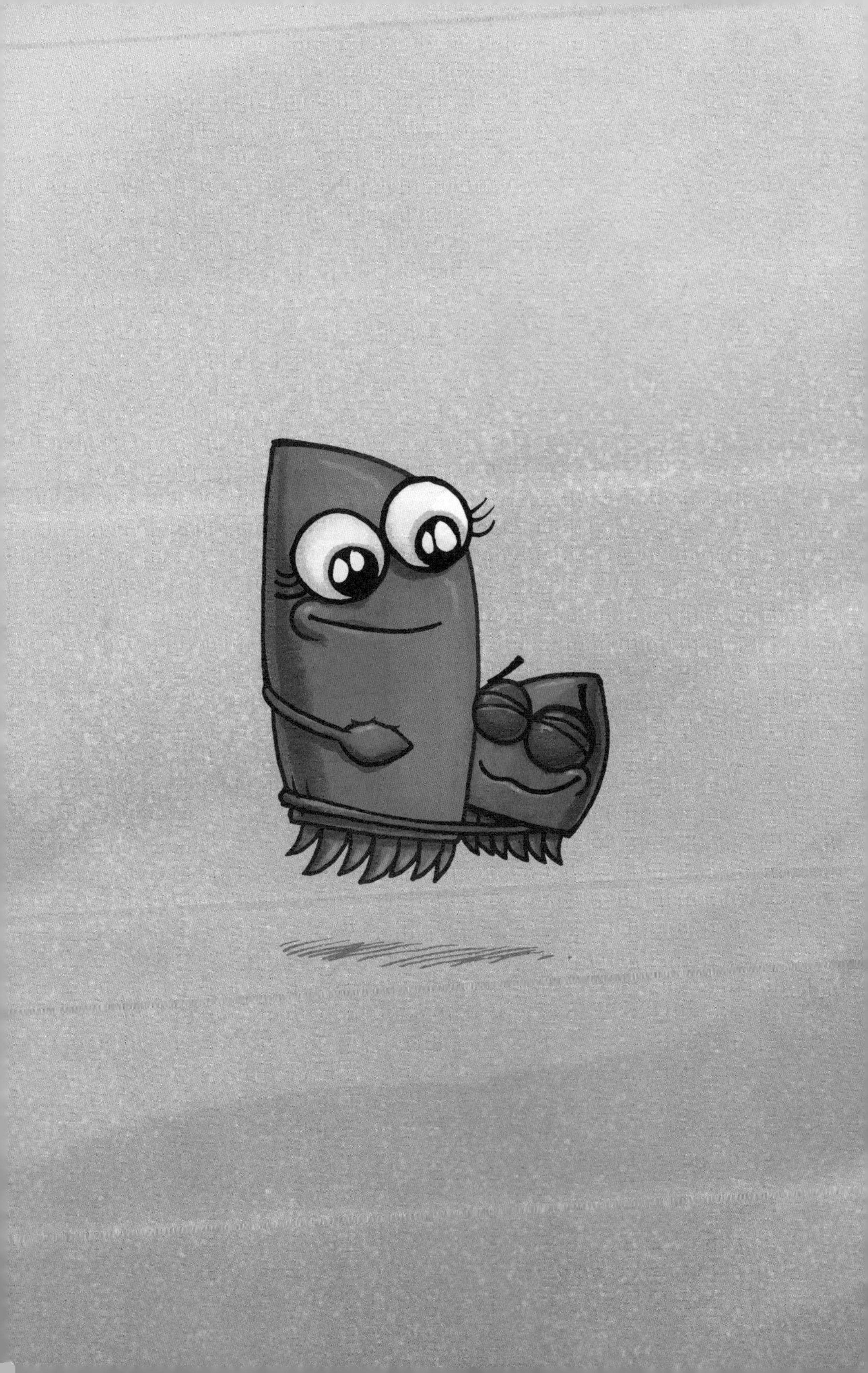

A CARNIVAL OF CORAL

Coral reefs are important underwater communities. They are structures made from the skeletons of tiny sea creatures called coral. Coral reefs cover less than 2% of the ocean floor, but around 25% of all ocean life depends on them for food and shelter. Pollution, rising water temperatures, and other factors are destroying coral reefs. Some scientists want to help by building artificial (ar-tih-FISH-ul), or man-made, reefs.

Artificial reefs can be made from all kinds of materials, like shipwrecks, sunken planes and lighthouses, concrete blocks, or even old tires. They give coral and sea plants a place to grow and fish a place to live and lay their eggs. If artificial reefs are not properly planned, they can pollute the ocean. It's a good thing Mr. Jaleel built his artificial reef carnival so carefully!

MAKE YOUR OWN NEWSLETTER!

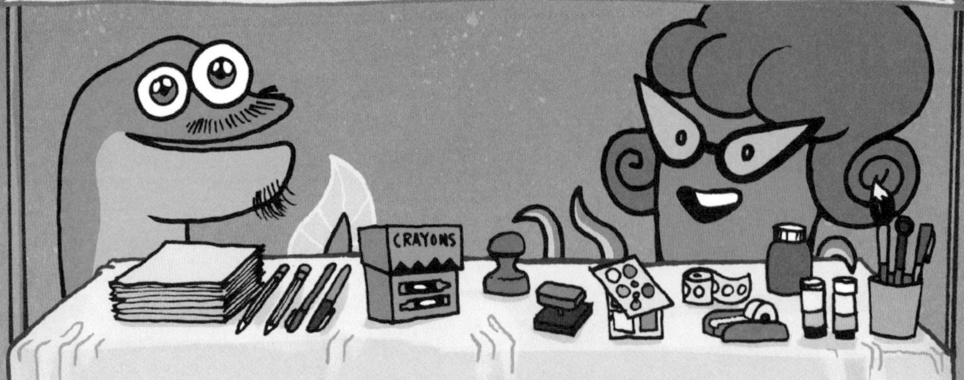
CRAYONS

You don't need to wait until you are an adult to publish your art and writing. You only need a pencil and paper! But ask a grown-up to help if you want to use other supplies: crayons, rubber stamps, stickers, tape, glue, and other art supplies.

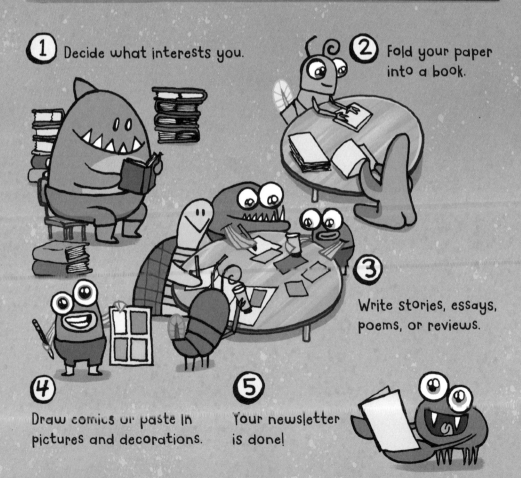

1. Decide what interests you.
2. Fold your paper into a book.

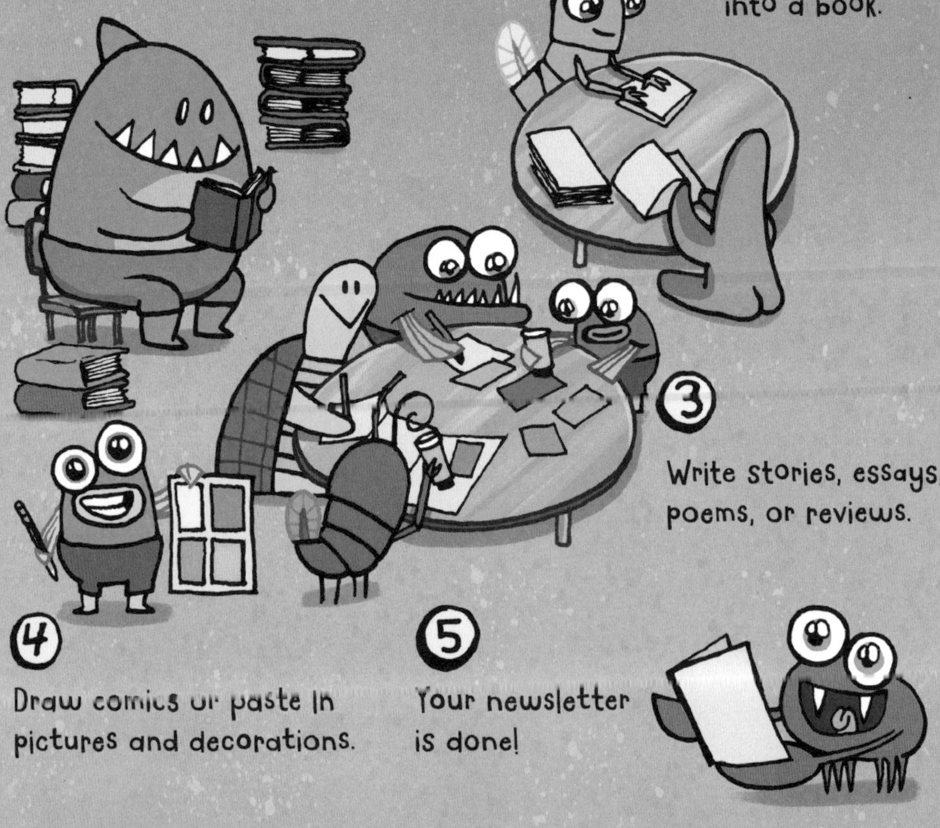

3. Write stories, essays, poems, or reviews.
4. Draw comics or paste in pictures and decorations.
5. Your newsletter is done!

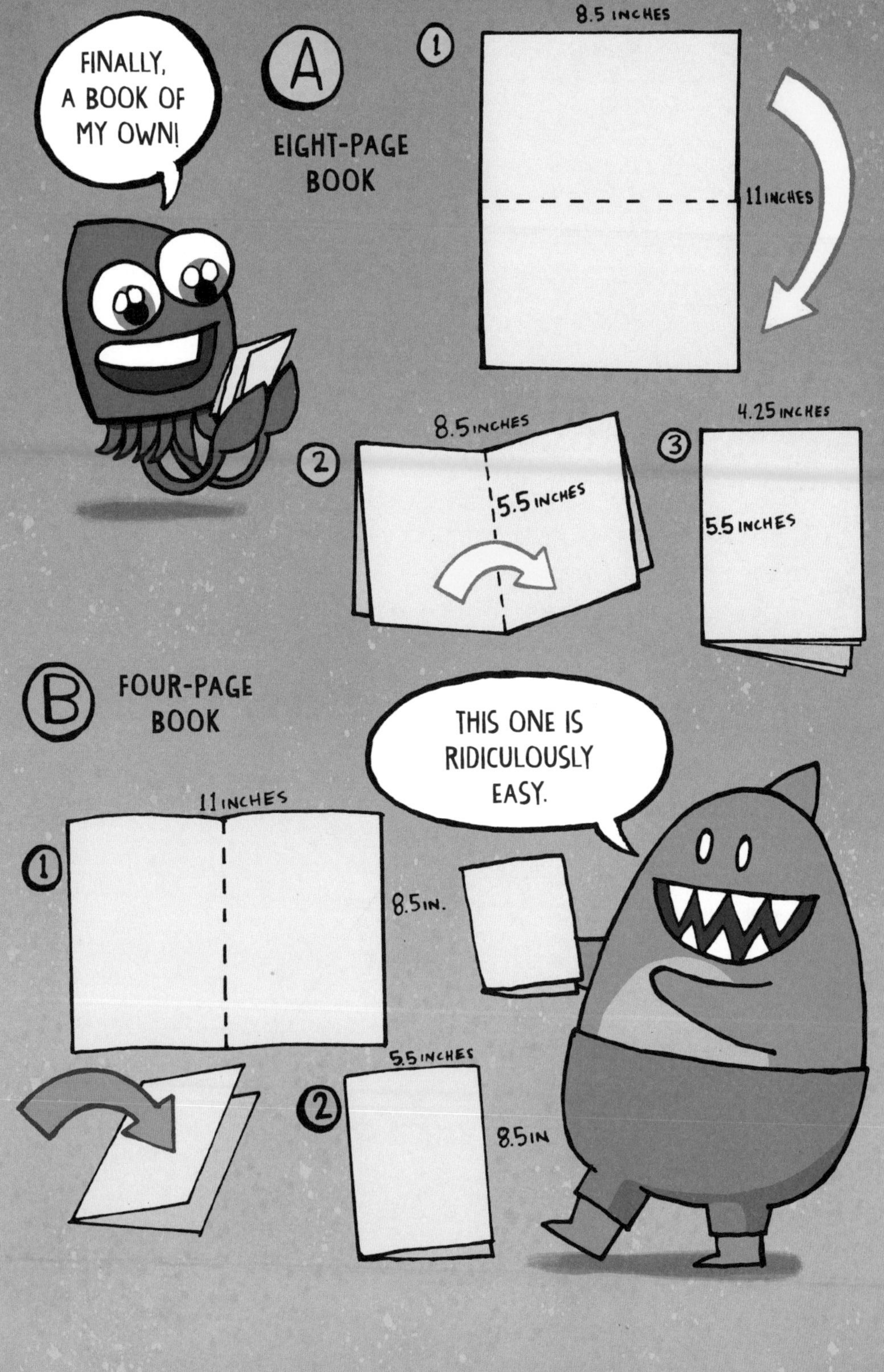
FINALLY, A BOOK OF MY OWN!
A
EIGHT-PAGE BOOK
1
8.5 INCHES
11 INCHES
2
8.5 INCHES
5.5 INCHES
3
4.25 INCHES
5.5 INCHES
B
FOUR-PAGE BOOK
THIS ONE IS RIDICULOUSLY EASY.
1
11 INCHES
8.5 IN.
2
5.5 INCHES
8.5 IN

KEVIN SHERRY is the author and illustrator of many children's picture books, most notably The Yeti Files and Remy Sneakers series, and the picture book I'M THE BIGGEST THING IN THE OCEAN, which received starred reviews and won an original artwork award from the Society of Illustrators. He's a man of many interests: a chef, an avid cyclist and screen printer, and a performer of hilarious puppet shows for kids and adults. Kevin lives in Baltimore, Maryland.

ACKNOWLEDGMENTS
Thanks To Rachel Orr, Cathy, James, Brian, Margie, Amelia, Dan, Al, Devlin, Gerrit, William, Sam, and Charlotte James. This book is inspired in part by the Zine Club at the Baltimore Design School, the Print and Multiples Fair that happens there, and Kevin's love of small press expos everywhere.

Kinkos

Ruby